A Savage Joy

Based on a True Story

DAVID LEE CORLEY

DEDICATION

To all the men and women that fought for their
country. Your sacrifices will not be forgotten.

Table of Contents

The rest of Coyle's regular aircrew were training CIA rookies also. The gunship was a new weapon platform and tricky to operate. The three miniguns fired in sync or could be designated to fire one or two at a time depending on the target. At 2,000 rpm, the Gatling-style guns burned through ammunition like grass through a goose. By using a cargo plane, the gunnery team could bring along plenty of extra ammunition and reload the weapons in mid-air.

As co-pilot, it was Coyle's job to act as navigator which was extremely difficult at night in the mountains. Still, Coyle was the best navigator available. He used a map with a red filtered flashlight to pinpoint the plane's position along a mountain ridge. He showed the map to Butler and said, "When you cross over this ridge, there should be a river in the valley below. With a little luck, the enemy has not heard our engines yet and will be surprised. You should be able to see the light from their torches for a few moments before they extinguish them. Look for two clumps next to each. That should be a river crossing where they are most vulnerable. That's your target area, but you gotta be quick before they scatter. Focus your fire on the crossing point then work your way wider into the surrounding jungle."

"Got it," said Butler. "What about anti-aircraft?"

"No way to tell what they have down there until they open fire on us. You're just gonna have to deal with it the best you can. We should be out of small arms' range, so anything coming up to reach us is anti-aircraft fire and needs to be taken seriously. You should take it out first if possible."

"But if I do that, I'll miss firing on the porters and troops."

"Yeah, you will. But we'll live to fight another day. I would prefer that."

"Alright."

"Do you see that mountain top coming up on your port side?"

"Yeah, barely."

"That's your pivot point where you'll cross over the ridge."

"I'll alert the gunnery crew to be ready."

When the aircraft reached the mountain top, it banked toward the West and flew over the ridge. In the valley below it was just as Coyle had said. There was a long line of flickering lights like a fire snake twisting its way through the valley and up a slope in the distance. As soon as the aircraft's engines were heard, the lights began to quickly extinguish.

Butler and Coyle peered through the windshield hoping to find the enemy before it was too late. "There," said Coyle pointing to two clumps of light at the bottom of the valley.

"Got it," said Butler keeping his eye focused on the two clumps as he flew toward them. "Turning."

As the last of the torches in the valley were extinguished, the gunship began its pylon turn over what Butler believed was the river crossing. "Guns up?" said Butler over the intercom as he checked the gun section switches.

"Ready," said the lead gunner as he and his assistant covered their ears and stepped back from the three miniguns leaving the rookies to wonder what was going on.

"Firing," said Butler and pulled the trigger.

All three guns whirled for a moment then erupted in a thunder of gunfire. The cargo hold lit up with a strobe effect from the miniguns chambers and barrels. The rookies were surprised by the roar of all three guns firing in unison. Hot empty casings bounced off the deck and rolled around. The rookies grabbed their snow shovels and scooped up the smoking brass, then dumped it into the lidless, empty oil drums.

In the valley below, the NVA troops and porters were scrambling for cover as they realized the dragon had found them even in the darkness. Its tongues of red fire reached down from the sky and chewed them to pieces as it touched them. Panic ensued. They dropped their weapons and supplies to scramble up the surrounding slopes into the trees. The circle of fire expanded outward gobbling up more and more of them. It seemed nowhere was safe. Many froze in fear waiting for their turn to die while others mumbled their prayers as if they would save them. They didn't.

In the aircraft, none of the crew could see the death they were delivering below as Butler kept circling. Finally, the miniguns ran out of ammunition and the thunderous noise stopped. The rookies' ears were ringing, and they seemed confused until the veteran gunners ordered them to reload. The rookies grabbed the next boxes of ammunition belts and dragged them over to the miniguns for reloading.

Butler kept the aircraft in a pylon turn while the weapons were reloaded. "I don't know if I hit anything," said Butler.

"Trust me. You hit something. And those that survive will tell stories of the night beast to others making it difficult to recruit porters. The psychological effect is almost as important as the physical effect," said Coyle.

"What's that?" said Butler pointing to a clump of lights on a mountain slope.

"I have no idea. Maybe it's a mountain stream crossing."

"Do you think they could hear our gunshots?"

"They heard them. But they also heard them stop, so maybe…"

"They lit their torches too soon?"

"Maybe…"

"Shall we have a look?"

"You're the pilot. It's your ship. You decide."

"I think we should have a look while our guys finish reloading the weapons."

Butler steered the aircraft towards the mountain slope and the flickering lights. Deep in thought, Coyle seemed quiet and distant as he stared at the approaching lights. And then it hit him… "Pull up and turn around!" said Coyle alarmed.

"What?! Why?!" said Butler confused.

"It's a trap. I'm taking control of the aircraft."

"You've got control," said Butler releasing the controls.

"It's like using fire to attract squid at night. The torches are bait…" said Coyle when the sky lit up with tracer rounds coming from the clump of lights on the mountain slope. Coyle gunned the engines and banked the aircraft hard as he evaded the stream of large caliber bullets.

Below an NVA gun crew operating a Russian-made ZPU-4 anti-aircraft gun fired into the night sky. It was difficult to see the black aircraft against the moonless backdrop, but the silhouette of the aircraft against clouds helped their aim. The ZPU-4 had four 14.5mm heavy machine guns firing in unison. An officer using binoculars guided the crew's aim by pointing and shouting instructions.

As the Black Widow turned, it exposed its underbelly.

In the cargo hold, bullets ripped through the deck hitting one of the rookies in the crotch and almost splitting him in half. Whimpering as he fell, he lived another twenty seconds before the blood loss was too much and he went silent.

Feeling the thump of the rounds hitting the aircraft, Coyle changed direction and put the aircraft in a dive toward the valley floor. "What the hell are you doing?" said Butler anxious.

"What they don't expect," said Coyle.

"What about the NVA on the trail? We'll be in small arms range?"

"Yep. Get the guns up and tell everyone to hang on to something."

Over the intercom, Butler ordered the gun crew to prepare to fire and grab onto something. Word of the rookie's death came over the intercom. "Jesus, he just turned twenty," said Butler.

"Stay focused," said Coyle.

"Where?"

"Everywhere. Just pull the trigger when I say."

"Okay."

Leveling out the aircraft just a hundred feet above the river, Coyle watched as enemy muzzle blasts winked from below the jungle canopy. "Fire," said Coyle.

Confused but obedient, Butler fired the miniguns. Coyle turned the aircraft into a spiral as he flew above the river. The minigun tracer rounds streamed like a pinwheel in all directions cutting through the dense jungle. In the cargo hold the gun crew was tossed around like ragdolls and shell casings tumbled through the air pelting them with hot brass. Coyle knew that the gunfire would be completely ineffective at killing the enemy troops, but the sight of the spinning tracer rounds would destroy them psychologically. The small arms fire ceased as the enemy dove for cover behind rocks and trees. "Alright. That's enough," said Coyle leveling out the aircraft.

Butler released the trigger and the miniguns went silent. Clear of the anti-aircraft gun on the mountain slope, Coyle pulled up and flew the gunship over the mountain. They were safe once again. "You've got the aircraft," said Coyle releasing the controls.

"I have the aircraft," said Butler taking the controls. "That was amazing."

"We got lucky. At least most of us did."

"I panicked," said Butler ashamed.

"No. You were just surprised. You would have figured it out after a moment."

"But you didn't hesitate. You knew what to do and did it. You saved us."

"Yeah, well… I hate to crash."

Coyle turned away and looked down at his right hand. It was shaking. He shook his head knowing that his nerves were shattered, but he was also exhilarated from the adrenaline like a drug addict. He had almost died… again.

Okinawa, Japan

After eight weeks of basic training, Marine Private Antwan Lincoln stepped onto Camp Butler's firing range on Okinawa. It was the farthest he had ever traveled from his hometown of Anniston, Alabama. It was in Anniston he had decided to join the military when he saw an Army officer stand up to a mob attempting to stop the Freedom Riders and almost getting lynched for the good deed. Lincoln never forgot him and the promise he made to himself. Even though he was only nineteen years old, he had the body of a man… a very big man with skin black as night and the muscles of a farm worker. He was no longer a young teenager that could be pushed around by the Klan in Anniston. Now, he did the pushing and the Klan avoided him.

Resting on his shoulder was the M60 machine gun he had been issued. Just as he was taught, he had stripped the weapon down and ensured that every part was clean and oiled when required. Now, he would check the site and make sure it operated correctly. His life and the lives of those in his squad would depend on it. The M60 would provide base fire for his unit during a firefight.

Beside him, carrying three bandoliers of ammunition and his M14, was his loader, Private Decan Turner from New Orleans, Louisiana. Also black, he was the opposite of Lincoln in stature. Short and lean, but scrappy in any kind of fight. The kinda guy that nobody noticed until it was too late. His face was oily and still pocked with pimples. His Marine uniform was the smallest size available and ill-fitting.

"I heard from a guy in headquarters that we're heading for Vietnam," said Turner struggling to keep up but not giving an inch.

"Is that right?" said Lincoln. "Sobeit."

"Why do you gotta say something like that for? It ain't our fight."

"It's our fight if the boss says it's our fight. That's the way it works."

"I don't see why we can't go someplace nice and quiet... like Hawaii. They got a Marine base there."

"Luck of the draw. This is where they need us."

"That's bullshit. Did you count how many Negroes are in our outfit? Just as many as the whites and spics. That ain't fair. It's fucking prejudice if you ask me."

"I didn't."

"Didn't what? Count?"

"No. Ask you. Why the hell did you become a Marine if you don't wanna fight?"

"I wanna fight. I just wanna make sure it's something worth fighting for."

"Maybe you should become a politician. They're the ones that decide."

"Maybe I will after I win me some medals. Voters like medals."

"Is that so?"

"Yeah. Look at Kennedy and Eisenhower. They got tons of medals from World War II."

"Yeah, but they were white. You ain't."

"Times are changing, Linc. You'll see."

"Well, if you run for office I'll vote for ya. Maybe I'll even help ya. Passing out flyers and shit like that."

"Yeah? I'm gonna hold you to that."

"I'm a man of my word."

"Do you really think I could do it… become a politician?"

"With your mouth? I don't see why not."

Lincoln checked in with the range master and waited until the firing line was clear before setting up his weapon. Lincoln took his time to make sure he got everything right. It was a luxury that he knew he wouldn't have once they were fully deployed. In the meantime, getting it set up right was more important than doing it fast. He loaded the first belt while Turner set up his M14. Turner needed the practice. Part of his job was to protect the machine gunner if need be. That and load the M60's ammunition during a firefight. He was a good assistant gunner and Lincoln liked him but wouldn't admit it.

The M60 was a beast of a weapon. It was gas-operated and weighed just over twenty-three lbs., unloaded. It didn't seem like much until the gunner had to carry it through dense terrain common to the Southeast Asian jungles. The M60 earned its nickname "The Pig" not because of its weight, but because it sounded like a hog grunting when fired. The M60 burned through ammunition which required every member of the squad to carry two 100-round bandoliers of the 7.62×51mm NATO shells in addition to their regular loads. Although it normally fired at a rate of 100 rounds per minute, it was capable of firing 550 rounds per minute if needed. The problem was that the barrel needed to be changed every minute when firing at that rate instead of the slow rate which only required a barrel change every ten minutes. The M60 was the most powerful weapon in a Marine rifle squad. As much as the Marines in the squad bitched and complained about the heavy ammo belts, they were grateful for the weapon whenever they faced the enemy.

At the hundred rounds a minute rate, the three belts that Turner had carried would be used up in three minutes. But Lincoln was disciplined. Whenever possible he fired his weapon in short bursts to conserve ammunition. There was no sense in continuing to fire the M60 when he was searching for a new target. He wasn't sure what he would do in an actual firefight with a live enemy firing back, but he figured it was better to practice the way he had been taught by his instructor.

Once the range master signaled open fire, Lincoln laid down on his belly in the prone position, aimed at the distant target, and fired a two-second burst using the bipod to steady the weapon. Turner used binoculars to spot for him. Lincoln adjusted the gun's sight by loosening the retaining screw, then adjusting the rear sight aperture with its wheel. When in combat, he would use the windage and elevating knobs to refine the sight for battlefield conditions. It took two hundred rounds before Lincoln was satisfied that the sight was properly zeroed.

For the final belt, Lincoln stood and fired the machine gun down range in short bursts. Firing the weapon while standing took a lot of practice because he wasn't using the sight. He was feeling the weapon and the target. It was surprisingly effective. But then again, Lincoln was bigger and stronger than most Marine gunners. The recoil of the weapon affected him less.

Once finished, Lincoln spotted for Turner as he fired and adjusted the sight on his M14. It was a lot less exciting than firing the pig, but fair was fair.

January 3, 1965 – Washington DC, USA

Standing before television cameras and reporters outside the Capital building, Senator Mike Mansfield, considered by many to be the most knowledgeable congressman about the Vietnam War, said, "While I support President Johnson and our military's efforts in South Vietnam, I believe we may be going down the wrong path with these bombing campaigns in the North. They're not going to work. The communists are not going to yield and change their policies of supporting the Viet Cong rebels in the South. We as a nation would do far better to negotiate a solution with the North based on the neutralization of South Vietnam that would eventually lead to elections and reunification of the two countries. It's the only practical solution on the table."

January 6, 1965 – Saigon, South Vietnam

Sitting at his desk inside the U.S. embassy in Saigon, Ambassador General Maxwell Taylor crafted a telegram about the current situation in South Vietnam to President Johnson which read, "We are faced here with a seriously deteriorating situation characterized by continued political turmoil, irresponsibility, and division within the armed forces, lethargy in the pacification program, some anti-US feeling which could grow, signs of mounting terrorism by VC directly at US personnel and deepening discouragement and loss of morale throughout SVN. Unless these conditions are somehow changed and trends reversed, we are likely soon to face several unpleasant developments ranging from anti-American demonstrations, further civil disorders, and even political assassinations to the ultimate installation of a hostile government that will ask us to leave while it seeks accommodation with the National Liberation Front and Hanoi."

Taylor was opposed to sending American ground troops to Vietnam. He felt they would only exacerbate the situation and create unnecessary tension at home. This was a South Vietnamese fight. It was their country after all. Not letting them take responsibility for their own freedom and liberty was a mistake that the South Vietnamese people could ill afford. Instead, Taylor recommended that the United States Air Force and Navy use graduated air assaults on the Ho Chi Minh Trail to cut off supplies and weapons to the Viet Cong and North Vietnamese Army (NVA) troops in the South. It was a strategy that showed continued American support of the South while keeping an arm's length to the fight on the ground. It was far better to risk the lives of a few brave American airmen than to let thousands of American ground troops tangle with the Viet Cong and NVA in the jungles of Southeast Asia.

Ban Ken Bridge

January 13, 1965 – Mountains, Laos

Like much of Laos, the Nam Mat River snaked its way through the steep mountains near the border between Laos and North Vietnam. Eight miles east of the town of Ban Ban on Route 7, the reinforced wooden Ban Ken bridge was the only structure crossing the Nam Mat River capable of handling the heavy Soviet-made trucks used to ferry war supplies down the Ho Chi Minh Trail. That fact made it a tempting target for American aircraft trying to interdict weapons and supplies being sent to the Viet Cong in South Vietnam. Each year, just as the rainy season ended, the Americans bombed the bridge. And each year, the NVA rebuilt it usually in just a few weeks or even days. It was a familiar cycle that both sides expected.

Near the end of 1964, the North Vietnamese received a large shipment of anti-aircraft weapons from the Soviets to protect Hanoi and to be placed strategically along the Ho Chi Minh Trail. The Ban Ken Bridge was the NVA's first thought. They knew the American aircraft would be coming when the rainy season ended. It was an opportunity to strike back with a vengeance at the American pilots that plagued their soldiers and porters like gnats.

Even though aerial reconnaissance revealed a large amount of new anti-aircraft emplacements, General LeMay, Chief of Staff of the U.S. Air Force, ordered the bridge destroyed anyway. Some under his command questioned the risk and value of bombing a bridge that the NVA could rebuild in a matter of days or weeks. But LeMay kept his own council and the order stood.

The strike force was made up of sixteen F-105 Thunderchiefs nicknamed "Thuds" and twelve F-100 Super Sabres nicknamed "Huds." Ten of the Thunderchiefs were loaded with 750 lb. conventional iron bombs on their hardpoints while the remaining six were loaded with AGM-12 air-to-ground missiles nicknamed "Bullpups." The F-100s were all armed with AGM-83 Bulldog missiles using blast fragmentation warheads and CBU-2 cluster bombs which dropped hundreds of bomblets onto anti-aircraft positions.

While the Thunderchiefs would be responsible for the destruction of the bridge, the Super Sabres were assigned MiG patrol and suppression of enemy air defenses.

Because of the agreement between the U.S. and the Thailand military, the majority of the strike force aircraft were armed, then flown from Thai air bases to Da Nang air base in South Vietnam where they were combined with the remaining aircraft. It seemed like an unnecessary redundancy, but the Americans wanted to keep a portion of their fighters in Thailand in the event that Laos fell to the communists and there was an invasion from North Vietnam or China.

At 1 PM on January 13th, an RF-101 reconnaissance jet roared over Route 7 in hopes of spotting an enemy convoy. There were none. The RF-101 proceeded to the Ban Ken bridge and did a fast low-altitude flyover to ensure there were no surprises for the flight of warplanes that followed. There were no vehicles on the bridge and the hidden anti-aircraft guns remained silent in hopes of better prey. They got it when four Thunderchiefs rolled in one after another to release their loads of 750 lb. bombs. Lieutenant Colonel Bill Craig was the lead aircraft and dropped his bombs on the west end of the bridge. The bombs were on target and shattered the bridge. The next three Thunderchiefs finished off what remained of the bridge.

The second flight of F-105s dropped their bombs on the already destroyed bridge with little further effect kicking dust and dirt mixed with smoke from the burning bridge. The next two flights held off dropping their bombs and headed for an alternative target – a small bridge downriver. That bridge too was destroyed. All seemed too good to be true when one of the Thunderchiefs was hit by a barrage from a Russian-made ZPU-4 14.5mm quad barrel anti-aircraft gun hidden on the slope of a nearby mountain. The jet's engine poured out black smoke. The pilot knew that if he bailed out near the bridge he would be captured, but he didn't have much time. He hugged the river and flew several miles then pulled up to gain altitude before punching out. He ejected. The jet continued skyward until it exploded showering the area with burning wreckage. Fortunately, none of the wreckage hit the pilot as he landed on a hillside shrouded with jungle just a few hundred yards from the river. He was alive and unhurt except for a few cuts and bruises. He used his radio to send his position as best as he could determine and by using the map he kept in the pocket of his flight suit. Then came the difficult part... not getting caught while he waited for rescue.

As expected, the pilots in the Super Sabres sought revenge for the downed aircraft. Having identified the location of the anti-aircraft gun, they dove one by one firing their rockets and dropping their cluster bombs before pulling up. The four-barrel gun and its four-man crew were obliterated. Only a smoking hole in the jungle remained. Seeing the weapon destroyed, the pilot of the final jet held his rockets and bombs hoping to find another target. He didn't have long to wait. A second anti-aircraft gun opened fire from the same mountain slope but farther down the river. The pilot, an experienced veteran of the Korean War, used all his skill to evade the gunfire climbing until he disappeared over the top of the ridge. He was safe, but not done. He banked his jet, then flew parallel to the ridge. He climbed back over the ridge and descended at a low altitude toward the gun. The gun crew swung their weapon around and again opened fire. The American aircraft was hit dead center. The control console in the cockpit was shattered and the electronics caught fire. The pilot had lost control and the plane was descending. He had no choice and ejected before he was burned alive by the fire. The pilotless plane pierced through the jungle canopy and exploded on impact with a thick tree trunk. The pilot landed on the same side of the river as the previous pilot but several miles apart. The second pilot was in far more danger of being captured because he was closer to the bridge and the enemy troops that protected it.

The strike force broke off their attack and headed for home in Thailand and South Vietnam depending on their home base. There was nothing more they could do except become cannon fodder for the enemies' anti-aircraft fire which was far more intense than expected. As much as the strike force pilots wanted to help their two missing comrades, the downed pilots were the rescue team's problem… except that the rescue team had been excluded from the mission's roster by accident. The strike force commander wasn't informed of his blunder until he landed back in Da Nang.

The NVA immediately started a search for the two downed enemy pilots. A platoon was sent out to scour the mountain slopes near the wreckage of each jet.

Both pilots moved away from their plane's wreckage and hid in the jungle. Trying to escape through the dense Laotian jungle was a good way to get hurt and a better way to get caught. They would hunker down in hopes that the NVA would pass them by as they searched. If they missed their prey on the first pass, the NVA were sure to double back. They would keep searching until the pilots were captured or killed. For the pilots, it was a matter of stalling until the rescue team could reach them. The American rescue teams were even more persistent than the NVA in finding the pilots.

Coyle landed his Pilatus PC-6 Porter on a new mountainside airfield created by Blackjack's SOG team and the Montagnard. Once the plane had stopped and the wheels were blocked on the steep slope, Blackjack and his team began unloading the supplies and weapons from the cargo hold in the back of the aircraft. Surprised by how quickly they were unloading everything, Coyle said, "What? No hug?"

"Sorry. We just got a radio call from HQ. Two American aircraft went down near the Ban Ken Bridge during an aerial assault. Both pilots ejected and are hiding in the jungle by the Nam Mat River," said Blackjack.

"Okay. So, the rescue team will pick them up."

"There is no rescue team in the area."

"Why the hell not?"

"Mission planners fucked up and forgot to include them."

"That's a pretty big fuck up."

"You're telling me? Anyway, we're the closest ground team. We'll head out as soon as you're unloaded."

"Fuck that. Go! I'll unload this stuff."

"Actually, we were hoping you could fly spotter for us. It's dangerous. The NVA have built up their air defenses by the bridge and along the river. They already downed two of our jets. I don't imagine your PC-6 will stand much of a chance if it gets targeted."

"You'd be surprised what this thing can do with the right pilot."

"And you're the right pilot?"

"Damned right I am."

"Good. Give me your map and I'll mark the pilots' last known positions."

Coyle handed him his map and Blackjack used a pencil to mark the last positions of the two pilots. "Keep your radio on," said Coyle. "Two clicks for affirmative."

"Will do," said Blackjack as he closed the door of the now empty cargo hold.

Coyle took off and headed Southwest along the mountain ridge.

Blackjack and his team left the supplies in the jungle, then grabbed their weapons and packs as they headed out in search of the pilots. Blackjack only had twelve Montagnard with his SOG team. It was a supply run, so he didn't think he needed more. Now, he wished he had the whole village of Montagnard. While there was no way of knowing exactly what he and his men were facing, Blackjack estimated that there was at least an enemy company guarding the bridge, maybe more. He and his men were outnumbered more than five to one, plus the pilots' could have been wounded from ejecting from their planes and could need to be carried. In all, it was not a good situation by a long shot.

As Coyle prepared to fly over the next ridge, he knew he would be entering the lion's den. While the Super Sabres were capable of reaching Mach 1.4 and the Thunderchiefs exceeding Mach 2, his single-engine prop plane had a maximum speed of 144 mph. He would be an easy target for the overabundance of enemy anti-aircraft weapons in the river valley. Even small arms fire was a threat. His only hope was to hug the contours of the terrain and keep moving.

Since the increase in traffic on the Ho Chi Minh Trail and the addition of anti-aircraft emplacements, the CIA technicians offered to outfit his PC-6 with two underwing pylons that could carry various armaments including rockets, bombs, and napalm canisters. Coyle declined. The problem was weight. The PC-6 could only carry an additional 2,300 pounds beyond the pilot and fuel. Two Mark 81 bombs weighed 500 pounds and two napalm canisters weighed over one thousand pounds. The addition of armament would dramatically reduce the amount of cargo he could carry which was the point of the supply missions to the SOG and Montagnard. Instead, Coyle drew on his experience in developing the AC-47 gunship. Since the aircraft had its wings on top, he asked for an M60 machine gun to be rigged on a pedestal and locked down in a fixed position so that it fired out the cargo door. The only problem was that he needed to fly the aircraft while firing the machine gun. He had them rig a shaving mirror above the control panel and a remote weapon trigger on the plane's steering wheel. It was a weird set up, but it worked. Like its big brother's miniguns, the single-barreled machine gun would be aimed by the pilot steering the aircraft. It took a few practice runs for Coyle to get used to aiming the gun with a mirror and steering wheel, but he got the hang of it. It was his own little gunship. He even had the CIA tech guys rig up a back door release so he could open the door in mid-flight without leaving the pilot's seat. The entire weapon system weighed under 200 pounds with a full load of ammunition. Coyle thought it was a good compromise.

As he flew over the ridge, he wished he had taken the CIA technicians on their offer for wing pylons. He knew they probably would make little difference against the NVA air defense, but he felt vulnerable and was less confident than usual. Everyone always thought that veteran pilots were invincible because of their experience. But what nobody wanted to talk about, especially the veteran pilots, was that precise knowledge about the enemy's capabilities could be a hindrance and a demoralizer. Sometimes, ignorance was bliss. Coyle was flying into a world of hurt and he knew it. He found it ironic that just a few weeks earlier, he had flown a full-blown gunship into a valley very similar to the river valley below. Although the AC-47 was more difficult to manure, it was far better protected with its three miniguns, than the PC-6 he was now flying. One hit from an exploding flack shell would instantly rip his little plane apart. There would be no surviving that kind of devastation.

Knowing that he could only fire his weapon out of the right side of his aircraft and that both downed pilots were on the western bank of the river, Coyle was downriver from the bridge. He suspected that there would be anti-aircraft weapons on both sides of the river. He also calculated that the majority of enemy troops hunting for the two pilots would be on the western side because that is where the smoldering wreckage was located. He knew the odds of using his machine gun to take out an anti-aircraft gun emplacement would be slim to none. But he thought he might have a decent chance at hitting some of the enemy troops or at least driving them to cover to buy the pilots more time.

As he descended into the valley, Coyle radioed the closest downed pilot and told him to click his radio button twice when his plane passed his position, then click for every ten yards his position was from the river. Out of breath, Blackjack and his team had made it to the top of the ridge just in time to see Coyle begin his run through the valley. The mountainside exploded with gunfire and anti-aircraft fire sending streams of tracer towards Coyle's plane. "Shit! Now we're gonna have three pilots to rescue if he's lucky enough to survive being shot down," said Blackjack.

As planned, Coyle didn't fly straight down the valley. He tried every trick in the book and a few not in the book. The anti-aircraft guns were on both sides of the river. Once he had entered the gauntlet, the anti-aircraft gunners couldn't fire at his plane without hitting their own troops. But that didn't stop the ground troops from firing their small arms at the American plane.

Coyle released the cargo door. It slammed open on its rails. He opened fire with the M60 and used the mirror to adjust the fire. His bullets strafed the banks of the river where the enemy troops were firing. Many dove for cover, others stood their ground and kept firing at his plane. Coyle had no idea if he had hit any of the enemy troops, but he figured it really didn't matter. There were too many of them to make a difference with just one poorly-aimed machine gun. Still, the chaos helped.

Multiple shells punched through-and-through holes in the skin of his aircraft and spider-webbed windows, but nothing exploded inside the aircraft and the engine kept running at full speed.

A SAVAGE JOY

As he passed a point a half mile down the river, he heard the clicks of the downed pilot's radio. He identified the position and radioed it back to Blackjack.

Knowing where the first pilot was located, Blackjack and his team traversed the mountain ridge to avoid contact with the bulk of the enemy troops. They knew the pilot didn't have much time before the NVA reached his position. But the jungle was dense and the footing was downright lousy with loose rocks and a steep slope. A twisted or broken ankle by any of the team members could put the team and the pilot in jeopardy. They moved as fast as they could, but not crazy. A measured pace.

Coyle flew farther down the river and the ground fire slackened, then went silent. He had made it. He radioed the second downed pilot and gave him the same instructions. But unlike the first pilot, the second pilot did not respond as Coyle passed the smoldering wreckage of the downed aircraft. Coyle wondered if the pilot was dead or possibly unconscious. The other possibility was that he had turned his radio off to keep from being discovered by the enemy. But surely, he would have turned it back on when he heard his plane's engine. Coyle figured that the pilot had not been captured. It was possible, but not probable. He was much farther from the bridge where the ground troops were stationed. But there was always the possibility of a patrol. Blackjack and his team could be walking into a trap when they went to find the second pilot. Coyle decided there were too many variables to know for sure. There was only one way to know what happened to the pilot… find him.

A couple of hundred yards beyond the wreckage, Coyle spotted an exposed sandbar on the west side of the river. Much of the sandbar was covered with gravel and a few small rocks. "Are you that stupid?" said Coyle to himself.

For Coyle, it was a calculation. The life of one CIA pilot versus the downed fighter pilot and maybe the SOG team and Montagnard warriors. "Yep, you're that stupid," he again said to himself.

He turned his plane around and steered toward the sandbar. "Dumb, Coyle. Really dumb," he said to no one.

Coyle knew the problem was not the gravel or even the small rocks. The PC-6 landing struts and wheels would probably handle them. It was patches of wet sand that concerned him. If one wheel hit a patch of sand, it would dig in and slow the wheel's momentum. With one wheel slower than the other, the plane could turn uncontrollably and tumble snapping the wings off and probably killing him. As he approached the sandbar, he drove the thought of failure from his mind and let his instincts take over. While the sandbar was long it was short for a runway. Coyle would have to time his landing perfectly. As the aircraft descended, Coyle cut power to the engine to slow it even more. They would be no touch-and-go for this landing. It was all or nothing.

The aircraft's wheels touched down on the sandbar kicking up gravel that pelted the underside of the fuselage. The plane rolled forward across the sandbar. Coyle saw the end of the sandbar approaching quickly. He was running out of runway. There was nothing more he could do about it, then disaster… Coyle saw a patch of wet sand directly in front of his aircraft. He steered using the aircraft's rudder. It was too little too late. The left wheel hit the patch of sand and he felt the aircraft turning sideways as if someone had nailed down the wheel. "Oh, shit," he said quietly.

The aircraft's momentum carried forward as it turned. The wheel was caught in the sand. The aircraft tipped and its right-wing dug into the gravel sending sparks into the air. But the plane did not flip. Instead, it stopped, then tipped back righting himself. The left wheel slammed down. Coyle wondered if it was damaged, but the plane was surprisingly level. He jumped out of the cockpit and examined his plane. It was intact. He laughed to himself and said, "See! Nothing to worry about."

Coyle heard a rustling in the jungle across the river. He saw leaves moving as if someone or multiple someones were sliding down the mountain slope. "Out of the frying pan and into the fire," said Coyle.

He climbed back into his aircraft and retrieved the M60 from its podium. He climbed back out and aimed at the moving jungle across the river. Then... the downed pilot appeared and said with his hands up, "I'm an American."

"No, shit," said Coyle. "Why the hell didn't your respond when I radioed you?"

"I kept my radio off so the enemy couldn't hear it."

"Yeah, well... you're an idiot. Get your ass in the plane."

The pilot waded across the river and climbed into the cargo area as Coyle replaced the M60 on its post. Coyle fired up the engine and taxied to the farthest point on the sandbar. He turned the plane and locked the brakes. He powered up the engine as far as it could go. The aircraft shook. He released the wheel brakes and the plane jolted forward. Landing was one thing, taking off was another. Coyle kept the plane moving forward and didn't try to take off until the very last second before he ran out of sandbar. His wheel touched the river as the plane lifted off. "You're pretty good at this," said the downed pilot.

Coyle just laughed as the plane gained altitude and he headed for the ridge. He radioed Blackjack and informed him that there was one less package to pick up. Blackjack had his hands full and double-clicked back his response. He was grateful that he and his team only needed to retrieve one of the pilots. Even so, it was still a risky mission.

Before turning down the mountain slope, Blackjack and his team had stopped one hundred yards short of where they thought the downed pilot closest to the bridge was located. If the NVA had already reached the pilot's position, they didn't want to meet them head-on. Instead, they would hit them in the flank as the team approached the valley floor. The SOG and Montagnard would be uphill from the enemy and even in the modern age of warfare that was still an advantage. Soldiers on the downhill side of a battle tended to misjudge their attackers' positions as they approached and undershoot. The charging Montagnard with their long knives drawn would unnerve the NVA.

The Montagnard preferred hand-to-hand combat. They felt surer of killing their enemy with their knives and arrows than with bullets from a rifle. Bullets were magical things and the Montagnard warriors didn't always know where they went when they entered the enemy's body. With a knife or poison-tipped arrow, they were sure their enemy had been mortally wounded or already dead.

During skirmishes with the enemy, the SOG would stop short of the melee and lay down a base of fire on the enemy while the Montagnard would press forward with the attack. Even though the SOG team had trained the Montagnard on how to use their rifles, the SOG team had more powerful weapons and better aim.

As they reached the valley floor and heard the river, they slowed. Through the dense jungle, they could see an NVA platoon already in the area and approaching where they believed the pilot was hiding. Blackjack ordered his men to wait and not reveal their position until the majority of the enemy patrol was squarely in front of them. Using hand signals, Blackjack designated that his SOG team would fire first, then the Montagnard would charge. He didn't want any of the warriors hit by friendly fire. Blackjack and the SOG team quietly moved closer and took up firing positions using trees and boulders to provide cover and stabilize their weapons as they aimed at the enemy passing below them.

On Blackjack's signal, they opened fire with a terrifying barrage. The Montagnard were disciplined and waited for Blackjack's signal. He was a great warrior and they respected him.

The NVA were completely caught off guard. Five went down in the first few seconds of the battle. But the SOG didn't stop. They kept pouring on their gunfire until guns ran empty. When their guns went silent, all five SOG team members tossed grenades at the clusters of VNA creating chaos and forcing them to keep their heads down. Blackjack gave the signal for the Montagnard to attack.

Most of the NVA were behind cover and were not prepared for the Montagnard charge. When they looked up, they saw the warriors with their long knives out and bows drawn. Arrows in the head and chest took out another two NVA. If the arrow didn't kill them, the fast-acting poison surely would. Terrified at the oncoming warriors several NVA broke and waded into the river trying to reach the opposite side. Others retreated down the riverbank toward the bridge. Those that remained met the full force of the Montagnard. A few got off shots from their rifles and killed one of the Montagnard.

One warrior ran into a group of three NVA raising their weapons to kill him. The warrior grabbed one soldier, slicing his arm with his long knife, forcing him to drop his rifle. The warrior whipped the soldier around and stuck the tip of his knife in the soldier's back forcing him to move forward toward the other two soldiers. Using the unarmed soldier as a human shield, the warrior closed his distance on the other two soldiers. They had no choice but to kill their comrade. It was too late. The warrior pushed the dying soldier on top of one of the remaining soldiers knocking him off his feet, then pivoted to slash his knife across the other soldier's face blinding him. The soldier dropped his rifle to grab his cut face. The warrior plunged his long knife into the wounded soldier's throat finishing him off. As he pulled his knife out of the soldier, he threw it into the left side of the chest of the remaining soldier piercing his heart. He dropped dead. The warrior again removed his knife and began the search for his next victim.

Another Montagnard pounced on an enemy soldier and hacked him to death with his long knife. As he prepared for one last strike from his knife, an enemy bullet blew off his hand holding the knife. The enemy soldier on the ground knew he had been mortally wounded by the warrior's blade. He pulled the pin on a grenade and blew himself up and the one-handed Montagnard. Both died.

Blackjack could see that while the warriors were ferocious in their attack, they were outnumbered and the NVA would soon regroup. There was no time to waste. He signaled the SOG team members to follow him and headed upriver to find the pilot. They moved through the jungle to keep out of sight. The mountainside was steep and made the going difficult. As they were moving past a tree, they heard, "Hey, I'm here," from an unseen voice.

They looked uphill and saw the pilot lying on his back with his leg tangled in the twisted roots of a tree. They moved beside him and Blackjack said, "We'll get you out of here."

The other SOG member kept guard as Blackjack tended to the pilot.

"I think I may have broken my ankle. It hurts like hell. Damned tree roots," said the pilot.

Blackjack examined the pilot's leg and saw that his ankle was at an impossible angle. "Yeah, it's broken. This is gonna hurt."

"No, wait," said the pilot.

"No time," said Blackjack as he reached down and pulled the pilot's leg out of the roots.

The pilot screamed in pain. "Suck it up or you're gonna get us killed," said Blackjack.

"Okay, okay. I'm sorry."

"Don't be. Just shut up," said Blackjack making a splint from fallen tree branches and the shoestrings from the pilot's boot. He used his knife to shorten the branches to the correct length.

As Blackjack straightened the ankle, the pilot stifled his scream. "That's better," said Blackjack. "Almost done."

Blackjack wrapped the shoelaces around the broken ankle and the shortened tree branches. He tied off the laces and said, "It ain't pretty, but that should get you back to the airstrip." Blackjack ordered the SOG team member to help the crippled pilot climb the mountain slope and wait for him at the top of the ridge. Blackjack headed back to check on the rest of the team.

By the time he got back, the battle was over. The surviving NVA had fled. The Montagnard had lost three warriors and two more were severely wounded. It was a big price to pay for two pilots, but it was done. He ordered the Montagnard to gather their dead and wounded. The SOG team would cover their retreat back up the mountain.

It was early morning before Blackjack and the team made it back to the new airfield. Coyle and the other pilot were waiting beside the PC-6. "Did you find him?" said Coyle.

"Yeah. We found him. Broken ankle but he's alive," said Blackjack.

Coyle could hear the sadness in his voice and said, "And your men?"

"My guys are okay, but the Montagnard lost three, plus two pretty shot up. Can you take them when you take the pilots?"

"No problem. I'll see that they're cared for."

"I appreciate it. Now, if you don't mind… I need some shut-eye. It's been a long couple of days. I'll see you next trip, Coyle."

Coyle nodded as Blackjack disappeared into the jungle.

January 26, 1965 – Washington, DC, USA

Having lost his bid for the presidency, former Vice President Richard Nixon kept himself in the public eye, by expressing his opinions on the war in Vietnam and at times criticizing the Johnson administration's strategy. He had a manner of explaining difficult concepts and policies. It made him seem like an expert on the wars in Southeast Asia and a man with a plan that could work. Nixon was explaining the Domino Theory in a way that the average American could understand while slowly but surely fighting his way back into politics and preparing for a potential future run against Johnson for the presidency.

During an interview with reporters, Nixon said, "I believe it is time for the American people to quit being defensive or apologetic about our role in Vietnam. We are not the aggressors in Vietnam. They are. What our policy is in Vietnam, is not to extend American influence, but simply to defend the right of people to be free and select the kind of government they want. It is the Chinese that are embarked on an aggressive course of action. And what it gets down to is this… unless we find a way to stop indirect aggression in a place like Vietnam our failure to do so will be the green light for the hardliners in communist China who are presently in the majority and the hardliners in the Soviet Union who are in the minority, to step up indirect aggression in the Congo, South America, and all over the world knowing that when the U.S. has a challenged cause we will not step in to stop it because of the risk of war. We must let the communists in China and the Soviet Union know that the United States will not stand by and allow any power, however great, to take over another country by direct or indirect aggression."

January 27, 1965 - Saigon, South Vietnam

As incredible as it was to believe, General Nguyen Khanh and the Armed Forces Council threw another coup to overthrow the civilian government of Tran Van Houng. It was a bloodless coup. People were hardly alarmed during the days when a coup was thrown by one side or the other. They simply locked themselves in their homes for a day or two until things settled down and it was safe to go out. Within a few days, a new prime minister or president would be assigned by the current coup leadership and life would return to normal. And so it was that civilian Nguyen Xuan Oanh came to power in South Vietnam once again as prime minister.

It was the South Vietnamese military that suffered the most. Despite everything that had happened over the years, most of the ARVN soldiers were patriots and anti-communists. They wanted to fight the communists and keep their country free. But with a new government every few months it was hard to know who they were fighting for and the rules they were pledged to follow kept changing.

By the end of January 1965, the ARVN soldiers and field commanders were completely demoralized. While the soldiers would still protect the cities and facilities they were tasked with defending, offensive operations to retake lost territory and villages were almost non-existent. The only offensive missions an ARVN commander was willing to undertake required heavy American air and artillery support. The ARVN troops would surround an enemy position, then wait until the American bombs, rockets, and shells had pulverized the enemy. In most cases, the enemy slipped away avoiding a ground conflict. But if the enemy chose to fight, the ARVN would usually break and run after any serious resistance. It wasn't that the South Vietnamese were cowards as much as they were confused, and morale was at an all-time low. Even their American advisors, who they normally respected more than their own commanders, could not get the ARVN to hold their ground and fight.

If the ARVN not fighting wasn't bad enough, the officials in the American embassy recognized an even more dangerous threat. A few months before the current coup, General Khanh had formed an alliance with the Buddhist Institute headed by Thich Tri Quang. Quang along with other Buddhist leaders was in favor of the neutralization of Vietnam. Ambassador Taylor was concerned with the direction of the current South Vietnamese administration. They seemed to be signaling the only way to end the war was through direct negotiations with the communist leaders in Hanoi. The American ambassador could foresee a situation in which the South Vietnamese government would eventually request that the American military would leave the country. Almost everyone recognized that without the American forces to protect it, South Vietnam would fall to the communists within a matter of weeks. All would be lost as the communist would have accomplished their goal of expanding their revolution into Southeast Asia. And, even worse, America would no longer be seen as a reliable ally in the international community.

Washington D.C., USA

In response to the coup and multiple cables from Ambassador Taylor, Secretary of Defense Robert McNamara and National Security Council director McGeorge Bundy sent a memo to President Johnson. The memo offered the president two options: use the U.S. military to defeat the VC and NVA insurgency or negotiate with the communists to salvage what little can be preserved in the South. Bundy and McNamara believed the first option was the best path. The only member of Johnson's cabinet to disagree with the military option was George Ball, Undersecretary of State. Ball felt it was time for America to withdraw before more damage was done and any escalation of the war including bombing or U.S. troop deployment in Vietnam was reckless. After listening to everyone's arguments, Johnson chose the military option. He drafted and sent a telegram to Taylor in Saigon saying, "The U.S. will spare no effort and no sacrifice in doing its full part to turn back the communists in Vietnam." President Johnson had psychologically crossed the Rubicon.

Vientiane, Laos

On the same day as Khanh's coup in South Vietnam, General Phoumi Nosavan once again tried to seize control of the government in Vientiane, Laos. Nosavan and his co-conspirators were opposed by the forces of General Kouprasith Abhay who supported the government. The armies fought for two days without either gaining the upper hand.

To make matters even more confused, on January 29th a second coup was independently launched by Colonel Bounleut Saycocie who also wanted to take over the government. After taking over Vientiane's radio station and a few infrastructure facilities, Saycocie agreed to a meeting with Kouprasith, then suddenly withdrew his troops and put himself and his army under the command of Kouprasith. Kouprasith then used Saycocie's additional forces to defeat Nosavan's army and control was returned to the original government.

Washington D.C., USA

When word reached the White House of the two coups in Laos at the same time as the coup in South Vietnam, McNamara was sitting with Bundy in a conference room going over possible troop unit assignments suggested by the Joint Chiefs. Bundy uncharacteristically burst out in laughter. "George, I fail to see in humor in this situation," said McNamara.

"Don't you see the absurdity of the whole thing? It's just a bunch of insane asylums run by clowns in uniform," replied Bundy.

"And we're the ringleader?" said McNamara.

"You said it, Bob."

"Regardless. What in the hell are we gonna do?"

"I see only one thing to do."

"And what's that?"

"We ignore the clowns and fight the communists ourselves."

"I'm no longer sure that South Vietnam and Laos are worth fighting for."

"I suppose it depends if we win."

"So, what do we do, just let the ARVN sit on their asses?"

"It's not as bad as all that. The ARVN can still protect the cities and their bases while our guys are freed up to go out and fight the bad guys. That's what we are good at anyway."

"And guarding stuff is what they're good at?"

"Kinda, yeah. I am not saying we can't use the ARVN at some point when things settle down politically."

"That may never happen."

"All the more reason to just let us handle the communists. That's why we are there… to stop the communists. Let's not forget that. If the president actually pulls the trigger and sends our troops in, I say we gotta be ready to fight independently of the ARVN. It's the only way to be sure of what we're doing. We can't trust our allies in Southeast Asia anymore, Bob."

"What about Laos?"

"It's the same. The Royal Laotian Army can hold the capital in Vientiane like they've been doing in between coups."

"That's not funny, George."

"It is a little. Anyway, the Montagnard have been doing most of the fighting in the mountains. Our SOG guys and the CIA supply them and control them. That's not going to change. We can still cut off supplies and weapons on the Ho Chi Minh Trail. We just don't rely on the regular troops in Laos. When you think about it, it's not a bad idea, Bob."

"I don't know how we're gonna sell the president on it. He still believes 'them Asian boys should be doing all the fighting.'".

"You'll figure it out. You always do. That's why we like you so much. Keeps the pressure off us mere mortals," said Bundy patting McNamara on the back.

"You're really pissing me off, George."

"I gotta laugh, so I don't cry."

The Beast Cometh

Camp Holloway, South Vietnam

Located just two miles east of Pleiku on Route 19, Camp Holloway was the new home of 81st Transportation Company. The 81st had been issued Bell UH-1 Iroquois helicopters nicknamed "Hueys" to replace their Piasecki H-21 Shawnees nicknamed "Flying Bananas." The Hueys had a thirty percent higher cruising speed and range, but they also carried fewer troops. In addition, the one main rotor helicopters had a 12,600 ft. service ceiling. The Hueys were true workhorses better suited for the mountains and jungles of Vietnam.

Scott Dickson, now a pilot, was returning from a ground support mission. It turned out to be a big ball of nothing like many of the missions the 81st was ordered to fly. The Hueys were the army's war wagons, good for hauling their troops around and providing air cover if needed. Everyone figured it was better to have some helicopter gunships flying overhead than to get into deep shit without them. At times, Scott felt like some of the missions were a waste of his talent and putting him and his crew in needless peril. The VC hated the American helicopters and took potshots at them with their small arms whenever the chance presented itself. Even the farmers would join in sometimes. A few weeks ago, Scott's crew chief had been hit in the thigh by a farmer's potshot. *Almost hit the guy's balls*, thought Scott. The door gunner killed the farmer and his water buffalo for good measure. There was little accountability for killing civilians, even unarmed. The American airmen were supposed to have higher moral and ethical standards than their South Vietnamese counterparts. Scott didn't like to see civilians hurt or killed, but this guy had clearly asked for it. He said nothing in the way of a reprimand and didn't report the shooting of the farmer and his water buffalo to his CO.

Staring out the bug-splattered windshield as he landed, Scott saw a familiar face – the man that claimed to be his real father, Tom Coyle standing by the runway. Scott wasn't thrilled Coyle had saved his life several times. He felt that accepting Coyle somehow betrayed the man that raised him, his mother's husband Colonel Dickson who had passed away. Scott knew it wasn't fair to Coyle, but his feelings were complicated, and he didn't feel the need to apologize for them.

Scott shut down his engine and turned everything over to his co-pilot. He stepped from the aircraft and Coyle approached. "You're getting pretty good at flying those things."

"Those things?" said Scott.

"Never could get used to them... helicopters."

"Did you ever fly one?"

"Yeah. A few years back. Let's just say it was a short relationship."

"You're good at those... short relationships."

"Ouch."

"Sorry, stupid mission. No VC."

"I'd say that's a good mission. Nobody shooting at you."

"Yeah, well... that's the difference between you and me, among other things."

"Let me start over again. I was hoping to take you to lunch. A couple of pork banh mi and some cold bottles of orange Nehi. Whatever you want. I'm buying. We can shoot the shit. Maybe get to know each other a little better."

"I appreciate it, but I think I'll pass. I'm not in a talking mood right now."

"I can understand that. Maybe another day. I'm down the road at the Pleiku Air Base. They just moved our operations there."

"They?"

"My bosses."

"At the CIA?"

"Can't really talk about it."

"I know the feeling. You have a nice day, Tom," said Scott walking off.

"You too, Scott," said Coyle feeling a little rejected.

Northern Mountains, Laos

Reconnaissance flights over Laos originated from air bases in Thailand. Capable of reaching speeds in excess of Mach 1.7, the McDonnell RF-101A Voodoo was outfitted with six high-resolution cameras in its nose and photographed the Ho Chi Minh Trail with high-speed overflights. The reconnaissance flights were just as dangerous as the bombing sorties with several Voodoos being shot down and crashing in the dense mountain jungles of Laos. But when things went well, the images they brought back were priceless to the Defense Intelligence Agency responsible for determining the flow of arms and supplies into South Vietnam by way of the Ho Chi Minh Trail.

Washington DC, USA

Once again, McNamara was tasked with giving the president bad news. Recently, it seemed like a daily occurrence and was wearing on McNamara. He always tried to soothe the president's mood with some good news, but it was getting harder to find as the war rolled on. Nothing good was happening in Vietnam, so he began looking for good news in other parts of the world just to maintain some sort of balance. It didn't work. Johnson was obsessed with Vietnam and Laos and took the bad news hard sinking into his own depression. His concerns over the sending of American troops to Vietnam kept him awake at night and the loss of sleep just made him more irritable. Johnson was beginning to understand that there was no way out of the Southeast Asia quagmire. It was his cross to bear whether he liked it or not.

McNamara briefed Johnson on a report from the U.S. Defense Intelligence Agency on the Ho Chi Minh Trail. The DIA analysts concluded that during the 1965 Laotian dry season the enemy was moving thirty trucks per day equaling ninety tons of supplies and weapons over the Ho Chi Minh Trail and into South Vietnam. Enemy improvements to the trail system included opening new routes that would connect to the Sihanouk Trail in Cambodia were having a dramatic effect on the trail's efficiency and capacity. The quantity of supplies transported in 1965 almost equaled the combined total for the previous five years.

During the year, interdiction of the enemy's supply system had become one of Johnson's top priorities, but operations against it were complicated by the limited forces available and Laos's supposed neutrality owing to the Geneva Conference of 1954 and 1962. U.S. and North Vietnamese interference in Laotian affairs was forbidden by the treaty. Since both sides secretly violated the treaty's articles, it led to a mutual policy of each ignoring the other, at least in the public eye. The North Vietnamese continued to protect and expand their supply conduit through Laos. They also continued to support their Pathet Lao allies in their war against the central government in Laos. U.S. intervention came in the form of a CIA-backed clandestine army in its fight with the communists, constant bombing of the trail, and support for the Lao government.

Listening to McNamara recount the statistics in the report, Johnson's mood soured. "Bob, I don't understand how that can possibly be true. What happened to Operation Barrel Roll? Are you telling me that it's actually had a negative effect on stopping the enemy's supply chain?" said Johnson.

"No. I'm not saying that. From all accounts, Barrel Roll has had a positive effect on curtailing existing enemy supply routes. The problem is that North Vietnamese have dramatically increased their efforts in both transporting troops and supplies into the South," said McNamara. "It's like they turned the tap all the way open and the South is getting flooded.

"So, why the hell can't we stop them?"

"I think eventually we will, but it's going to take time and more effort."

"More effort? How much is enough to whip their commie asses?"

"Honestly, I don't think anyone knows for sure. But I know that you can't win a battle if you don't fight it. We've got to hang in there and do whatever is necessary."

"Okay, that's fine. Now, answer my question. How much is enough to win?"

"I don't know."

"Well, if you don't know, Bob, then who does? You're my damned Secretary of Defense."

"It's like a bad fog on a highway, Mr. President. We don't know what's ahead, but we have to keep going if we ever want to reach our destination."

"That's not very reassuring, Bob."

"I know, Mr. President. But it's the truth."

"So, what do we do? How do we keep moving forward?"

"We could increase our interdiction efforts with more bombing sorties and ground missions in Laos. That will undoubtedly put more pressure on the North Vietnamese."

"So, we continue with Barrel Roll?"

"In Northern Laos, yes. The Joint Chiefs are working on a new operation for Southern Laos called, 'Steel Tiger.' It will focus on the passes that the North Vietnamese are using to crossover into South Vietnam. The North Vietnamese have transported such a large quantity of supplies and weapons that they are a victim of their own success. They can only push so much through the passes with their existing infrastructure. The passes are becoming a bottleneck. The Joint Chiefs see that as an opportunity to hit them hard."

"I like the sound of that... hitting them hard. It's what I've been asking for."

"Yes, Mr. President. And everyone is trying to get you what you want. Steel Tiger and Barrel Roll combined should have an intense effect on the enemy's supply trail."

"When can I see the details?"

"In a couple of weeks. They're still collecting and analyzing intelligence. They want to make sure they get it right."

"Alright. But let's not let perfect become the enemy of good enough. We need to do something pronto before we lose any more of the South to the Viet Cong."

"I understand that, Mr. President. I assure you we are working as fast as possible on a credible solution."

As McNamara left the Oval Office, he began to wonder if accepting the position of Secretary of Defense had been a wise move. He wanted to serve his country, but it didn't feel like he was doing any good. He yearned for the days when he was president of Ford Motor Company and all he had to worry about was making enough profit to satisfy the company's investors. He too was in the middle of the quagmire and felt like there was no way out. McNamara was no longer confident that sending American troops into Vietnam would be successful and win the war. But until he had a better idea, he would keep his doubts to himself and that was Robert McNamara's biggest mistake. The better idea remained elusive.

New York, USA

The anti-war movement was growing, and Karen Dickson's photographs were growing along with it. She had left the financial security of being a photojournalist for a newspaper and had struck out on her own. She no longer had the protection of her editor and the newspaper's legal team. If something went south, it was all on her. In exchange, she had gained her freedom. She could photograph who and what she wanted without concern of being censured by corporate America. She could sell to whomever she chose. She missed her paycheck and often lived off Campbell soup and peanut butter and jelly sandwiches until she sold her next photograph. Her New York apartment was the size of a postage stamp and in a rough neighborhood, but the rent was cheap. She didn't mind. She knew she could ask her mother for a small loan to hold her over, if necessary, but she resisted the temptation and decided early on that she was going to deal with her problems and not offload them on her family and friends. She was growing and she was confident she would find a way to make it through.

The founders and organizers of the various movements learned to trust her and allowed her to photograph their meetings as long as she didn't reveal the plans for their protests. She didn't. But at the same time, she would not prejudice her photographs on their behalf. She prided herself on capturing the reality of the situation no matter which side benefited or was damaged. The truth was the higher cause to her.

She had been roughed up several times as the police and the protestors clashed. But it was still early in the war and nothing was too serious. She couldn't afford a doctor's visit or a trip to the emergency room, so she learned to bandage her wounds. A kitchen towel filled with ice kept the swelling down and butterfly bandages closed the more serious cuts. She didn't hold back. She had to be in the center of what was happening to get the shot... to find the truth of the moment.

She was slowly developing a network of newspaper and magazine editors that would buy her photos. Many of the photojournalists employed by newspapers and magazines were hesitant to place themselves between the police and the protestors. Karen wasn't, plus she always seemed to know when and where the protests were taking place and who was behind them. She was becoming a valuable resource and could be relied on. To keep in her good graces, many of the editors offered her paid photo assignments which she turned down unless she was getting low on soup cans or peanut butter. She wanted to always be available for an unplanned protest or newsworthy event concerning the war.

She often thought of Scott, her twin brother serving as a helicopter pilot in South Vietnam. He went into harm's way daily, and she feared for him even though she believed he could handle himself. She had given up on religion and prayer with it, but she believed her thoughts could somehow comfort and protect the people she loved. It was a stupid concept really, but she hung on to it despite logic. Everyone needed something to believe in when times got dark. Karen was no different.

The protests against the war were increasing in number and attendance. In 1965, there would be three times as many protests as the previous year and the audiences were growing exponentially. The rhetoric of the protest speakers was growing more intense as they accused the Johnson administration and the Pentagon of lying to the American public about the war. They weren't wrong, but their evidence was flimsy.

The police were usually outnumbered many times over and that just made them more aggressive as they attempted to control the crowds through intimidation. Snarling and snapping police dogs were a particularly strong deterrent when things got out of hand at a demonstration. But most of the protests were still peaceful even when large. That wouldn't last. As the war grew more intense, so did the protests.

There was a rumor that Johnson was going to send the Marines to Vietnam. The movement organizers believed sending in troops would galvanize the American public, the majority of which still trusted their government and supported the war effort. The organizers were biding their time and growing their movements daily. They armed themselves with their own team of lawyers attempting to sue the government for not telling the truth and undermining the will of the people. Soon, they believed, everything would explode out onto the streets and the government would be forced to listen. They weren't wrong, but their timing was off. It would take a lot to turn the American people against their government. They were still naïve and believed in America's superiority when it came to the moral high ground. They wanted it to be true.

At night families would gather around the television as Dad watched the nightly news and Mom finished making dinner. Walter Cronkite was one of the first broadcast journalists on American television. He became the anchorman and managing editor of the CBS Evening News which expanded its nightly news show from fifteen minutes to a half hour. It was considered a bold move by the other network executives that felt it would be impossible to hold the interest of the average American beyond fifteen minutes. They were wrong and Cronkite quickly became America's favorite. Americans trusted Walter Cronkite.

When images of American advisors fighting alongside ARVN troops appeared on television, parents were required to answer the questions of their young children and belligerent teenagers. It wasn't easy. Most Americans were not well-informed on what was happening and why American soldiers and pilots were fighting halfway around the world. It was the communists trying to take over the world and our boys were there to stop them and keep America safe. That was the go-to answer. But the parents knew it was more complicated than that, they just didn't know why or how. Americans would remain in the dark a while longer, but the day of reckoning was coming.

Northern Mountains, Laos

A well-worn caravan of Russian-made GAZ-51 trucks weaved their way through the switchbacks of the Laotian mountains. A triple-canopy jungle and camouflage on their roofs made the trucks invisible to the American reconnaissance jets that flew overhead several times a day. It was a deadly game of hide-and-seek with the North Vietnamese hiding and the American fighters seeking.

The driver of the lead vehicle was Chau, late thirties, attractive. She knew the way better than most and was trusted by her commander. Chau was from a small village near Lao Cai in the Northern Highlands. She had long black hair that she kept tucked under the hat she had been given as part of her uniform. When the day's work was done, she would let her hair fall and untangle it with a small comb she carried in her rucksack. Like so many Vietnamese women, she was proud of her hair and plucked out any strands that had turned grey.

Twenty years ago, she had lived with an American named "McGoon" in Hanoi. She liked him, maybe even loved him, but would never mention the relationship to her communist comrades who would see her as a traitor. They didn't understand that things were different back then and snagging a foreigner was considered good luck. It was her secret and she kept it well. After McGoon had died, she and her housemate, Nguyet, McGoon's other lover, left the bungalow they had called home for so many years. The French had lost the war and the communists were coming to take over Hanoi. The girls were in their late teens and didn't know politics, but they had heard the stories of what the communists did to girls that had comforted foreigners. They each went their separate ways to the villages where they grew up, Nguyet in the South and Chau in the North. They would lead boring lives compared to their lives in Hanoi, but they would be protected and have enough to eat. The village elders always took care of their people.

Chau and the other drivers in the caravan were part
of the North Vietnamese 559th Group commanded by
General Phan Trong Tue. The group had six truck
battalions, two bicycle battalions, and a boat battalion.
Eight engineer battalions maintained and expanded the
trail when possible. When the American warplanes
bombed the trail, the engineers and their work crews
would repair the road with amazing speed. They kept
tools and supplies at the forty-five commo-liaison
stations all along the trail. They also built hidden
underwater bridges across streams and rivers at fords
to prevent the trucks' wheels from sinking into the
muddy bottoms.

In all, General Tue commanded 24,000 men and
women. The group's motto was "Build roads to
advance, fight the enemy to travel" which lost
something in translation, but the soldiers and porters
seemed to like it.

By 1965, the Ho Chi Minh Trail had become an
intricate maze of eighteen-foot-wide dirt roads. Unlike
the early years of the trail that used reinforced bicycles
pushed by porters for transportation, trucks did most
of the heavy lifting of weapons and supplies. Many of
the road sections were covered with gravel and
corduroyed with wooden poles where mud would have
bogged down the trucks. There were numerous storage
bunkers, barracks, hospitals, communication bunkers,
and command-and-control facilities used to keep the
army of porters and soldiers moving along the trail.

Chau valued her job. She was good at it and her
village appreciated the money she sent back every two
weeks when she got paid. She kept a little from each
paycheck for herself, mostly to buy the sweets she
loved or oil for her hair at the group's commissary at

the head of the trail. She didn't need much and felt good supporting her village with the cash needed to buy medicine and seeds for their crops.

The weather in Laos came to play a large role both in the North Vietnamese supply effort and in the U.S. and South Vietnamese efforts to interdict it. The monsoon from mid-May to mid-September brought heavy precipitation of over 100-inches of rain. The sky was usually overcast with high temperatures. The dry season from mid-October to mid-March was relatively waterless with lower temperatures. Since the majority of the road network was generally dirt, the bulk of supply transport was conducted during the dry season.

The consolidated time frame for transport on the trail was like open hunting season for the American and South Vietnamese aircraft. Dozens of sorties would be flown each day during the dry season. Hundreds of tons of bombs and rockets would blast craters in the trail and occasionally take out trucks that could be seen through the thick canopy. Much like farmers, the porters faced the risks bravely to harvest what they could before the rains once again slowed the flow of supplies and the ever-present cloud cover frustrated the American and South Vietnamese fighter pilots. It was an endless cycle. A deadly cycle for truck drivers like Chau.

February 7, 1965 - Camp Holloway & Pleiku Air Base, South Vietnam

It was just past midnight, and the air base mess hall was empty... almost. Coyle sat at a table sipping the hot coffee that was available twenty-four/seven. He couldn't sleep and the coffee wasn't helping the situation. He didn't care. Relationships were not Coyle's strong suit although he tried and in the case of his son, Scott, he failed miserably. He couldn't blame Scott for rejecting him. Coyle appeared in his son's life after more than twenty years of Scott believing that another man was his father.

It wasn't Coyle's fault either. He didn't know he had two children. After their brief time together as lovers, their mother had cut Coyle off and never told him of the twins' existence until she needed Coyle's help in protecting her son. Still, it hurt. It wasn't like he wanted to recapture Scott's childhood and play catch or teach him how to fish. It was too late for all that. Coyle just wanted to get to know the man. A man... his son was a man now and a pilot. Weird. He wondered if the desire to be a pilot was somehow in Scott's blood. Something he inherited from Coyle without knowing it. Maybe...

Two miles away at Camp Holloway, Scott and the rest of his aircrew were asleep. A battalion of South Vietnamese Rangers and a thirty-foot-tall barrier of concertina wire protected the perimeter of the airfield and the barracks along with other facilities in the American advisory compound. There were also five regional force companies and an armored company protecting the base. Even with all the personnel, there were only forty guards on duty that night which wasn't much when considering the size of the base and its importance to operations in the Central Highlands.

The airfield's importance was why the leaders in Hanoi had chosen the American base as a target. Although their numbers were growing, there still were not a lot of helicopters in South Vietnam and the American 81st Transportation company had to handle the tremendous load of continually ferrying South Vietnamese troops into battle and giving them air support. Even though the ARVN troops were demoralized because of the government's behavior in Saigon, their commanders, prodded by their American advisors, still carried out patrol-type missions around government and American facilities.

If the VC sapper company of the 409th battalion could destroy the aircraft and kill the pilots, the VC and the NVA would have free rein in the highlands.

Nguyen Thanh Tam, the commander of the 409th battalion, took over command of the VC 30th sapper company he had assigned to the mission. He was honored that his unit was chosen to assault the American air base as a demonstration of the Viet Cong's military progress to the new Soviet Premier Alexei Kosygin who was visiting the North Vietnamese leaders in Hanoi. Tam and his men would do everything in their power to make a good impression. He and his men were serving the revolution, not to mention, that it was the kind of opportunity that could mean a big promotion and propel a commander into the upper echelons of the military or even the communist party leadership.

While the VC sapper company was outnumbered by the South Vietnamese guarding the base, the enemy's numbers were not his biggest concern. It was the wall of wire that surrounded the base that was most daunting. The problem was that his men needed to breach the wire wall without alerting the ARVN guards. Explosives were out of the question. The wire would need to be cut by hand. The concertina wire had been strengthened with oil during its manufacture which made it much more difficult to cut. Thin electrical lines had been strung within the wire loops that would set off alarms if cut or severed by an explosion. He assigned his bravest and best sappers to create the breech. Tam also divided the assault force in two. One team would be responsible for destroying the aircraft while the other team would kill the pilots and their aircrews. Both teams waited in the nearby jungle as the sappers carried out their mission to breach the wire wall.

All was going well until one of the sappers accidentally cut one of the electric alarm lines in the third layer of the concertina wire. It was a disaster and Tam's men prepared for the worst. But the worst didn't happen.

The U.S. Military Police showed no interest in the alarm which frequently went off creating false alarms. They simply looked out at the wire fence from a distance. Everything seemed okay, so they shut off the alarm and carried on with their duties. It was a huge mistake and dereliction of duty. It was a lucky break for Tam's sappers who after a few tense minutes continued their work on cutting through the wire.

Penetrating the last barrier by 1:50 PM, the Viet Cong assault teams rushed through the breach and opened fire with their AK-47s on the guards. Grenades were hurled back and forth as the on-duty guards attempted to fight off the assault and buy time for the off-duty troops to assemble and join the fight.

At Pleiku air base, Coyle heard the grenade explosions in the distance. Realizing what was happening, he ran outside and looked east. The sky was turning red in the direction of Camp Holloway. The airfield was under attack and that meant that Scott was at risk. Coyle ran to the barracks, awakened his crew chief, and said, "Holloway's under attack. Wake the others, get to the gunship, and load the weapons. I want us airborne in five minutes."

"Will do, boss," said the crew chief.

Coyle ran toward the hangar and pushed open the doors revealing the CIA's black gunship. He removed the wheel blocks and climbed into the aircraft's cockpit. He went through a truncated preflight check and fired up the two engines which sputtered, then roared to life. Still without a crew, he taxied the plane out of the hangar and stopped. He looked through the side windshield and saw his co-pilot and crew running across the tarmac toward the plane. Two minutes later, they were loading crates of ammunition stored in the hangar through the aircraft's cargo hold door. They climbed in and started loading the three miniguns. As soon as his co-pilot's ass hit the seat, Coyle reeved the engines and taxied onto the runway. The co-pilot radioed the tower for permission to take off. Without prior notification, permission was denied, and the pilot was ordered to return to the plane's hangar until things could be sorted out. "What should we do?" said the co-pilot.

"Fuck 'em," said Coyle as he gunned the engines and rolled the plane down the runway picking up speed.

A minute later, the CIA gunship was in the air. Coyle banked the plane east and headed for Holloway.

Below at Camp Holloway, the Viet Cong assault team advanced toward the aircraft parked on the airfield and engaged the Rangers guarding them. Dozens of explosive devices had been prepared by the VC engineers. Thanh Minh Tam, a VC Sedang soldier carried eight explosive charges. While under fire from the ARVN Rangers, Tam single-handedly placed all eight charges, alternating to every second aircraft so the explosion would not only destroy the target aircraft but hopefully the aircraft next to it. After placing each charge, he lit the fuse, then ran to the next aircraft. The resulting explosions destroyed or badly damaged sixteen U.S. helicopters. It was a major blow to the Americans.

It was a short trip lasting only a minute to Holloway airfield only two miles away. The gunship gained altitude as it flew, its engines straining to reach 2,000 feet. Coyle could see the gunfire and explosions below. Based on what little he knew about his son, Coyle figured he would be in the middle of the fight below. Scott had turned his helicopter around during the Battle of Ap Bac to save a downed helicopter crew and had left the safety of his helicopter to retrieve the bodies of his fellow soldiers during another rescue operation. Like his stepfather and real father, Scott was no coward. At that moment, despite being incredibly proud, Coyle wasn't sure unbound courage was the best thing for his son. "Launch two flares," said Coyle over the intercom.

The crew chief launched the flares as the aircraft began its pylon turn over the airfield. Coyle continued to ease the plane upward as it approached the proper altitude to accurately aim the miniguns. Illuminated by the powerful flares, the ground lit up and Coyle saw the Viet Cong flooding through the breach in the wire.

"Let me know as soon as the guns are up," said Coyle over the intercom as he checked his altitude, leveled the plane out while continuing the pylon turn, then aligned the gun site on his side window on what he thought was the Viet Cong. He said a silent prayer that he was right and wouldn't accidentally kill his son or any American soldiers when the miniguns were unleashed.

Tam the VC sapper heard the thrum of the engines and looked up into the dark sky just as the two flares ignited. He saw the silhouette of the beast he had heard so much about from his comrades. It seemed like a shadow or ghost. But he knew what it was and whispered in his native dialect, "Dragon."

Tam was brave and willing to sacrifice himself for the good of his country. But he did not want to be devoured by the foul beast. It was bad providence, and he imagined the gods would never allow him in the afterworld even if his spirit survived the demon. Like many of his comrades he broke and ran back toward the breach in the fence with the helicopters he had destroyed burning in the background.

Hearing the explosions from the grenades, Scott and his aircrew, armed with M16s, had made it out of their barracks and were headed toward the airfield. The plan was simple. Get their helicopter in the air. They were too late and watched as their helicopter was blown up, then landed in a fiery heap on the airfield. One of Scott's door gunners took fire from a VC. The gunner was riddled with five bullets. He fell to the ground. Scott picked him up in a firemen's carry while the rest of the aircrew provided covering fire. He carried the mortally wounded gunner into a maintenance hangar where he died two minutes later. The rest of Scott's crew joined him in the hangar where they fought using tool chests and engine parts as cover. They were outnumbered, but in a good defensive position for the moment. He also heard the thrum of the gunship's engines but saw nothing in the sky above as he peered through the open hangar doorway. But the sound was familiar – the engines of an AC-47. A gunship from Pleiku he hoped.

With explosions erupting around the airfield and tracer rounds streaming in every direction, the second VC assault team approached the airmen barracks which were surrounded by three layers of seven-foot-tall stacks of sandbags to prevent shrapnel from mortar attacks from penetrating the barrack's walls. The VC's mission was assassination. They took no prisoners and killed anyone in their sight.

Unable to reach their helicopters, a group of American airmen barricaded themselves inside their barracks and defended their position by firing through the windows and out the front and back doorways. When the Americans saw the onslaught of Viet Cong troops rushing toward their barracks, they closed the reinforced doors and used their metal beds as makeshift buttresses against the doors. The Americans continued to fire out the windows as the enemy surrounded their position.

This is what the Viet Cong hoped would happen. The Americans had trapped themselves. A VC sapper carrying a satchel charge ran toward the front door. As he prepared to pull the wire that started the charge's fuse, a U.S. Military Police soldier shot him in the side. Mortally wounded, the VC sapper stumbled to the ground, but not before pulling the wire on the charge. The charge smoked for a few moments as it lay ten feet from the barracks. The airmen saw the charge and rushed to move away from the front doors of the barracks. The explosion was massive, and flames burst through the barrack's windows and the seams in the doors. But the reinforced doors held, and the sandbag walls protected the Americans from injury.

Above in the gunship, Coyle kept the aircraft aligned with his target – a group of Viet Cong fighting near the airmen's barracks. He had no idea where Scott was or if he was still alive. He drove the thought from his mind and focused on the task at hand. "Guns up," said the crew chief over the intercom.

Coyle immediately fired the aircraft's weapons hearing the high-pitch whirl of the barrels, then a thunderous cacophony of gunfire.

Streams of orange tracer rounds descended from the gunship and licked the ground consuming anything or anyone in their path.

The remaining VC broke and retreated toward the breech in the wire firing their weapons behind them to keep the Americans and the Rangers away.

Tam was almost at the fence when he saw the soldier in front of him consumed by the dragon's fire. The man was torn to shreds and fell in a bloody pile of broken bone and flesh. Tam looked up. The fire was coming from a black hole in the sky, but he knew in his heart it was the beast and that he was next. He slowed to a stop, then dropped to his knees and mumbled his final prayer. But the dragon's tongue moved off toward another group of Viet Cong running for the jungle. For whatever reason, the beast had chosen to let him live. One did not dare question fate, especially when it was in one's favor. Tam climbed to his feet and ran through the hole in the wire. Tears streamed down his cheeks; he was alive.

As the last of his targets disappeared in the jungle, Coyle released the trigger and the miniguns went silent. It was over. There was nothing more that he could do to protect his son. He turned the gunship back west and headed for Pleiku.

Below, Scott looked up into the night sky and watched as the silhouette of the gunship flew away. He couldn't help but wonder about the pilot. Was it Coyle? He felt a deep guilt at the way he had treated his father. He hadn't asked for his help, but it seemed Coyle was there when he needed him most… just like a real father.

Seven U.S. soldiers and airmen were killed and 104 were wounded during the attack on Camp Holloway. The South Vietnamese guards also took heavy casualties. Ten helicopters were destroyed, and another dozen were heavily damaged but would fly again. It was a bad night for the U.S. Army. It was lucky it wasn't worse.

The next day, General Westmoreland, McGeorge Bundy, and Ambassador Taylor flew out to Pleiku, then took a jeep to Camp Holloway to survey the damage. They were shocked by what they saw. The enemy force had been overwhelmingly outnumbered and yet they still caused extensive damage and loss of life. Westmoreland was beginning to question how reliable the South Vietnamese were at protecting American bases and personnel. Bundy called President Johnson and put force behind MACV's request for immediate retaliatory air strikes against North Vietnamese military bases. Bundy said, "The situation in Vietnam is deteriorating and without new U.S. action defeat appears inevitable—probably not in a matter of weeks or perhaps even months, but within the next year or so... There is still time to turn it around, but not much."

It was sobering news for Johnson. He felt like a floor painter that had backed himself into a corner with no way out. The president began to reconsider his position on sending troops now rather than later. Bombing didn't seem to have much of an effect on the North Vietnamese and Viet Cong. Perhaps American boots on the ground would make them think twice.

Later that afternoon, General Khanh arrived in Pleiku to meet with Westmoreland and Bundy. They informed Khanh that recommendations for air strikes against North Vietnam had been made to the President of the United States. Khanh was elated. The Americans were entering the war slowly, but surely. President Johnson's actions would be a major morale boost for the South Vietnamese military. It was a show of confidence that the Americans believed South Vietnam was worth saving.

Flaming Dart

Just twelve hours from the attack on Camp Holloway, Johnson retaliated by ordering Operation Flaming Dart. On February 7th, forty-nine sorties were flown targeting North Vietnamese army bases around Dong Hoi and Viet Cong logistics and communications near the Vietnamese Demilitarized Zone (DMZ).

Because of bad weather, the strike against Vit Thu Lu was canceled. The weather over Dong Hoi wasn't much better. The Americans launched their aircraft from two aircraft carriers – USS Coral Sea and USS Hancock. South Vietnamese junta leader Air Marshal Nguyen Cao Ky was among the pilots that flew for the RVNAF from South Vietnamese airfields.

Dong Hoi was the home of the PAVN 325th Infantry Division. Twenty-Nine A-4 Skyhawks from the USS Coral Sea flew in strike formation at 500 knots as they approached their target.

North Vietnamese anti-aircraft gunners threw a curtain of 37mm shells in front of the attack aircraft. Swatow gunboats on the Kien River fired their automatic weapons into the sky above the PAVN base.

The American attack squadrons VA-153 and VA-155 hit the ARVN barracks with hundreds of 127 mm Mk 32 Zuni rockets and 250-pound bombs. Several barracks exploded killing dozens of PAVN soldiers and wounding hundreds. An ammunition depot was also destroyed sending a huge ball of fire into the sky. More bombs and rockets hit the division command headquarters and the base mess hall. The few Soviet-made vehicles the North Vietnamese possessed were smashed with rockets and bombs making them useless and beyond repair.

During the raid, Lieutenant Edward Dickson's A-4 was hit by anti-aircraft fire but he continued his attack. His missiles took out the division's communications tower and his bombs ignited the fuel tank that powered the base's generator. When he finally ejected from his crippled plane, his parachute failed to open and the American lieutenant plunged to his death.

Right behind the Coral Seas formation of aircraft came 17 A-4s of VA-212 and VA-216 from the USS Hancock. They dropped their ordnance on already burning and smoking camp facilities. A squadron of F-8 Crusaders suppressed fire from the enemy's anti-aircraft emplacements. When the mission was over and the aircraft were returning to their carriers and airfields, an RF-8A reconnaissance aircraft photographed the scene for naval intelligence analysis. The results were disappointing. Considering the amount of ordnance dropped, the attack had destroyed only twenty-two of the 275 buildings in the camp. While some of the buildings were key to operations, they could be rebuilt and reequipped in a matter of days.

February 10, 1965 - Hanoi, North Vietnam

The Soviet government was infuriated that the Americans had chosen to step up bombing attacks on North Vietnam during Soviet Premier Kosygin's stay in Hanoi. As a result, Kosygin and North Vietnamese Prime Minister Pham Van Dong issued a joint statement that highlighted the Soviet's resolve to strengthen North Vietnam's defenses by giving it all "necessary aid and support." It was a major improvement in Soviet and North Vietnamese relations.

Qui Nhon, South Vietnam

On the same day as the Soviet and North Vietnamese announcement, the Viet Cong mounted a retaliatory attack on the four-story Viet Cuong Hotel in Qui Nhon. The hotel had been turned into an enlisted men's billet which was protected by U.S. Military police and South Vietnamese guards. Many of the sixty American servicemen staying in the hotel came from the 140th Transportation Detachment who provided maintenance support for the 117th Assault Helicopter Company based at Qui Nhon Airfield.

At 8:05 PM, the Viet Cong began their assault on the hotel. Their mission was to kill as many Americans as possible by demolishing the hotel. Two VC sappers with explosive charges were killed by machine-gun fire from U.S. sentries on the roof of the hotel. Two South Vietnamese guards were killed by more VC sappers as they charged the hotel's front entrance. Charging into the hotel's lobby, the VC sappers placed one hundred pounds of plastic explosives at the base of a staircase that provided the building's main structural support. When detonated, the massive explosion caused the entire hotel to pancake to the ground killing twenty-one American soldiers and seven Vietnamese civilians. Their mission accomplished, the remaining VC sappers escaped through the city and were hailed as heroes when they returned victorious to North Vietnam.

After the Viet Cong's terrorist attack on the hotel, all American military dependents were ordered to return to the United States. With the increase in VC attacks on American personnel, South Vietnam was too dangerous.

Chanh Hoa, North Vietnam

Refusing to back down from the communist terrorist attacks which he found repugnant and cowardly, Johnson ordered more air strikes by expanding Operation Flaming Dart. The next aerial assault was twice the size of the February 7th mission with ninety-nine fight-bombers from three American aircraft carriers: USS Hancock, USS Coral Sea, and USS Ranger. The mission mix was made up of A-1 Skyraiders and A-4 Skyhawks. The Skyhawks were small which allowed better maneuvering at slower speeds. This trait was ideal for the terrain in Vietnam which often required flying low in mountains and valleys. The aircraft delivered tons of rockets and bombs to their target: the barracks at Chanh Hoa in North Vietnam.

Protecting the fighter-bombers were American F-8E Crusaders and F-4B Phantoms assigned to take out enemy anti-aircraft emplacements around the military base. Using AGM-12 Bullpup air-to-ground missiles and 20mm Vulcan cannons, the aircraft strafed the enemy's anti-aircraft emplacements, killing their gun crews and destroying their weapons.

Enemy anti-aircraft gunners damaged a Coral Sea A-4C, forcing the pilot to make an emergency landing at Da Nang Air Base. Unused bombs still on the wings exploded when the pilot landed at Da Nang, destroying the aircraft. Miraculously, the pilot survived.

Also hit by anti-aircraft fire, Lieutenant Commander Robert Shumaker of VF-154 ejected from his damaged F-8 over Chanh Hoa. When an American rescue team was unable to reach him in time, Shumaker was captured by PAVN troops and taken to a Hanoi prison to sit out the remainder of the war.

Thirty-three F-8s, F-4s, and A-1s protected the attack force from the North Vietnamese MiGs based near Hanoi. Knowing of the massive air cover, the MiGs did not interfere with the American operation.

While U.S. naval aircraft bombed and strafed Chanh Hoa, the RVNAF and the U.S. Air Force (USAF) hit Chap Le. The RVNAF used twenty-eight propeller-driven A-1s in their attack, while the USAF used an equal number of jet-powered F-100 Super Sabres to assault their targets.

The United States' reaction to Communist terrorist attacks was not restricted to just bombing North

Vietnam. With White House approval, the Pentagon also escalated its use of air power when it authorized the use of U.S. jet attack aircraft to engage targets in South Vietnam. The North Vietnamese and Viet Cong considered the use of jets by the Americans as a major escalation of the war. On February 19th, USAF B-57s Canberra tactical bombers conducted the first jet strikes flown by Americans in support of South Vietnamese ground units. On 24 February, the USAF jet bombers struck again, this time breaking up a Viet Cong ambush in the Central Highlands with a massive series of tactical air sorties. The Viet Cong ended up fleeing the battlefield.

While undeterred, the leaders in Hanoi were concerned about how far the Americans would go and if China would keep its word in defending North Vietnam from a U.S. invasion. They continued with their tit-for-tat retaliations against the South and the Americans but wanted the conflict to cool down before the U.S. military overreacted. The steady escalation of the war was what Le Duan wanted. With almost everything going his way, Le Duan did not want a large number of American troops on the ground in South Vietnam. Not yet at least.

Pleiku, South Vietnam

Two weeks had passed since the attack on Camp Holloway. But things were far from settling down. Saigon wanted more air missions against Viet Cong positions. Coyle saw the escalation like the generals of MACV were finally taking the gloves off. While that seemed like a good thing, he wasn't sure. It would mean more missions for Scott once their helicopters were replaced.

Coyle was in the middle of examining a batch of aerial reconnaissance photos that had been sent to him for his opinion. The photos showed a buildup of NVA and VC forces in various areas around the Central Highlands. He didn't like the look of it. There was a knock at the conference room door and a private peeked his head in and said, "Are you, Tom Coyle?"

"Yeah. Why?" said Coyle.

"I got a delivery."

The private set a box on the conference table. Coyle waited until he left before opening it. Inside, were twelve bottles of orange Nehi. Coyle was stunned. There was no note, but he knew who had sent it. He pulled out one of the bottles and examined it like it was a fine bottle of wine. He thought for a moment, then gathered up the photos placing them back in the manilla envelope in which they had arrived. With the photos in one hand and the box of soda bottles in the other, he left the conference room.

On his way back to his room in the officer's barracks, Coyle dropped off the envelope with the photos to the intelligence group that had sent them. Outside the perimeter fence, he purchased a block of ice wrapped in banana leaves from a Vietnamese woman that sold ice to the airmen living at the base. Ice under one arm and box of soda under the other, he walked to his barracks. With both hands full, he used his elbow to open the door to his quarters. He set the box and block of ice down on the floor. He pulled out his knife and used it to chip a large groove in the top of the ice block. He opened the box of soda and removed one of the bottles. He set the bottle in the groove and carefully placed the chipped ice pieces around the bottle. He sat, staring at the bottle for thirty minutes. He touched the glass to ensure it was sufficiently cold. It was. Using the back of his knife blade he pried off the bottle cap. It fell to the floor and rolled under his bed. Coyle knelt, reached underneath, and retrieved the bottle cap. He studied it for a moment, then placed it in his pocket where it would remain for the rest of the war. He sat down on the bed, picked up the bottle, then after a moment of contemplation took a drink. As he had thought, it was the best orange Nehi he had ever tasted.

February 8th, 1965 – Da Nang Air Base

Concerned about Hanoi's new air force of MiG fighters and growing North Vietnamese aggression, Westmoreland wanted more protection for American facilities around South Vietnam. He was particularly concerned about the air bases which seemed to be a regular target for Viet Cong sappers. In addition to once again stepping up perimeter security, the USMC 1st LAAM Battalion based in Okinawa arrived at Da Nang Air Base.

The next day, its HAWK SAMs were operational at the base and were soon expanded to Hill 327 on a ridgeline three miles west of Da Nang Air Base.

Raytheon's MIM-23 HAWK ("Homing All the Way Killer, commonly referred to as "Hawk") was an American medium-range surface-to-air missile capable of shooting down any aircraft in the North Vietnamese air force. However, the complexity of the system, and the quality of tube-based electronics, gave the Hawk's radars a mean time between failures of only forty-three hours. Ongoing maintenance was required to keep the missiles operational.

The Hawk missiles had slender cylindrical bodies with four long chord-clipped delta-wings. Each wing had a trailing-edge control surface that steered the missile while in flight. Each missile weighed 1278 lb. with a 119 lb. high-explosive fragmentation warhead. The missiles had a maximum range of sixteen miles and a maximum altitude of 36,000 feet. When detonated near the target, the missile's warhead produced 4,000 fragments moving at 6,600 feet per second.

The Hawk missiles were transported and launched from the M192 towed triple-missile launcher. Each missile was propelled by a dual thrust motor, with a boost phase and a sustain phase. A parabolic reflector inside the missiles was used to track incoming targets.

It was believed by many that it was the Hawk missile system that prevented the North Vietnamese air force from attacking the Da Nang Air Base during the war.

February 9, 1965 – Washington DC, USA

As a result of the U.S. bombing of North Vietnam, China issued a statement through its embassy in Washington DC that stated, "We warn U.S. imperialism: You are overreaching yourselves in trying to extend the war with your small forces in Indochina, Southeast Asia, and the Far East. To be frank, we are waiting for you in battle array."

While an alarming threat, the Johnson administration did not respond directly. Instead, National Security Adviser Bundy told Senator Mansfield that President Johnson was willing to run the risk of war with China if an invasion of North

Vietnam was deemed necessary. Their conversation became public. Bundy's assertion was not what the Chinese leaders were looking to achieve by their statement.

Moscow, Russia

Desiring to curtail the current trajectory of events in Vietnam, the leaders in Moscow wanted to send a message to the United States about their continued bombing of the North. They also wanted to draw international attention to the bombing in hopes of putting pressure on the Americans.

A mob of 3,000 Asian and Russian students surrounded the U.S. Embassy to protest the American military's bombing of North Vietnam. As Russian police watched from the sidelines, the mob of students smashed over 200 windows in the building. Hoping that the police would eventually intervene, the American Marines guarding the embassy showed restraint and only took aggressive action when any of the students tried to enter the building. Two international journalists were injured during the protest – Adam Clymer of the Baltimore Sun and Bernard Ullman of the Agence-France news agency. After several hours, the Russian police finally intervened and drove the students away from the American embassy when things looked like they might get out of hand and the building might be set on fire by Molotov cocktails that some of the students had brought.

Although unlikely to affect the Johnson administration, the Soviet message had been sent and received.

February 16, 1965 – Vung Ro Bay, South Vietnam

The writing was on the wall. The U.S. Marines were coming to Vietnam and that meant that Granier would be out of a job. MACV had never appreciated the paramilitary teams that Colonel Lansdale had created. The generals saw them as a CIA intrusion on U.S. military forces. When Lansdale left Vietnam, MACV took over the paramilitary teams and let them languish except for a few covert missions. Now that the Marines were coming, MACV would most likely dissolve the teams, and Granier as a team commander would be reassigned, then forced into retirement because of his age.

Granier was not ready to return to America. He knew what would happen. He would become an instructor at CIA headquarters or become an advisor/analyst at the Pentagon. Neither sounded appealing. He liked being in the field. Besides, there was more to do in Vietnam. The war was kicking into high gear, and he wanted to play his part. He wanted to help America win.

He decided to make a preemptive move. He resigned from MACV and rejoined the CIA. There were no age limits with the CIA. If you were an experienced veteran of clandestine operations, the CIA would find you a position that best suited your skills. In Granier's case that meant intelligence gathering and, at times, assassination. He was comfortable with both. The CIA was grateful to have an officer with Granier's experience back in the fold. And the fact that he didn't want a cushy job in Europe but preferred to stay in Vietnam was a bonus.

His first assignment was to gather intelligence on a report from Vung Ro Bay on the eastern coast of South Vietnam. Through heavy cloud cover, an American pilot returning from a mission had spotted what looked like a 100-ton trawler unloading cargo on a beach.

As the sun was setting, Granier was sent to investigate. It only took him an hour by small plane to parachute near the beach. Parachuting at night was always a challenge and Granier was anxious to avoid a tree branch, or a fence post up his ass.

Studying his map after landing safely, Granier used a red-filtered flashlight to determine his location, then selected a nearby hillside where he could observe the beach undetected. Even though he was in friendly territory, Granier carried his sniper rifle. It was like his security blanket and gave him an extra dollop of confidence... as if he needed it.

Approaching the top of the hill, Granier belly-crawled the final ten yards to ensure he wasn't spotted. Settling in, he used his sniper scope to survey the area. Just as the pilot had reported, the crew of a trawler was unloading cargo on the beach. Several civilians armed with AK-47s were picking up the cargo and moving it off the beach using bicycles reinforced with bamboo and equipped with racks. Viet Cong thought Granier. He could not see any flag or name on the trawler but imagined it was North Vietnamese or perhaps Chinese. If the ship was Chinese that would be a much bigger deal with diplomatic consequences. He decided to move closer to get a good look at the crew to determine their nationality and maybe spot some kind of identification on the vessel. Granier was a stickler for accomplishing his mission to the full extent as ordered.

He crawled down the hillside until he reached some dunes. He doubted the crew or porters could see him in the dark, especially with the camouflage uniform and dark face paint he was wearing. To be safe, he kept low only exposing his head and rifle as he once again surveyed the ship and crew. The crew seemed Vietnamese, but in the dark, it was hard to tell for sure. He scanned the bow of the ship and spotted what he thought was the ship's name. Although he couldn't read Vietnamese, he could identify the difference in the shape of the letters from Chinese. It was a Vietnamese vessel. That made things much easier. He wanted a look at what they were unloading. That would be tricky, but he was determined to at least give it a try.

Keeping low, he followed one of the Viet Cong with a bicycle loaded down with a large crate. The Viet Cong were moving the cargo to a nearby road where several trucks were waiting. When the truck was full, it would take off down the road without waiting for the other trucks. Granier imagined this was in case the smugglers were caught. At least some of the cargo would make it to their hideout.

Granier could not afford to be seen. The Viet Cong would scatter, and the ship would most likely make a run for it back out to sea. But he also needed to be sure before reporting back his findings. A pile of crates was sitting in the sand next to the trucks waiting to be loaded. That would be his target. He set down his sniper rifle and pulled out his knife. Granier was good with a knife, but at the moment he would use it as a crowbar to pry open one of the crates. He belly-crawled up to a sandy knoll next to the crates. Two Viet Cong grabbed a heavy crate and carried it to a waiting truck. Granier crawled toward the pile of crates when he saw writing on the side of one of the smaller crates. It was hard to make out in the dark, but he was sure it was Chinese. He opened the crate with his knife and reached inside. The top of the interior of the crate was covered with a thin sheet of wax paper. He tore it open, reached through the hole, and pulled out several shells. It was Chinese small arms ammunition. That was enough evidence. He closed the lid on the crate as best he could without making too much noise, then crawled back to his sandy knoll where he retrieved his rifle.

Ten minutes later, he was back where he had originally landed. He radioed the pilot flying in a big circle and relayed the information about the trawler and its contents.

Just before dawn, a company of South Vietnamese naval commandos landed on the beach in rubber boats using paddles to keep silent. An American destroyer at the mouth of the bay cut off the trawler from escape. The commandos used mortars to attack the crew and the Viet Cong unloading the cargo. Moments later, a fierce firefight ensued, but the commandos were far better armed and outnumbered the enemy forces.

Sitting in the bay, the trawler was an easy target for the RVNAF aircraft that swooped in and staffed the vessel's hull with 20mm cannons and Zuni rockets. Filled with holes and water flooding in, the ship sank in the shallows of the bay. The crew jumped overboard and swam to shore to join their comrades in their fight against the commandos.

Within ten minutes, the entire trawler crew and Viet Cong were dead or wounded. The survivors threw down their weapons. Prisoners were taken and would be interrogated by the South Vietnamese.

Watching from the hillside and munching on the beef jerky he usually kept in his shirt pocket, Granier was satisfied with the operation. He had considered joining in with his sniper rifle but thought better of it. He was a spy once again and needed to keep a low profile. Besides, the South Vietnamese commandos were handling the situation just fine. He walked down the hillside and disappeared into a nearby jungle.

Making his way through the jungle, Granier felt calm and sure of himself. This is what he was supposed to be doing. It was what he knew, and he was good at it. He didn't want to deal with life back in the states. It was too complicated and there were too many rules. He wasn't ready to become civilized again. Vietnam was a strange country, even somewhat barbaric, but Granier had grown used to it over the years. It wasn't home. It was something else. What was it? He wasn't sure, but he didn't care either. It was where he belonged.

Moscow, Russia

The official English-language broadcasting station of the Soviet Union, Radio Moscow, warned the international community that continued U.S. bombing raids on North Vietnam could lead to another World War when it said, "The flames of war starting in one place could easily spread to neighboring countries and, in the final count, embrace the whole world. The responsibility for the dire consequences of such a policy rests with America."

White House – Washington DC, USA

A short time after the Soviet broadcast, President Johnson was buried with cables from international leaders asking for restraint. While Johnson understood the dangers of the bombing campaigns, he also believed that the campaigns were in fact, a restrained response to North Vietnamese and Viet Cong aggression against American bases in the South.

Johnson's VP Hubert Humphrey sent a private memorandum to the president saying that expanding the war would hurt America's image overseas, destroy any hope of improving relations with the Soviets, and undercut the president's favorite domestic program, the Great Society. Johnson did not respond to the memo and wondered why Humphrey felt the need to put his beliefs in writing, instead of sitting down and talking with the president. It seemed many members of Johnson's administration felt the need to go on the record with their advice. It pissed off Johnson.

February 17, 1965 – Congress – Washington DC, USA

During a speech on the Senate floor, Senator Frank Church said, "The Saigon government is losing its war, not for lack of equipment, but for lack of internal cohesion. The best solution would be the negotiation of a neutral South Vietnam."

Church's speech for a neutral South Vietnam echoed similar statements by French President Charles de Gaulle, the Pope, and the Secretary General of the United Nations.

At the same time, former President Eisenhower and several Republicans supported Johnson's policy. Calling the president a short time after Church's speech, Eisenhower recommended Johnson not to negotiate from weakness but stay the course until the North Vietnamese approached the White House suggesting peace negotiations.

February 19, 1965 – Saigon, South Vietnam

For months General Khanh, the head of South Vietnam's ruling military junta, had been losing support among the military. Khanh had been securing the support of the Buddhist leaders in South Vietnam. The Buddhists supported talks with the Northern leaders in hopes of ending the war through the Neutralization of Vietnam. This approach seemed counterintuitive to many of the Buddhists because everyone knew that Buddhists would be persecuted under any type of communist regime. The communists were devout atheists and rejected all religions, even Buddhism which ninety percent of the Vietnamese in the South practiced. But the Buddhists also believed in peace and were against violence whenever possible. They saw no other practical way to stop the war other than neutralization which would most likely result in an eventual communist takeover of the government in the South.

The Americans were dead set against neutralization calculating that it was akin to surrender. They knew that if neutralization in South Vietnam was realized, the American military would be ordered to leave Vietnam by the South Vietnamese government. If that happened, the communists were sure to take over one way or another. Vietnam would be lost and eventually much of Southeast Asia with it. The dominos would begin to fall and there would be nothing to stop them.

For this reason, Ambassador Taylor encouraged the South Vietnamese generals to plot against Khanh. While the Americans wouldn't out and out endorse a coup of any kind in South Vietnam, they didn't discourage it either. They subtly indicated that the United States would support any new government as long as it was stable and continued to persecute the war against the North. More and more the Americans were focused on the war and ignored the happenings in Saigon. To them, it really didn't matter who was in charge as long as they supported U.S. goals to keep the South out of communist hands.

Thao, who was General Khiem's aide, was ordered by the military junta to return to South Vietnam. Thao suspected that Khanh wanted him killed hoping to eliminate one of Khiem's key liaisons with the ARVN military. Upon arriving in Saigon, Thao immediately went into hiding and continued to organize a coup against Khanh and replace him with Khiem.

On the morning of February 19th, ARVN elements under the command of General Lam Van Phat and Colonel Pham Ngoc Thao launched a coup against General Khanh. Their goal was to install General Khiem, Khanh's rival who had been sent to Washington as South Vietnam's Ambassador to the United States to prevent him from seizing power from Khanh.

Taylor and the Americans at the embassy were not prepared for Catholics Phat and Thao to seize power by establishing an explicitly religious platform. Phat supported the previous policies of deceased President Diem and his family. No matter how ineffective the current government and military in South Vietnam were, the Americans had no intention of going back to Diem's regime which in their mind was a complete disaster.

Though still bloodless, the coup quickly reached a stalemate with both sides having equal military resources and possessing an equal number of key infrastructure facilities. Neither side could seize or maintain control over the government without the other side surrendering.

At the American's prompting, a third group of officers led by General Nguyen Chanh Thi and Air Marshall Nguyen Cao Ky entered the fray. Thi and Ky were against the coup organizers but also wanted Khiem removed from control of the junta and government. During the initial attack, Thao and Phat tried to capture both Khanh and Ky. Although some of their colleagues in the Armed Forces Council were arrested, both Khanh and Ky narrowly escaped.

Late in the night, Thao and Phat met with Ky in a meeting arranged by the Americans. Ky was able to convince Phat and Thao to remove their forces from the capital in return for Khanh being removed from power.

With Ky in complete control of the air force, Khanh recognized that he could not win. He stepped down and retired gracefully with a military parade in his honor. Dr. Phan Huy Quát became prime minister.

From that point on, Thi and Ky took control of the government. Fearful of retaliation, Thao and Phat went into hiding and as they predicted, they were both sentenced to death in absentia. Thi sent hit squads in search of Thao and Phat. Thao found refuge in Catholic villages and began planning his return to the government by assassinating Quat and kidnapping Thi and Ky.

Hue, South Vietnam

A few days after the end of the latest coup, Granier was in Hue for what he thought was another intelligence-gathering assignment. It wasn't. It was something far more nefarious.

After arriving by plane, Granier headed for a go-go bar that he had previously visited. The beer was cold and the girls dancing were scantily clad. He sat down at the bar and ordered. An American dressed in plain clothes sat down a few stools down and also ordered a beer in English. "Rene Granier?" said the American turning to Granier.

"Yeah. Who's asking?" said Granier.

"A friend from Langley."

"Okay. Why not just say that instead of all the cloak and dagger?"

"Because I'm not here… officially."

"You at least got a name?"

"Choose one."

"Okay. I'll call you… sheepfucker. Is that alright with you?"

"How about Bill?"

"Sheepfucker is easier to remember."

"Let's find a table in the back so we can talk."

"Okay, Bill. But you're buying from this point on."

"Fair enough."

Both rose and moved to a table in the rear of the bar. The bartender brought over their beers. Bill paid her and she left. "Okay, Bill. The beer's paid for. What's on your mind?" said Granier.

"Are you familiar with the coup that just happened in Saigon?"

"Sure. Three-ring circus if you ask me, but I'm not paid for my political opinions."

"Colonel Thao was one of the organizers."

"Okay. I'll take your word for it."

"Do you know him?"

"I've seen him once or twice."

"So, you know what he looks like?"

"Sure. I could pick him out in a crowd."

"Good. You need to kill him."

"Excuse me?"

"You heard me correctly."

"Colonel Thao is an officer in the South Vietnamese Army. Our ally in case you've forgotten."

"Colonel Phạm Ngọc Thao is a sleeper agent working for the North Vietnamese."

"That's a bit of a stretch, Bill."

"Yeah, but it's true and you need to kill him before anyone finds out."

"I thought he was on the run since the coup failed."

"He is. That's the problem. When General Thi finds him, he will most likely torture him before he kills him. Thao may very well give up his secret during torture in hopes of somehow saving himself. We can't let that happen. You've got to kill him before it does."

"Bill, I don't mean to insult you, but we just met. Being in my line of business, I'm skeptical. I'm not going to kill anyone on the word of a stranger."

"I didn't think you would... and neither did my boss."

"Who is?"

Bill reached into the shirt pocket, pulled out a folded envelope, handed it to Granier, and said, "Sorry about the creases. It was a long flight."

Granier opened the sealed envelope and examined an enclosed letter which had the seal of the CIA on the top of the letterhead. The letter read, "To whom it may concern, you are hereby ordered to obey the instructions given by the officer carrying this letter. Signed, John A. McCone, Director of the Central Intelligence Agency."

"Nice," said Granier laughing. "I still don't buy it."

"Okay. What will it take?" said Bill.

"How about an order from my boss at the Embassy?"

"John Hart?"

"Yeah. Bill, I'm not trying to be difficult, but I'm just a cog in a great machine. I get my orders through the chain of command and I execute them."

"Yeah. This time is different. Nobody can know about this assignment, except for you and me and Director McCone."

"This is bullshit. I ain't doing it."

"Yeah, you are. You just don't realize it yet."

Another man sitting alone at a table in the opposite corner got up and walked over. Granier recognized him... It was General Edward Lansdale dressed in civilian clothes and he said, "Hello, Granier. Been keeping busy?"

"You could say that. What the hell are you doing here, General?"

"Visiting a few old friends and vouching for this man."

"You can't be serious?"

"Do you think I would fly all this way if I wasn't serious?"

"Okay. But do you even know this guy?"

"Actually, I don't. But I know his boss and he asked me to come here because it's important and not the normal protocol. So, I came."

"Do you understand what he's asking me to do?"

"No, and I don't need to know. As I understand it, the fewer people that know about the assignment the better."

"Now, I don't know what to think."

"Well, I'm sure you'll figure it out. It was good to see you, Granier."

Lansdale walked out of the bar. Bill turned to Granier and said, "Need more?"

"No. But that still doesn't mean I'll do it."

"I suppose skepticism is a good thing, but it sure as hell is annoying. Your country needs you, Granier."

"You mean the CIA needs to cover up its mess."

"There's some truth in that. A colonel in the South Vietnamese Army is a deep-cover spy. Not sure how we missed that one. My guess is that some heads are gonna roll in counterintelligence. But that doesn't matter at the moment, now does it?"

"I guess not."

"The only thing that matters is that you agree to take the assignment."

"Do you know where he is?"

"We suspect he's in a Catholic enclave somewhere in the South."

"That's not much to go on."

"I'm sure he'll pop up at some point."

"And I'm supposed to blow his head off when he does?"

"Something like that."

"It's one hell of a clusterfuck you're asking me to fix, Bill."

"I know. It never should have happened. But it did. And now guys like you and me need to deal with it."

Granier thought for a long moment. He had never turned down an assignment before, but this one was different. Assassinating a South Vietnamese officer crossed the line for Granier. And yet, he saw the need for the mission and the need for keeping it quiet. The South Vietnamese military would be embarrassed by the revelation that they had been harboring a North Vietnamese spy for over a decade. The South Vietnamese government had a lot of problems at the moment and this admission surely wouldn't help the situation. And the CIA would be damaged too. While it was primarily the job of South Vietnamese intelligence to detect enemy agents, as the South's intelligence partner, the CIA was sure to catch some of the flak. But what was the clincher for Granier was that if Thao truly was a traitor, he needed to be eliminated to stop the damage he was creating. By taking the assignment, Granier would be a judge, jury, and executioner. But then again… that was what he did. He said, "Alright. I'll do it."

"Good. I'm sure the director will be pleased."

"Well, knowing that just makes me feel all warm and fuzzy inside. Tell me one thing, Bill."

"Why you?"

"Yeah. Why me?"

"Because you're good at your job and you know how to keep your mouth shut. McCone remembers you from the Kennedy days. He's a fan."

Granier laughed. Signaling the waitress with his hand, Bill ordered another couple of beers.

February 28, 1965 – Saigon, South Vietnam

A brigade of South Korean soldiers along with their equipment departed a ship at Saigon Harbor. Known as the Dove Force, the Koreans were support personnel that included engineers, liaison staff, medical teams, military police, and a Navy LST. The engineers helped build schools, roads, and bridges in Ben Hoa and the surrounding area. The medical unit treated over 30,000 South Vietnamese civilians and was seen as a countermeasure to the Viet Cong's efforts to discredit the South Vietnamese government as uncaring and unresponsive to the suffering of the Vietnamese people. The fact that the soldiers were Korean and not Vietnamese didn't seem to matter. They were Asian and helping. That was enough and those they helped were grateful.

February 28, 1965 – Hanoi, North Vietnam

When the United States and South Vietnam announced that they would begin bombing the North, the leaders in Hanoi ordered an evacuation of the elderly and children from Hanoi and other large cities. Spider holes were constructed on the sidewalks of busy boulevards to protect passing pedestrians during bombing raids. In addition, more troops and weapons were assigned to the anti-aircraft batteries across the country. The North Vietnamese had no intention of bowing to pressure from the South. They hoped that

China and the Soviet Union would intervene on their behalf as they had promised.

While the Chinese and the Soviets were strong on rhetoric, they were cautious in their responses. Nobody wanted World War III, especially if the Americans were involved. With nuclear weapons in the mix, the stakes were much higher than in a third-world country like Vietnam. The Chinese did offer more aircraft and more support personnel to free up North Vietnamese soldiers for defensive duty and the Soviets sent more advanced anti-aircraft systems by train. Both the Chinese and the Soviets wanted to hurt the Americans but were careful not to provoke them into an expanded war.

The Soviets sent Mikoyan-Gurevich MiG-17s, while the Chinese sent Shenyang J-5s which were basically the same aircraft. They were subsonic at maximum speed which was a great disadvantage against the American and South Vietnamese jets. In fact, the Soviet MiG-17s flew at roughly half the speed of the American F-105s which could fly in excess of Mach 2. Armament was also a major problem for the MiG-17s and J-5s. The communist jets were equipped with three Type 23-1 23 mm aircraft cannons. The American 105s only had one gun - an M61A1 Vulcan 6-barreled Gatling cannon firing 20 mm shells at an incredible rate of 6,000 rounds per minute. The American jet also had Sidewinder air-to-air missiles on its hard points. The Sidewinder could be fired at a target twenty-two miles away and traveled at Mach 2.5 guided by an onboard infrared homing system. The Sidewinder carried a twenty-lb. fragmentation warhead with a proximity fuse. In fighter aircraft design and manufacture the Soviets and Chinese were playing catch up to the Americans.

March 2, 1965

After months of debate, planning, and target selection, Operation Rolling Thunder began. The operational objectives were simple: while destroying infrastructure and military installations the systematic bombing raids would boost the morale of the South and destroy the morale in the North. The White House and the Pentagon hoped that sooner or later the North would cry uncle and cease their support of the Viet Cong in exchange for an end to the bombing. President Johnson insisted on complete secrecy. The American public would not be told that there had been a major shift in the administration's policy from retaliatory air strikes to the systematic bombing in North Vietnam.

One hundred and four American fighter-bombers and nineteen RVNAF aircraft struck targets in North Vietnam. It was the largest bombing raid to date in the Vietnam War. Five U.S. planes and one RVNAF plane were shot down by the North Vietnamese anti-aircraft defenses which now included surface-to-air missiles. The operation was designed to last eight weeks but ended up lasting over three years.

While the international community pleaded for restraint, North Vietnam, China, and the Soviet Union were all furious at what they perceived as a major escalation by the Americans. They immediately stopped all talks concerning the possible neutralization of Vietnam. It was exactly what the Americans wanted to happen. The neutralization of Vietnam would have been nothing more than a defeat on the installment plan for the Americans. They were happy to see the end of the negotiations. Both sides in the war were now in it for the long haul. There would be no comprise until victory or defeat by one side or the other.

As expected, South Vietnamese and American intelligence reports suggested a large increase in potential terrorist attacks against U.S. advisors and aircrews. The closer to the border between the North and South, the higher the risk of an attack. All government and military installations and facilities were put on alert and troops guarding the perimeters were vastly increased. The bombing of the North would not pass without repercussions. Anti-communists had raised the stakes and the communists were doing their best to meet the new challenges with equivalent force.

The Request

Known for his calm nature during battle, Westmoreland was concerned about the growing number and intensity of terrorist attacks. He had over 25,000 advisors in the country all of which were targets for the Viet Cong and NVA bent on revenge for the bombings in the North. While the majority of the advisors were veterans in the field and could take care of themselves, the airmen at the American air bases were not experienced in fighting ground combat and therefore at risk during the Viet Cong assault. In addition, America had a large number of aircraft spread throughout the country. Aircraft, especially jets, were one of the more expensive weapons in America's arsenal and were not easily replaced. Every time an American aircraft was destroyed on the ground, he heard an earful from General LeMay, the U.S. Air Force commander. LeMay let it be known that he expected Westmoreland to keep his aircraft safe.

At the moment, the biggest target in all of Vietnam was the bombers stationed at Da Nang Air Base. They were all designated to bomb the North. The South Vietnamese military was in charge of protecting the air base, but the ARVN had become less and less effective as trouble in the capital continued to erupt. It was getting to the point where Westmoreland could no longer trust them to carry out their mission to protect the American aircrews and their aircraft. He increased the U.S. Military Police as much as possible but there were too few resources spread too thin. There were just too many American facilities that needed to be protected.

Seeing no other way to carry out his mission, Westmoreland sent in an official request to the Joint Chiefs of Staff for two battalions of U.S. Marines to protect the airbases. Naturally, the generals at the Pentagon were all for the idea. They had been pressing for ground troops in Vietnam for several years. But it wasn't up to them. It was up to their Commander and Chief – The President of the United States Lyndon B. Johnson. It was his call, and everyone knew it, including Westmoreland.

Johnson had been expecting such a request for some time. He was surprised that it took this long, especially after the multiple Viet Cong attacks against the airbases. But Johnson was holding out as long as he could before sending ground troops to Vietnam. Ambassador Taylor who was originally for sending in ground troops was now against it, told Johnson, "Once you put that first soldier ashore, you never know how many more are going to follow."

Johnson felt like he was up a creek and had finally lost his paddle. He felt he had no choice but to accept Westmoreland's request or be blamed if more American advisors and aircrewmen were killed. And he was sure more would die if he did nothing. As he continued to struggle with the decision, Johnson told one of his cabinet members, "I feel like a Jackass caught in a Texas hailstorm. I can't run, I can't hide, and I can't make it stop."

In the end, Johnson agreed to Westmoreland's request and ordered McNamara to send him the two battalions of U.S. Marines. McNamara made it happen.

That night, Johnson called his friend Senator Richard Russell of Georgia and said, "I guess we have no choice, but it scares the death out of me. I think everybody's going to think, we're landing the Marines. We're off to battle. Of course, if they come up there, they're going to get them in a fight. And if they ruin those airplanes, everybody is going to give me hell for not securing them, just like they did last time they made a raid. What do you think?"

Russell replied, "Well, Mr. President, it scares the life out of me. But I don't know how to back up now. It looks to me like we just got in this thing, and there's no way out. A man can fight if he can see daylight somewhere down the road."

"There ain't no daylight in Vietnam, Bill. Not a bit," said the president.

The government of South Vietnam was not even consulted about more foreign troops entering its country. The South Vietnamese were so dependent on American aid and military assistance, that there was little they could do if they objected. The White House had larger concerns and was tired of the South Vietnamese revolving door of who was in charge. Why bother informing the South Vietnamese government when in just a few months it would be replaced?

Instead, the Americans ignored the South Vietnamese and did what they felt was necessary to save South Vietnam from communist expansion. In a secret memorandum prepared by Assistant Secretary of Defense John McNaughton, he wrote, "Our interest in the war in Vietnam is seventy percent to avoid America being humiliated, twenty percent to stop communist expansion, and ten percent to protect South Vietnam."

The United States military was taking over the war effort and it was time for action. While MACV still expected the South Vietnamese military to play their part, they would no longer be the spearhead in offensive operations. As time went on, the ARVN troop's main responsibility, unless called upon by the Americans, was to protect the cities and infrastructure such as highways, bridges, railways, ports, and airfields. It was an important job, but mostly out of harm's way. It was what most of the South Vietnamese generals wanted... to conserve their troops for an invasion should it happen, and everyone believed that eventually, it would.

As usual, the U.S. Marine Corps was ready. The generals had made their plans and logistics had been thrown into high gear. The requested two battalions for the U.S. 9th Marine Expeditionary Brigade were already forward deployed to Okinawa and were chopping at the bit. Within a week, they would be in Vietnam, and for America, the real war would begin.

March 8, 1965 – Da Nang, South Vietnam

Like most of the thirty-five Marines with him in the LCM-8 nicknamed "Mike boat," Private Antwan Lincoln was both excited to be going into combat for the first time and terrified of being shot or dying. It was Vietnam and he had heard the stories. His sergeant had told him to believe he was already dead and that the fear would leave him. But that didn't any sense to Lincoln. Where were Jesus and the pearly gates? It was fucked up that was for sure. He puked. He was seasick from the landing craft bobbing up and down in the waves. They weren't even big waves. But it was enough for someone like Lincoln. Fortunately, he wasn't the only Marine that spewed his breakfast. That would have been embarrassing.

His assistant gunner Private Turner stood beside him. Some of Lincoln's regurgitated scrambled eggs and bacon got on Turner's boots, but Lincoln knew that Turner wouldn't care. He had other things on his mind. Turner always talked fast and a lot when he was nervous. Ever since reveille aboard the ship, Turner had been spouting off about the stupidest things. Lincoln had stayed quiet as usual and just let his friend release his tension through his mouth and kept him from forgetting anything as they prepared to board their landing craft. Turner had two ammunition belts wrapped around his neck and was carrying two ammo boxes in addition to his rucksack and M14. Lincoln was sure his friend was going to sink to the bottom of the ocean once they jumped out into the surf. It was just the way Turner was… a klutz. Lincoln lifted the two ammo belts from around Turner's neck and put them around his neck. "What the hell are doing?" said Turner as if insulted.

"You're too short. I don't want the shells dragging through the ocean," said Lincoln. "Saltwater will corrode the inside of the gun's barrel."

"Oh, yeah. Good thinking," said Turner. "But I want 'em back once we get ashore."

"Yep. They're yours."

Turner seemed satisfied.

"Everyone listen up," said the sergeant leading the platoon from the front while the lieutenant led from the rear. "When we hit the beach, I don't want to see anyone lollygagging or building sandcastles on the beach. You get your asses up to the first berm, find the enemy, and kill 'em. If you see any of our guys get hit, you call for the medic and keep going. He'll take care of the wounded while you fight. That's the best thing you can do for him. If everyone does their job the way they're supposed to, we're gonna accomplish our objective and everyone's a hero. Keep your heads down until the ramp is lowered and you can step off. And remember… don't shoot me in the ass. I don't like that. Got it?!"

The platoon shouted "Oorah!" in their husky voices. The landing craft reversed its engines to slow its momentum and not strand itself on the beach. The ramp whined as it lowered. Everyone tensed. Lincoln peeked over the ramp and caught a glimpse of the beach. "Get your nigger ass down, Lincoln," said the sergeant.

Lincoln obeyed and crouched down in the well bay. He held no animosity toward his sergeant. The sergeant was from the Deep South and accustomed to calling black folks derogatory names. It wasn't right, but at that moment Lincoln was more concerned about staying alive than social justice. The sergeant was a veteran and knew how to keep the men under his command as safe as possible. Lincoln was grateful.

As the ramp hit the water and stopped, everyone followed their sergeant and poured out of the landing craft in front of Red Beach. When Lincoln and Turner reached the edge of the ramp, they looked down. The water was murky with sand and mud that had been kicked up by the Marines already moving toward the beach. They could see that their fellow Marines were wading up to their balls in water. Lincoln could see that Turner was hesitant. He wasn't a strong swimmer. Lincoln jumped off the ramp, bounced off the sandy bottom, and stood up. He was in Vietnam, he thought. Turner followed him but misstepped and fell. "Dammit, Turner," said Lincoln grabbing his friend by the harness on his rucksack and pulling him up to his feet. "You better pray those ammo cases don't leak."

But Turner's hands were empty. He had dropped the two ammo cases. "Fuck," said Turner as he reached back down into the murky water trying to retrieve the cases.

"Leave 'em," said Lincoln. "We gotta get to shore." But Turner wouldn't give up. "Shit," said Lincoln and went back to help Turner.

After several tries, Turner finally came up with one of the cases and held it up with a smile. "That's enough," said Lincoln turning back toward the beach.

Turner followed gripping the ammo case like his life depended on it. Lincoln saw that the rest of the platoon was already on the beach and the sergeant was yelling for them to haul ass. Lincoln pushed ahead and Turner dropped in behind him. When they reached the beach, they were both out of breath. Lincoln was sure they were both gonna be cut down by enemy fire until he looked around and saw that nobody was firing at them. There were no explosions from mortars or even grenades. It was just peaceful. Like paradise with palm trees lining the sand. "Where the hell are they?" said Turner.

"I don't know, and I don't care as long as they ain't shooting at us," said Lincoln. "Let's go."

Lincoln and Turner scrambled up the beach and joined the rest of the platoon lined up behind a sand berm. "Get that fucking gun up, Marines," said the sergeant.

"Yes, Sergeant," said Lincoln and Turner in unison.

Lincoln opened the bipod legs, then laid the machine gun down on the berm. Turner pulled one of the ammo belts from around Lincoln's neck and laid it across the gun's chamber being held open by Lincoln. Lincoln carefully lowered the top of the breach, locked it in place, and chambered the first round. The weapon was ready. "Up, Sergeant," said Lincoln.

"About damned time," said the sergeant.

"Where are they?" said Turner.

"How the hell am I supposed to know?"

"Probably hiding, right, Sergeant?" said Lincoln. "Setting a trap. Sneaky bastards," said Turner.

"Shut the fuck up and keep an eye out," said the sergeant.

"There!" said Turner pointing.

Lincoln swung his gun around and watched as a man's head peeked above another sand berm in front of the Marines. He wasn't an American. Lincoln put his finger on the gun's trigger. "Wait," said the sergeant.

The man waved to someone behind him like he wanted them to move forward with him. *This is it*, thought Lincoln. *It's the Viet Cong.* Lincoln watched steely-eyed as the man stepped forward and reached the top of the berm. He seemed unarmed and was wearing a white shirt and tie with black slacks. The man was followed by a teenage Vietnamese girl wearing a white Ao Dai and holding several homemade necklaces of local flowers. She was followed by another girl, then another until fifteen young girls stood at the top of the berm looking around. "What the hell is this, Sergeant?" said Turner.

"Just stay where you are and don't shoot unless something bad happens," said the sergeant.

The man that seemed to be in charge of the group spotted the Marines and pointed to them. The first girl walked toward the Marines. "What do we do, Sergeant? Is it a trap? Do we shoot?" said Turner holding his M14 at the ready.

"She's just a kid," said Lincoln watching her approach.

"You don't know. She could have a grenade," said Turner.

"Keep your damned fingers off the trigger," said the sergeant to no Marine in particular.

The girl stopped in front of Lincoln still on the ground. He looked up into her face. She smiled. Lincoln rose. The girl's expression changed to surprise mixed with fear. Lincoln was the biggest man she had seen in her life. Lincoln just stood there looking down at her, half expecting her to run away. But she didn't. Instead, she pointed at the bandolier of shells around his neck. Lincoln removed the belt and handed it to Turner still on the ground. "What are you doing, Lincoln?" said the sergeant.

"I think it's okay, Sergeant," said Lincoln.

The girl motioned for Lincoln to bend down so she could reach his head. He followed her instructions, carefully, cautiously. She took one of the flower necklaces and placed it over Lincoln's head. Lincoln stood back and said, "Thank you."

The girl nodded and smiled. Her teeth were white and perfect. Lincoln smiled back. More girls stepped forward with flower necklaces. The Marines rose cautiously and let the girls put the necklaces around their necks. More Marines came ashore, and the girls ran out of necklaces, so they kissed each marine on the cheek and flashed them a big welcome smile. The Marines didn't seem to mind the lack of flower necklaces.

Lincoln stood on the sandy berm and looked around at the countryside. He was stunned by the beautiful green landscape of rice paddies and groves of trees. Through the morning haze, the blueish mountains appeared off in the distance. The smell of rotting vegetation from the jungle mixed with the cooking fires of a nearby village. A farmer used his water buffalo to plow his field. It was surreal. Vietnam was nothing like what Lincoln had expected. It was paradise.

Just two hours before the landing, Prime Minister Quat had discovered that the U.S. Marines had arrived and were preparing to come ashore in Da Nang. He was naturally angry that he had not been informed by the American Ambassador. Rather than lose face, Quat decided to make the best of the situation and welcome the Marines. They were, after all, there to fight the communists.

The teenage girls were from a local high school. Their principal, the man in the white shirt and tie, had received a call from the prime minister's office asking if some of his students could go out and greet the American Marines that were flooding ashore.

That night, Lincoln, Turner, and the other Marines bivouacked on the beach listening to the gentle waves lap against the sand. Nobody bothered setting up their two-man tents or even rolling out their sleeping bags. It was too hot and the sand was soft. A gentle breeze and the smoke from their campfires kept the mosquitos away. The nearby villagers sold a dozen pigs to the Marines and roasted them on spits as part of the deal. The BBQ, seasoned with local herbs and sauces, tasted far better than the rations they have stowed in their rucksacks.

As they prepared to sleep, lightning stuck over the mountains, and lit everything for a brief moment. Dark clouds were rolling in and the Marines were wondering if it had been a mistake not to set up their tents. It was. Within a few minutes, it began to pour in sheets and continued for over an hour. Everything and everyone was soaked. However, by morning everything was completely dry. The heat hit early, and the Marines wished the rain would come back and cool them down. Vietnam was going to take some getting used to.

After a breakfast of fresh fruit and leftover roasted pork wrapped in banana leaves, the Marines stuck their camp and climbed into the South Vietnamese military trucks that had arrived. On the beach, the landing craft were busy unloading the Marines' tanks and other vehicles from the ships. Their vehicles and gear would catch up to them once the Marines had reached their final destination – the Da Nang Air Base.

Hanoi, North Vietnam

The North Vietnamese propaganda machine made great use of the Marine landing. It was an invasion of South Vietnam by an imperialist army, much like the French two hundred years previously. That was their hammer point – the Americans were like the French. Most people in North and South Vietnam hated the French and feared another foreign government once again ruling them. The North Vietnamese encouraged those in the South to join the Viet Cong and expel the foreign army. Many did.

Da Nang Air Base, South Vietnam

The Da Nang Air was a sprawling facility with dozens of hangars, aircrew quarters, mess halls, hospital, commissary, radar and communication facilities, operational buildings, and a separate camp for the Marines. The entire base was surrounded by a tall perimeter fence capped with layers of concertina wire. Block houses and machine gun emplacements were spaced every hundred feet. Mines and hidden foo gas canisters covered no man's land. Well-protected gates with heavy machine gun emplacements covered the entrances and exits to the base.

Within a month almost 5,000 U.S. Marines replaced the South Vietnamese guards that protected the base. The American Marines had been ordered to "not, repeat not, engage in day-to-day actions against the Viet Cong. The Marines would only fight when under attack and did not leave the air base.

From the jungle and hills in the distance, the Viet Cong watched and waited for their opportunity, but it was different with the Marines. They were far more vigilant and organized than the South Vietnamese guards. The American Marines continually changed their patrol routines and routes making it hard to plan any kind of attack without being discovered. The Marines were far better armed too. They had the latest weapons and plenty of them.

Lincoln and Turner stood behind three layers of sandbags looking out beyond the perimeter fence for signs of the enemy. There were none. Their machine gun was set up and ready to rock and roll but day after day nothing happened, and boredom set in. Turner's M14 leaned against the sandbags always within his reach. In addition to loading the machine gun, Turner was responsible for security if there was an attack from the rear or flanks. They kept their weapons clean and oiled but there was no need. Nothing happened. "This is bullshit," said Lincoln. "The Viet Cong are out there in the jungle. That's where we should be."

"It's too damned hot in the jungle. I can't breathe. At least here we can feel the breeze from the ocean," said Turner. "Besides, any day we don't get shot at is a good day in my book."

"It ain't why I came. I wanna fight for my country, not sit on my ass."

"VC heard the U.S. Marines had arrived and headed for the hills. Smart move."

"That's my point. We gotta go out and find 'em."

"I'm fine right here."

And so it went day after day... a whole lot of nothing. Their sergeant came around periodically to check that they were awake and on the lookout. He always brought a set of extra canteens and watched as they drank deep from them. Each visit he would hear their report on anything that remotely seemed like enemy action, then impart a dirty joke from the hundreds he had learned over the years of serving in the Marines. Some were funny. All were filthy. The sergeant was like that – half gruff, foul-mouthed boss and half nursemaid. Lincoln and Turner knew him as a Southern bigot, but they also knew he would do everything in his power to keep them alive as long as they performed their duties and that included drinking enough water so they didn't get dehydrated by the Vietnamese heat.

March 16, 1965 – Detroit, Michigan, USA

Karen snapped her camera's shutter as one by one a group of six men burned their draft cards. She was disappointed. It was nothing that the American public hadn't seen before and the protest was small. Only two local cops had shown up to keep the peace but stood by and watched as they smoked cigarettes and drank coffee out of paper cups. There would be no confrontation. Passersby did not even stop on their way home from work. It was all anti-climactic in Karen's opinion and a waste of round-trip airfare. She doubted that any of the national newspapers would buy her photographs of the event and she was getting low on peanut butter. But it was history and she felt it was her obligation to record the protest even if it was small.

When she was finished and the protesters dispersed after cleaning up the ashes they had created, Karen heard a voice that said, "Are you, Karen Dickson?"

Karen turned to see an eighty-two-year-old woman, short in stature, standing behind her and said, "I am. Do I know you?"

"No, but I know you. I've seen your photographs."

"Really?"

"Yes. They are quite good."

"Well, thank you. It's nice to know I have a fan."

"I'm sure you have more than me. But that's neither here nor there."

"What do you mean?"

"There's going to be another anti-war protest tomorrow."

"Here in Detroit?"

"Yes. If you meet me tomorrow morning at 9 o'clock, I will show you."

"I'd like to, but I booked a flight back home this evening."

"Stay one more day. Please. I promise you it will be worth your time."

Karen considered for a moment as she studied the woman's face. There was something about it. *Wisdom*, she thought, then said, "Alright. I'll stay."

The woman handed Karen a piece of paper with her name "Alice Herz" and the address of an intersection in downtown Detroit written in pencil. On the other side of the paper was a short biography. Eighty-two-year-old Alice Herz was born in Germany and escaped the Nazis with her daughter Helga. She lived in France before coming to America. She objected to America's role in the Vietnam War. "Bring plenty of film, dear," said Herz as she turned and walked away.

Karen smiled to herself and thought the meeting the next day would lead to another disappointment. "In for a penny, in for a pound," she said to herself.

The next morning, Karen arrived at the intersection with her suitcase in hand. She had rebooked her flight for noon and hoped to leave straight for the airport after the protest. Her camera was around her neck and her other hand was occupied with a coffee cup and a cherry danish. She was a multi-tasker.

She looked around and saw Mrs. Herz across the intersection waving with a smile. Karen set her suitcase down and waved back. Herz walked towards her crossing the street. Karen realized she would probably want to shake hands. She set down her coffee and danish on top of her suitcase. When she turned back, she saw Mrs. Herz had stopped in the middle of the road like she had forgotten where she was going. Karen thought it was cute and snapped a photo of the old lady standing in the middle of the street. There was little traffic and Karen didn't feel that the woman was in any danger, until she saw Herz pulling what looked like a can of cleaning fluid from her handbag. Karen cautiously snapped another photo. Herz twisted the lid off the can and poured it on the top of her head. Streams of the clear liquid poured down her face and onto her dress. Realizing what was happening, Karen felt like screaming but didn't. Instead, she snapped another photo. Herz pulled out a box of table matches from her purse and removed a match. Karen took another photograph. Herz smiled at Karen, then lit the match setting herself on fire. She was immediately engulfed in flames.

Herz didn't run. She turned from side to side and bobbed her head up and down as if trying to find air. There was none. The fire was consuming the oxygen around her burning face. Tears streamed down Karen's face as she continued to advance the film in her camera and snap more photos. A car stopped next to Herz. A father and his two teenage sons leapt out of the car, pulled off their jackets, and put out the flames. Herz lay on the street shaking, her hair gone and the skin on her face blackened to a crisp. She no longer looked human. Karen shot the last of the film in her camera. Hearing the last click of the camera's shutter, the father turned and looked at Karen as if she were some kind of monster. Lowering her camera, Karen wondered if he was right.

Still alive, Alice Herz was given oxygen by the ambulance driver before being taken to a nearby hospital. Karen had stopped snapping photos. She was in shock and couldn't bring herself to load another roll of film. Instead, she watched the ambulance pull away. She picked up her suitcase letting her coffee and danish drop to the sidewalk. She was no longer hungry.

As the airliner took off, Karen sat quietly. Her camera bag was tucked under the seat in front of her. After calming down, she removed the film and replaced it with a new roll as she always did. The exposed film canister was placed in a container and the lid secured.

Karen was sure of two things. First, once developed and put on the wire, her photographs of an American woman's self-immolation to protest the Vietnam War would sell to every major newspaper and magazine across the world. She would be rich and no longer need to be concerned with her peanut butter supply. The second thing she was sure of was that upon seeing her horrifying photographs others would follow Alice's footsteps and burn themselves to death in protest of the war.

Halfway through the flight, Karen reached into her camera bag and retrieved the container of film. She unscrewed the lid and took out the canister of exposed film. She grabbed the strip of film that she always let hang out from the canister for the lab to use and pulled. As the film was exposed to the sunlight, the images on the cellulite were destroyed. The man sitting next to her turned and said, "You know, that ruins it."

Karen smiled a little and said, "Yeah. I've heard that."

Alice Herz died of her injuries ten days later.

White House – Washington DC, USA

Once again President Johnson was not happy and McNamara was sitting in the hot seat across from him. The CIA and Defense Intelligence Agency had prepared a report for the Joint Chiefs of Staff. The report estimated the armed forces in South Vietnam to be around 567,000 which were made up of ARVN, Regional, and Popular Force militia. That wasn't the problem. The problem was that the Viet Cong had vastly increased in size and now had 60,000 regulars and another 100,000 in militia. And that was not including the North Vietnamese troops that had entered South Vietnam through Laos and Cambodia using the Ho Chi Minh Trail.

To add salt on an already painful wound, General Johnson offered his analysis that it would take five years of fighting and 500,000 American troops to win the war. The Joint Chiefs of Staff were now recommending a mission change for American troops in Vietnam. The American military would no longer simply withstand the Viet Cong but would gain operational superiority and assume the offensive. The JCS wanted two divisions of combat troops sent to South Vietnam to accomplish that purpose. "To turn the tide of war, requires an objective of destroying the Viet Cong, not merely keeping pace with them, or slow their rate of advance," said the JCS memo.

McNamara had just presented a synopsis of both the intelligence report and the JCS memo to the president. "What the hell happened? I thought you said our interdiction strategy was having an effect?" said Johnson.

"It has and will continue to have an effect. The problem is that the North Vietnamese and the Viet Cong are outpacing us," said McNamara.

"You make it sound like a damned horse race."

"Well, it kind of is. The South Vietnamese still outnumber their enemy three to one."

"Yeah, but our allies don't wanna fight. They're just gonna sit on their asses behind the barbed wire where it's nice and safe."

"Well, that's the problem in a nutshell."

"I know that. Tell me something I don't know, Bob."

"It seems pretty clear that the only way we are gonna win this thing is if our guys get out in the field and stomp some VC."

"Yeah, except it ain't a field where they're hiding. It's a jungle."

"We've fought in jungles before. Our Marines can handle this if we just unleash them."

"Well, I believe that. So, maybe you're right. Let's unleash them. But I want air and artillery support wherever our guys go."

"Absolutely, Mr. President."

"But as far as the additional divisions… well, I'm gonna have to give that some deep thought. It's a big commitment."

"Of course, Mr. President. It's a big decision."

"My real question is will it be enough or are they really serious about 500,000 troops?"

"I think they're serious, but that doesn't mean you have to give them what they want. Maybe something less…"

"How much less? People keep talking about what it will take to win, but they never tell me exactly what they need. At least the Joint Chiefs had the balls to come up with an exact number. It's way too damned much, but at least they committed to the number. Now we got something to argue about."

March 22, 1965 – Ann Arbor, Michigan, USA

Organized by a group of professors, 3,000 students participated in a Teach-In at the University of Michigan in Ann Arbor. Many students and professors believed the war was immoral, while some argued it was unconstitutional or not in the national interest. It was a lively discussion.

As usual, Karen was there with her camera. Unenthusiastic, she was still in shock from witnessing Alice Herz's sacrifice for the anti-war movement. Karen was also tired. She hadn't slept much lately. Her mind was preoccupied with the anti-war protests and what they meant to the nation and its military. She didn't want to harm anyone, but as a photojournalist, she knew that was not always possible. She thought a lot about her brother, Scott. They wrote to each other once a month. That seemed to be enough to catch up on what was happening in their busy lives. She worried about him and he worried about her. They both believed in what they were doing and pushed themselves. It seemed to be a family trait. Karen asked her brother about Tom Coyle. Coyle had written her a letter, but Karen never responded. She didn't feel the need to correspond with a man claiming to be her real father. He wasn't there when she was growing up. He had no place in her life and she wanted to keep it that way.

Scott wrote back and said that he had run into Coyle a few times and that he was a good guy, but he also understood how she felt. There was something about accepting Coyle that betrayed the memory of the man that raised them. Still, Scott did reach out with a case of orange Nehi as a sort of peace offering. He wasn't interested in a full-blown father-and-son relationship. It was too late for that. But he did want to know more about Coyle and was willing to let him ask questions if he wanted. He just wasn't sure what his answers would be.

Scott's openness toward Coyle gave Karen pause. Scott was usually more reserved and cautious like her. Both had trouble including others in their lives. Close relationships were even more difficult. As Karen lifelessly snapped more photos of the professors and students at the Teach-In, she decided to respond to Coyle's letter. The truth was important if they were going to have any kind of relationship at all. It had been over a year since the letter had arrived. She would start off by apologizing for... No. That was wrong. She had nothing to apologize for. She would just acknowledge that she had received his letter, then explain that she had mixed emotions about responding. Yes. That was good. Coyle had not been part of her life growing up and she felt a strong allegiance to the man that raised her. Colonel Dickson could never be replaced, no matter what. Hmmm... She wondered if that might be too strong. No. It was the truth. But maybe something lighter should follow. She would explain her career as a photojournalist and that she was documenting the anti-war movement in the U.S. She wondered how Coyle would feel about that. He might think she was some kind of anti-war hippie. She knew she wasn't, but she wasn't sure if Coyle would understand. She decided she didn't care. He could accept her for who she was or not. It was up to him. He was the one that chose to make contact after all these years. It occurred to her that she knew little about what he did as a career beyond that he was a pilot. But for whom? That's good. She would ask a question. She had an honest curiosity about him. Again, the truth. No facades or hidden agendas. Honesty. She decided the first letter would be short. One page. First letter? Was she planning on writing more? Was that what she wanted?

She snapped out of her conversation with herself and looked up to see a man with short hair and wearing a white shirt and tie standing at the podium presenting a counterargument to the anti-war rhetoric of the last couple of days. Karen had heard that pro-government anti-protesters were going to be allowed to speak to the crowd of students and present their views as a counterpoint. Just a few minutes into his impassioned speech, a few students in the crowd started shouting that he was a liar and a pathetic government stooge. More joined in the taunts until finally, nobody could hear what the man had to say. Balls of paper flew across the room hitting the man. He finally flipped off the students and left the stage. Everyone cheered. They believed they were right and didn't need to hear contrary opinions.

Karen snapped dozens of photos of the confrontation. She wasn't sure if anyone would buy them, but she felt they should be part of the historical record. America was becoming polarized. The anti-war movement was still far outnumbered by pro-government supporters. But things were changing. People were becoming more passionate about their beliefs. Some were becoming curious and questioning their beliefs. At times it seemed like a person would lean to one side of the argument, then snap to the other side just a short time later. It was a confusing time for everyone, including Karen.

Pleiku Air Base, South Vietnam

Returning from an early morning mission, Coyle walked across the tarmac toward the officer's quarters where his room was located. It wasn't much, but it was his. He didn't have to share. He didn't mind sharing, but he knew he snored at night and didn't want the grief from a roommate. Being CIA had its perks. Private quarters were one of them.

As he entered his room, he saw a letter sitting on his bed. He picked it up and read the return address. "Karen Dickson?" he said to himself.

It took him a moment to realize the letter was from his daughter. He froze. He wanted to put the letter down but knew that wouldn't be right. She had written. It took a year, but she had written him. He had been heartbroken as the months had passed without receiving a response from her. He dared not write a second letter. But finally, here it was… an envelope from his daughter. Her handwriting was strong like a man's. Strange. What if she was angry? What if it was his letter returned? Her way of saying she didn't want to hear from him again. There was no upside to opening that envelope. He feared the contents more than death… and yet…

He sat on the bed holding the envelope. He looked over at the case of orange Nehi the bottles more than half gone. From Scott… at least he had Scott, sort of… He mustered his courage and carefully opened the envelope, so he did not tear the back flap. He pulled out the letter and studied it. It wasn't the letter he had sent. Thank, God. He read and with each word his mood lightened. She wasn't accepting him. But he wasn't expecting that she would. That would take time. She was asking questions which meant she expected him to write back. She wanted him to write back. Holy Shit! He had a daughter.

March 25, 1965 – White House – Washington DC, USA

President Johnson called the Joint Chiefs of Staff, his cabinet, and his advisors together in the Cabinet Room. It was crowded and the layer of cigarette smoke didn't help. The Chinese government had just announced its intention to "send its personnel to fight together with the Vietnamese people to annihilate the American aggressors."

"Folks, I feel like I just stepped in a wet cow pie. If the Chinese troops enter the war in a big way we will have no choice but to increase our own troop commitment and all bets are off. We could have another Korean War on our hands. I thought I made it clear from the beginning, I didn't want this thing to get out of hand. Somebody clearly fucked up and I want to know who it was," said Johnson staring down a long table of government officials that did not want to make eye contact.

"Mr. President, if I may?" said General Earle Wheeler, the Chairman of the JCS.

"Of course, General. Very brave of you."

"The Chinese are not going to invade South Vietnam."

"And why is that?"

"They don't want to expand the war any more than we do. Nobody wants World War III. We both have nuclear weapons. The only difference is that we have a lot more of them and ours are on missiles while theirs are in the back of trucks."

"I fail to see the humor at the moment, General."

"I'm serious, Mr. President. They have no way to deliver a nuclear weapon except by driving it across the border. And even if they did, we could pulverize every major Chinese city within a couple of hours. They can't win World War III and they know it. This announcement is just more bravado. A way of saving face. At most, they will increase their commitment of support personnel and anti-aircraft crews."

"And what about the Soviets? Their nukes are on missiles too."

"Yes, Mr. President, they are. But note that the Soviets did not make a similar announcement. Both China and the Soviet Union will support communist Vietnam, but they are not about to take the lead in any kind of invasion. That's a bad strategy and they know it."

"I sure hope you're right, General."

"You can have my resignation if I am wrong, Mr. President."

"If you're wrong, General. I don't think I'll be needing it."

"Of course, Mr. President. But I'm not wrong."

"So, what do we do? Wait and see?"

"No, Mr. President," said McNamara. "General Wheeler is right. We ignore the Chinese announcement and continue with our current strategy."

"More bombing?"

"Yes, Mr. President. It's having an effect."

"Are you sure about that, Bob? Hanoi hasn't said squat and ain't about to cry uncle. The Viet Cong are getting more weapons and supplies than ever."

"We always knew it would take time, Mr. President."

"Seems somebody forgot to tell me that little detail when I signed off on this thing."

"In hindsight, we should have been vocal about our expectations."

"Ya think, Bob?"

"Yes, Mr. President."

Within twenty-four hours, Johnson was hit with another bombshell report. This time from Westmoreland who informed the president through the Pentagon that the South Vietnamese military was beginning to show evidence of fragmentation and there was no longer an effective chain of command. "Beginning to show fragmentation? If that doesn't take the prize at the county fair, I don't know what does.

Where has our dear field general been for the last six months?"

"Mr. President, I am sure General Westmoreland is well aware of the situation and is just putting his observations in writing for the historical record," said McNamara.

"Really. Seems like everyone around here has been doing that lately. When do I get to do that, Bob, putting it in writing for the historical record?"

"When you write your memoirs, Mr. President."

"Don't be a smart ass, Bob. It doesn't suit you."

"Yes, Mr. President."

Johnson thought for a long moment, then said, "Bob, send a cable to Westmoreland and remind him that we sent him there to solve problems, not to put them in writing for the historical record."

"Right away, Mr. President. Although…"

"What is it, Bob? Spit it out."

"It might be better received coming from someone else. You were correct that sarcasm is not my forte."

"I wasn't being funny, Bob. If Westmoreland can't turn this thing around, then we need to find someone who can. Pronto."

"I'll start a list of candidates."

"No. It's too soon for that. We gotta give the man enough rope to hang himself. We owe him that. We certainly dumped him in a world of hurt."

"Westmoreland's tough. He can take it, Mr. President."

"I expect nothing less, Bob. And you send the cable yourself."

Sovereign Ground

March 30, 1965 – Saigon, South Vietnam

Granier crossed the street and entered the U.S. Embassy in Saigon. Moments later, a Citroen sedan pulled up in front of the building and parked. The driver got out and started to walk away when the two South Vietnamese guards called after him and told him to move his car. Saying that he would only be a minute, the driver began to argue with the two-armed South Vietnamese guards who were adamant that he move the car.

Stepping off the elevator, Granier approached the receptionist in front of an unmarked office and said, "I have an appointment with Mr. DeSilva."

"Your name?" said the receptionist.

"Rene Granier."

The receptionist picked up her phone, called her boss, then said, "You can go right in."

Granier walked into a large office with a hefty wooden desk and a sitting area. CIA Saigon Station Chief Peer DeSilva motioned for Granier to sit in one of the padded chairs in front of his desk and said,

"Thank you for coming, Officer Granier. A record of our conversation will be recorded."

DeSilva turned to his secretary sitting by the window and nodded. Wearing a green skirt and a yellow blouse, twenty-one-year-old Barbara Robbins sat at her steno machine and began typing. "Last night I received a cable from Langley saying you were to be given one month's leave and that the leave was to be extended until I was notified otherwise. There was no other explanation," said DeSilva. "What the hell is going on, Officer Granier?"

"I can't say," said Granier.

"I am your superior."

"Not in this case."

"How is that?"

"I can't say."

"This is bullshit."

"I agree. Maybe you should discuss it with your boss."

"My boss is the Director of the CIA John McCone."

"I am aware of that."

There were several loud pops from out in front of the Embassy. "What the hell is that?" said DeSilva, annoyed.

Robbins rose and looked out the window. "The guards are shooting at a man running away from his car. Wait… another man on a scooter is shooting at the guards."

DeSilva and Granier both moved toward the window. There was a loud thud and the windows imploded shredding Robbins with glass and the mangled iron grate that had covered the window hit her in the chest. She flew backward and landed on the carpet. DeSilva and Granier were knocked off their feet, but Robbins had taken most of the flying debris from the blast. After a moment to clear the fog from his head, Granier looked over at Robbins lying on her back, her skirt and blouse turning dark from blood. Knowing he was unable to help her and seeing DeSilva crawling toward her, he rose, headed out of the office, and took the stairs down to the lobby.

DeSilva crawled next to his secretary. Her face was perforated with glass shards, and several ends of iron rods from the grate pierced her stomach and chest. She was in shock. "It's okay, Barbara. I'll get help," said DeSilva knowing there was little anyone could do to save her.

She died a few moments later in a pool of blood.

Out in front of the embassy, Granier saw the mangled corpses of a dozen Vietnamese and two hundred others severely wounded, some were children. He looked up at the embassy. All the windows had been shattered and there was extensive structural damage. There was a large hole in the street where the car bomb holding 300 pounds of high explosives had gone off. The injured were moaning in pain, some were screaming seeing their loved ones dead beside them. Granier did what he could to help the survivors pulling them from the rubble that had fallen from the five-story building.

It was a good day for the Viet Cong. They had struck America's greatest symbol in Saigon and made clear that nobody was safe. Two Americans and nineteen Vietnamese had died in the terrorist attack. Almost 200 Vietnamese and Americans were wounded, and the American embassy was heavily damaged.

Born in South Dakota, Robbins had come to South Vietnam to help fight the communists. She was a patriot through and through. Barbara A. Robbins was the youngest and first female CIA employee to die during the Vietnam War. She was given a star on the CIA's Wall of Honor and her name was written in calligraphy in the Book of Honor.

Pleiku Air Base, South Vietnam

Scott was taking advantage of his weekend pass. He had no plans but decided to visit Bangkok in Thailand. It was close and he had never been there before even though he had heard stories… wild stories. It sounded like fun.

While waiting for a flight at Pleiku Air Base, he stopped by to see Coyle. Coyle was happy to see him and showed him the letter from Karen. He asked Scott's advice on how he should respond since he was close to his sister. "Just be yourself. She'll see right through you if you try to impress her," said Scott. "Karen's a stickler for honesty."

"Yeah. I got that from her letter. Anything else?" Coyle asked.

"Complimenting some of her photographs wouldn't hurt. You have seen them, right?"

"Honestly, no. I'm not big on reading newspapers."

"Well, you'd better start. She's becoming a big deal… or at least she thinks so. I've got some clippings of her photos in my quarters at Camp Holloway. I'll bring them to you when I get back."

"I'd appreciate it."

Coyle's crew chief dunked his head through the door and said, "Coyle, there's a phone call for you."

"Did they say who it is?"

"Some guy named Dung. He said you knew him."

"Okay, thanks."

The crew chief left and Coyle turned back to Scott and said, "I should probably grab that. Do you have time for lunch?"

"No. I gotta get going. I just wanted to stop by and say 'hi,'" said Scott.

"I'm glad you did… Scott."

Things became even more awkward when Scott offered his hand to say goodbye. Coyle wanted to give him a hug but knew it was probably too early for that. They shook and Scott left.

Coyle went into the officer's common area and grabbed the receiver sitting on top of the wall phone that everyone shared. "This is Tom Coyle," said Coyle.

"Mr. Coyle, I don't know if you remember me. I'm Mr. Dung, the owner of the Bui Lam Dung Detective Agency. You hired me in Hanoi to find two girls," said Mr. Dung over the phone.

"I remember you. I also remember you took my money and never found squat."

"That happens sometimes. It's the nature of my business. But I always do my best."

"Hmm… I am sure you do. How can I help you, Mr. Dung?"

"I found one of the girls, Nguyet."

"What?"

"Do you remember her?"

"Yes, of course. But it's been so long. Where is she?"

"She's living in a small village in the Mekong Delta."

"What's the village name?"

"Before I give it to you, there is the matter of your bill."

"What bill?"

"Technically, you never fired me and I have continued working even without being paid. As I said, I always do my best for my customers."

"Right. Of course. How much?"

"Five thousand American dollars."

"Are you insane? I'm not giving you five thousand dollars."

"I see. Perhaps we could negotiate a lesser amount."

Coyle reached into his pocket and pulled out three dollars and some change. "I got three dollars and fifty-nine cents. How's that?"

"Be reasonable, Mr. Coyle."

"I don't know if this is some kind of hustle, but it sure sounds like it."

"It is not a hustle as you say. I have found Nguyet as you had requested."

Coyle thought for a moment, then said, "I can give you one thousand U.S. dollars, Mr. Dung, and not a penny more. If it turns out to be a hoax, I will turn you over to the police."

"You don't need to threaten me, Mr. Coyle. I am an honest man. In the name of diplomacy between our two great nations, I will accept your offer."

"And that includes any information you might have about Chau."

"I have no information about Chau, Mr. Coyle. The last I heard she had stayed behind in the North."

"Can you find her?"

"It will be difficult, but I still have contacts. I will see what I can do."

"Alright. I will give you a bonus if you find Chau."

"That's very reasonable of you, Mr. Coyle."

"I'm a reasonable man unless I am dealt with dishonestly."

"When we meet and your bill is paid, I will give you the name of the village where Nguyet is living."

"Alright. Where and when?"

"I don't suppose you will be coming to Hue anytime soon? That's where my office is located."

"I can be there Thursday afternoon. I'll need your address."

Dung gave Coyle the address of his office and said, "There is one more thing you should know, Mr. Coyle."

"What's that?"

"Nguyet has a daughter… a tall daughter with fair skin."

Coyle was stunned by the news and said, "How old is she?"

"Ten years old."

"Sweet Jesus."

"She could be James McGovern's daughter, yes?"

"I suppose. I'll see you Thursday, Mr. Dung."

Coyle hung up the phone and wandered back to his quarters deep in thought. Sure, she could be McGoon's daughter. But as Coyle remembered back, she could also be his daughter. When Coyle had arrived in Hanoi to fly for the French Army, he had stayed at McGoon's bungalow for a month while trying to find himself a place of his own. Nguyet was one of two Vietnamese girls McGoon had inherited from the previous owner, a French man.

During his stay, Nguyet grew to like Coyle and slipped into his bed one night. It was a long,

125

memorable night. One of many. The next morning, Coyle could barely keep awake while flying a supply mission to an outpost near Sapa.

McGoon didn't mind that Coyle was shagging Nguyet. He believed in sharing. The girls had voracious appetites for sex and McGoon couldn't handle them both on a regular basis. He said Coyle was doing him a favor. Coyle was happy to oblige until he met a French journalist, Brigette Friang.

McGoon had died at Dien Bien Phu a short time later. The two girls had left the bungalow when they heard of his death before Coyle could get back and take care of them. Even though he no longer had a desire for Nguyet, Coyle believed he owed McGoon his life, and looking after his two whores was the least he could do.

Later that night, Coyle couldn't sleep. Three children that he didn't know about? He began to wonder if there were more. He got out a pencil and paper. He made a list of every woman he had sex with, at least those that he could remember. Some had names, while others just had faces. He would give those women names like Girl #3 at Madam Vinh's Houseboat or Waitress at the café near the statue of the general in Seoul, South Korea. It was a longer list than he had imagined, and he felt a little embarrassed... and a bit proud. He had never considered himself a great lover, but maybe he was wrong. When the list was done, Coyle faded off to sleep and had a dream...

He was flying with McGoon, who was sitting in the pilot's seat made of rattan that he had custom-made to fit him better. The mountains swept below them. Flying also made Coyle happy, especially when he was with McGoon. "Honey," said McGoon. "Liquid gold if ya ask me."

"Is that right?" said Coyle playing devil's advocate.

"Damned right. People pay good money for honey, especially honey from Vietnam. And it grows wild, just sitting up in the trees waiting to be harvested."

"What about the bees?"

"What about 'em?"

"Don't they get mad?"

"Sure, they do. That's why we hire some locals to collect the stuff. They know how to do it without getting stung or maybe they just don't mind cause they're getting paid. I don't know. The point is we could export it back to the states and maybe Europe."

"How do you know Americans will buy it? I mean, they got honey in the states already."

"Yeah, but have you ever tasted Vietnamese honey?"

"Can't say I have."

"It's sweet and fragrant cuz of all the tropical flowers. Americans want variety on their toast and biscuits."

"I see. So, we fly it back?"

"Why not?"

"Cuz it's a long way and will cost a ton in fuel."

"There you go with the negativity, Coyle. Why don't you start coming up with ideas to help me, instead of coming up with objections on why my ideas won't work?"

"I just don't wanna see you get hurt when you fall flat on your face, McGoon."

"I ain't gonna fall flat on my face, Coyle. I'll make it work."

"Okay. I believe ya."

"Good. It's time for you to go."

Coyle rose and slipped on his parachute, "Are you gonna be okay?"

"I'm always okay, Coyle. That's what's so great about positive thinking."

"Take care, McGoon. Thanks for the lift," said Coyle as he exited the cockpit.

Coyle slid open the cargo door and looked down. There was a battle below with a lot of tracer rounds going back and forth between the lines and explosions that lit up the night. He jumped.

As he pulled the rip cord on his chute and drifted downward toward the battleground, he looked at the aircraft, the Dora May, that McGoon was piloting. An anti-aircraft shell burst next to the right engine, and it began smoking. Another shell took out the left engine and the plane was falling fast. He watched the damaged aircraft skid across a runway and break apart. Coyle landed and ran toward the wreckage.

When he reached what was left of the aircraft, Coyle made his way inside the cockpit. He pried the door open and saw McGoon bleeding badly from where the control panel had wedged him into his seat. He was trapped. "Hey, buddy. You made it," said McGoon surprisingly chipper.

"I always make it, McGoon," said Coyle looking for something to pry his friend loose.

"Yeah, ya do."

"I'll get you out."

"No, you won't."

"What do you mean?"

"We both know I'm a goner."

"I suppose you're right. I'm sorry, McGoon."

"Not your fault, Coyle. But you will look after my whores, won't you?"

"Of course."

"Thanks, Buddy."

McGoon's sleeve caught fire and he said, "I hate this part."

Coyle tried to pat the fire out. "Don't do that, Coyle. You're just delaying the inevitable," said McGoon as the fire grew bigger and traveled up his arm.

"I don't want you to go, McGoon," said Coyle with tears welling up in his eyes.

"I appreciate that, but it ain't in the cards to save me. You go on, Coyle. I don't want you to see this next part."

"Bye, McGoon."

"Bye, Coyle."

Coyle climbed out of the cockpit and looked back through the doorway. McGoon was engulfed in flames and screaming. Coyle closed the door.

As always, Coyle woke up in a cold sweat and heaving for breath. He hated it when McGoon died.

Moscow, Russia

Sitting in his office in the Kremlin, General Secretary of the Communist Party Leonid Brezhnev was less than pleased with China's Mao Zedong's response to his cable. Brezhnev had asked Mao to allow Soviet trains to travel through China to deliver military and financial aid to North Vietnam. Brezhnev saw this as a simple request to his junior partner. Mao did not see himself or his country as a junior partner, but rather as a sovereign nation that had every right to protect its borders. Mao had agreed to allow Soviet trains to transport aid to North Vietnam but refused to allow Soviet cargo planes or any other aircraft into Chinese airspace. The Soviets were not above treachery and Mao was not going to test them. This wasn't the first time the Chinese had refused what Brezhnev considered a reasonable request. The Soviet leader's patience with China was wearing thin.

The Soviets did not have many allies. At least not yet. They couldn't afford to just cast aside China. The two countries shared a long border and both were nuclear powers. Brezhnev would once again bite his tongue for the good of the communist revolution that both countries believed in.

April 1, 1965 – Hanoi, North Vietnam

Le Duan and Ho Chi Minh wanted the same thing – the reunification of Vietnam. Ho Chi Minh was on board with Le Duan's plans to expand the war, or at least he wasn't going to stand in his way. Ho knew that Le Duan was the future and that he was the past. Vietnam needed a strong leader. Ho would help Duan achieve his goals for the revolution whenever possible, but also council caution when necessary. Ho had fought Duan for control of the politburo and lost. However, the aging Ho maintained the title of President of North Vietnam.

As president, it was Ho's responsibility to see that the military had enough soldiers to carry out the objectives of the communist party. At Duan's request as the party's first secretary, Ho decreed an updated military service law throughout North Vietnam. Enlistments were automatically extended indefinitely for soldiers and previously discharged soldiers were recalled. In addition, the number of young people inducted into the military was greatly increased. In 1965, the North expanded its army by 290,000 personnel and its self-defense militia from 1.4 million to 2.0 million. An army of women was recruited to repair the damage to the North from the American bombing campaigns. Hundreds and even thousands of women worked at an incredible speed to repair buildings, factories, bridges, and roads astonishing American intelligence analysts. It was a massive commitment. The North Vietnamese would serve until the war was won.

April 3, 1965 – Hanoi, North Vietnam

There was little doubt by either side that the American jet fighters were superior in technology and performance to any of the jets in the North Vietnamese Air Force. The American aircraft were faster, more maneuverable, and far better armed than the MiGs provided to North Vietnam by the Soviets and the Chinese. The North had no capability to manufacture or even repair heavily damaged aircraft. Everything had to be sent over the border to China and that took time leaving the North with fewer and fewer aircraft. The North Vietnamese still had not received the MiG-21s promised from the Soviets and had to make do with MiG-15s and 17s.

To prevent sabotage, the North Vietnamese MiGs had been based across the border in southern China instead of the North Vietnamese's own Phuc Yen Air Base near Hanoi. But the Gulf of Tonkin Incident and the start of the American bombing changed all of that.

The North Vietnamese Air Force was needed to defend Hanoi and returned home.

The American bombing of the North was a major threat to the fledgling air force. The North Vietnamese pilots knew they were facing an uphill challenge when it came to defending Hanoi. They were far outnumbered, and their aircraft were inferior to the American aircraft. But technology and numbers did not always win the day. On April 3, the North Vietnamese pilots set out to prove they could defeat the Americans with bravery and clever thinking.

Four U.S. Navy F-8E Crusaders took off for the USS Hancock stationed just outside of the Gulf of Tonkin. The aircraft were loaded for bear with their underwing hardpoints carrying eight 500 lb. bombs and their two-side fuselage mounted Y-pylons carrying LAU-10 rocket pods filled with four Zuni rockets each. For air-to-air defense, the F-8E had four Colt Mk 12 20 mm cannons in its lower fuselage. It was a heavy load, but the Crusaders could handle it. Once in formation, they headed inland.

Soviet-made radar installations picked up the inbound American fighter-bombers. Eight North Vietnamese MiG-17s were scrambled and moved to incept the American jets before they could drop their loads on targets near Hanoi. The MiG-17s hid in the clouds until the Americans were directly underneath, then they pounced.

Like most dogfights, the confrontation was brief and furious. The MiGs opened fire with the 23 mm cannons and raked two of the F-8s. One of the F-8s was seriously damaged and caught fire. Out of ammunition, the MiGs ducked back into the clouds. The damaged F-8s headed for Da Nang. With one of the aircraft still on fire, the pilots landed their jets safely. The rest of the group continued with their mission, dropped their bombs, then returned to the USS Hancock where they landed without incident.

April 4, 1965 – Thanh Hoa, North Vietnam

The next day, the North Vietnamese Air Force and the U.S. Air Force had another confrontation. A group of U.S. Air Force F-105 Thunderchiefs also loaded down with a heavy bomb load took off from Da Nang Air Base and headed North. A flight of F-100 Super Sabres flew air cover for the fighter-bombers. All the pilots kept an eye on the clouds. They believed the North Vietnamese pilots had been lucky the day before, but they weren't going to give them a second chance.

As they approached their target; the "Dragon Jaw" bridge outside of Thanh Hoa, the F-105s were attacked by MiG-17s which had approached through a thick layer of morning haze below the fighter-bombers. The F-100s who were flying above were too late to defend the bomb-laden F-105s which were unable to maneuver effectively. The North Vietnamese shot down two Thunderchiefs while an American F-100 shot down one of the MiGs. All three downed pilots died. The remaining MiGs retreated into the haze before more F-100s engaged. It was a clear air-to-air combat victory for the North Vietnam air force.

Although it was hard to admit, the American commanders were forced to acknowledge they had grossly underestimated the North Vietnamese air force. The Americans were still confident that their aircraft were superior to the North Vietnamese aircraft and their pilots were far better trained, but they needed to change their strategy… and fast. Using the two aerial confrontations to remind the pilots of the North Vietnamese capabilities, the commanders admonished their pilots to always be on the lookout for multiple points of attack and prepare for the unexpected.

Steel Tiger

Operation Barrel Roll was having limited success interdicting the North Vietnamese supply convoys on the Ho Chi Minh Trail. The mountain jungles in Northern Laos provided perfect cover for the North Vietnamese trucks and reinforced bicycles used to transport supplies. The fact that the North Vietnamese mostly traveled at night didn't help the American pilots in acquiring clear targets. During monsoon season, pilots were almost assured to encounter rain, drizzle, overcast, or fog which made effective bombing almost impossible. During the dry season, Laotian farmers used slash-and-burn techniques to clear their land for crops. The resulting smoke and haze also hindered bombing.

The North Vietnamese convoys hid during the day under huge camouflage nets at truck parks and supply depots constructed along the trail. The North Vietnamese often redistributed the weapons and supplies traveling down the trail toward South Vietnam. The trail was chopped up into sections where the most efficient means of transportation was used for the terrain in that area. This meant that the loads needed to be redistributed often. The redistribution points were the most fruitful targets for the American bombs because the supplies, trucks, and porters were clustered. But the redistribution camps were also expertly camouflaged, and movement was kept to a minimum during the day when American reconnaissance aircraft flew overhead.

The most frustrating element of the American bombing campaign was how fast the North Vietnamese engineers repaired the damage from the American bombs. A road cratered by fighter-bombers was often repaired overnight. A bridge downed by multiple bombs or rocket hits could be repaired within a few days. It seemed the North Vietnamese had an endless supply of labor and kept resources and tools nearby key points along the trail.

On top of the physical issues of interdicting the weapons and supplies, the airmen also had to obey an array of ever-changing air restrictions imposed by politicians to minimize the danger of causing civilian casualties and over-escalating the air war. The bombing raids were being micro-managed to the point that pilots often didn't know where or if they were allowed to attack the enemy caravans.

The commanders of the Laotian interdiction effort decided to split the bombing campaign into two separate operations. Operation Barrell Roll would continue in Northern Laos, while Operation Steel Tiger would be responsible for Southern Laos. Convoy targets in southern Laos were considered more valuable than targets in northern Laos. The Northern Vietnamese incurred great expenditures in resources and manpower to transport weapons and supplies along the Ho Chi Minh Trail. The closer they were to their final destination in South Vietnam the more valuable the shipment.

Steel Tiger also used different attack aircraft than Barrell Roll. Barrel Roll's arsenal was almost exclusively leftover bombs from missions in North Vietnam as part of Operation Rolling Thunder. If the original target could not be destroyed because of overcast skies or some other reason, then the bombers were diverted to targets in northern Laos. With Steel Tiger, many of the bombs used were from South Vietnam targets such as Viet Cong camps or supply convoys already over the border. Steel Tiger could also use South Vietnamese aircraft stationed in Saigon.

Since Westmoreland's command center was responsible for dispatching bombing missions in Vietnam and Laos, it could slice and dice the bombers however it saw fit. Unfortunately, both bombing campaigns were unable to cut off the flow of weapons and supplies completely. At times, the American bombers were more effective and slowed the North Vietnamese supply lines to a crawl.

The one method that did work consistently for the Americans in Laos was gunships. Mostly used at night, the gunships with the bottoms of their aircraft painted black were almost invisible to the North Vietnamese anti-aircraft guns and soldiers firing small arms into the darkness. If the anti-aircraft gun crews chose to use powerful their spotlights to find the American ghost planes, they could be quickly dispatched by the very prey they were hunting. The gunships on the other hand could use parachute flares to illuminate their targets. The miniguns that the gunships generated easily penetrated the jungle canopy and struck terror in the enemy below. The American aircrew could see their results when ammunition was ignited, or truck gas tanks exploded. Unlike the jet fighters and bombers, the gunships could linger above their targets at 2,000 feet in pylon turns for hours on end. When targets were found, it was death by patience, destroying one target and then moving to the next. It was hard to deny the gunship's effectiveness even when the jet pilots made fun of the fixed-winged aircraft's sluggish style of attack.

The CIA kept their own small fleet of gunships that were stored in hangers and flew out of Pleiku Air Base. Since they technically did not exist, the CIA gunship pilots disregarded many of the rules of engagement and picked their targets without restriction. Coyle and his aircrew had trained all of the gunship pilots and crews. They were like his own little air force to be metered out when assignments were received. He often took the most promising missions for himself. It was good to be a CIA prince.

Coyle's pacifism leftover from the Indochina War was gone. He had rejoined the war effort in Vietnam and was determined to win it. After the death of his fiancée Bian, Coyle had lost much of his compassion and had become cold. He blamed the North Vietnamese that had blackmailed her into becoming a spy. For that, he sought his pound of flesh and the gunship crews he trained were his tools of vengeance. He wondered what he had become… a true predator as he had been in World War II and the Korean War? Coyle had realized that war was prolonged and suffering continued unless an all-out effort was made by both sides to win. The faster a victor could be determined, and a war ended, the better it was for the civilians caught in between the warring factions. As a patriot, Coyle would do everything in his power to ensure that America was the victor. If that made him a killer, then sobeit.

Of course, if nuclear weapons were used, all bets were off, and everyone would lose. It did little good to irradiate a battlefield when the lethal effects would last for a decade and prevent the occupation of enemy territory even after victory, not to mention the horrific human toll.

April 5, 1965 - Moscow, Russia

North Vietnam was reeling from the American bombing campaign Rolling Thunder with multiple daily attacks on military facilities and civilian oil and gasoline storage tanks. While the North Vietnamese were far from giving in to the American's demands that they stop helping the Viet Cong, they were feeling the effects of the ongoing onslaught of air raids.

Seeking help, Le Duan, the communist party's first secretary in North Vietnam, went to Moscow. Duan was a confident and proud man. But he was also a patriot and would do what he needed to get the Soviet's help in acquiring weapons to fend off the American bombers. He met directly with his Soviet counterpart Brezhnev, and they had a frank conversation. Brezhnev liked Duan's passion for the communist revolution and his desire to bring the war in Vietnam to a swift conclusion in his favor. He listened carefully, then verbally approved Duan's request for anti-aircraft missiles that would be used to shoot down the

American aircraft invading North Vietnamese airspace. Duan was elated. North Vietnam would now have the means to stop the Americans without giving in to their demands.

Hanoi, North Vietnam

Construction on the Russian-made SAM missile sites began immediately, even before Le Duan's returned to North Vietnam or the arrival of the missiles from Russia. There was no time to spare.

A U.S. Navy RF-8 reconnaissance aircraft photographed the SA-2 surface-to-air missile site under construction. The revelation that North Vietnam would soon have SAMS "sent shivers down the spines of task force commanders and line aviators alike." With a maximum range of twenty-eight miles and a 440-pound warhead with high explosive fragmentation, the SA-2 anti-aircraft missiles were a game changer. Even so, the U.S. military would not authorize the destruction of the site so close to the civilian population of Hanoi. It would take the loss of several American aircraft to change its mind.

April 17, 1965 - Washington D.C., USA

Karen had finally recovered from the death of Alice Herz and was back photographing the anti-war movement with relish in Washington D.C. Activist organizers from Students for a Democratic Society had put together a protest that had attracted 25,000 anti-war demonstrators in the largest anti-war demonstration to date. Ironically, the number of protestors exceeded the number of U.S. soldiers currently deployed in South Vietnam.

Many tourists had come to the capital to view the blooming of cherry blossoms. Groups of high schoolers had also come to Washington DC for their senior trip. The city was already packed when the long line of marching demonstrators blocked the streets creating traffic snarls.

The protest started with a picket line and demonstration in front of the White House, then moved to the National Monument where Karen and other photographers could capture a clear image of the massive rally as both sides of the long fountain were covered with students. Folk singers Joan Baez and Phil Ochs played for the crowd and gave impassioned speeches to stop the war.

But the message was not always clear, as some speakers tried to connect other causes such as poverty and equal rights to the anti-war movement. It seemed everyone wanted their cause to climb onboard the peace train. Karen burned through a half dozen rolls of film during the day-long demonstration.

Saigon, North Vietnam

Granier made regular visits to the South Vietnamese counterintelligence unit. Having top secret clearance, he was allowed to view surveillance reports and photographs taken of individuals suspected of collaborating with the Viet Cong and NVA. Even when asked by the South Vietnamese intelligence staff who he was searching for, he never told them Colonel Thao. Instead, he made up an individual called, "Wei Li" who was supposedly an undercover Chinese agent.

Granier didn't expect that Thao would appear in any of the photographs taken by intelligence officers. Thao was far too smart to reveal himself. Instead, Granier was looking for something out of place that might lead him to Thao's whereabouts.

Granier also checked with U.S. military counterintelligence which was constantly monitoring radio calls in South Vietnam. He knew it was a long shot, but everything seemed like a long shot. Although he didn't give them Thao's name, Granier did ask the analysts to be on the lookout for anything that might indicate an individual was hiding or on the run, perhaps requesting help or transportation across the border. He said it would probably not be from a big city where there were lots of soldiers, but rather a village or hamlet. The individual he was searching for might speak in French which Thao spoke fluently. It was a broad net Granier was casting and he caught everything, all of which was useless.

Finally, Granier spent some time each week viewing aerial reconnaissance photographs of the countryside. Granier's instincts told him that Thao would avoid anyone in the military that might recognize him and therefore would seek refuge in the less populated countryside rather than a city. Granier wasn't sure exactly what he was looking for but sought things that looked out of place. The American analysts helped him by cross-referencing photos taken since General Khanh had once again taken power and contained his criteria. Again, it was a long shot. There were thousands of photographs almost all of which were of rice fields or jungles. But it was the photographs of villages and hamlets that most interested Granier. If

Thao was still in South Vietnam, a village or hamlet would most likely be where he was hiding.

Ho Chi Minh Trail – Mountains, Laos

It was 3 AM and Chau's eyes were dry and itchy, but she knew better than to take her eyes off the road in front of her truck. She would rest when the night and the driving were done. She knew her section of the route well. She had driven it hundreds of times since she joined Group 559 several years ago. She had joined the North Vietnamese Army to protect her village and family from the South. She also needed the money the government paid her for her service. She would send most of it home to her family and village.

It had been twenty-two years since she had left her village to find work in Hanoi. She didn't have an education, but she was attractive. She worked as a waitress in a restaurant for a month but found the work too hard on her back, plus the manager kept part of her pay as an incentive to keep him from firing her.

Next, she was a dancer at a bar. Late at night after the police had left the area, she was required to take off her clothes while dancing. She had a cute figure and her breasts were larger than most Vietnamese girls, so she didn't mind too much. She made good tips from the coins thrown on stage and customers often bought her drinks after her performance. That was how she had met a Frenchman. He lived with another girl in the bungalow before the American McGoon. The Frenchman thought a second girl would make a nice threesome. Chau was invited to stay with them and, after the Frenchman bought her a new pair of shoes, she accepted.

When she first met Nguyet, they fought like two alley cats. But after a couple of really big fights, they settled down and became best friends.

When the Frenchman finally left to go back to France, he left the two girls in the bungalow with some money and rent paid until the end of the month. McGoon, the new tenant, arrived just in time to pay the next month's rent and they convinced him that it would be in his interest to let them stay. The other American, Tom Coyle came later.

Everything fell apart when McGoon died. The French had lost the war and the communists were taking control. Hanoi was no longer a safe place. Nguyet went to the South and Chau stayed in the North.

When Chau volunteered for the army, she had been lucky. Many people wanted to join Group 559 but didn't have the required skills. The American Tom Coyle had taught her and Nguyet how to drive a jeep while he was staying at McGoon's bungalow where they all lived. When off duty, McGoon was usually too busy drinking or working on his next business idea to teach the two girls. Coyle volunteered to be their instructor and McGoon begrudgingly agreed. It wasn't that McGoon didn't want the girls to learn to drive, he just didn't see the point. He was taking care of them and felt that should be enough. But both girls wanted to learn to drive and fantasized about one day owning their own automobiles which they would race through the streets of Hanoi.

When Chau told the North Vietnamese recruiter that she could drive, she was immediately put behind the wheel of one of the Russian-made trucks to test her skill. It wasn't a very proud moment for her as she ground the truck's gears loudly, then released the truck's clutch too fast making the engine stall. But the fact that she eventually drove the truck out of the recruiting facility lot and onto the street without crashing was all that was needed to qualify her to join Group 559. She would learn to drive the treacherous roads of the Ho Chi Minh Trail under the tutelage of a veteran driver who was missing one eye, part of an ear, and two fingers. Eventually, she would be given her own truck to drive when she was ready.

When she was given leave before being sent to her section of the trail where she would drive, she spent her time visiting her family and friends in her village. She was treated with a strange reverence by everyone including the village elders. She was a driver on the great trail of Ho Chi Minh and was doing her part to help win the war to reunify her country. The village's deference made her feel old and like she no longer belonged in the place where she grew up. Why couldn't they see she was the same girl that had thrown rocks at chickens and swam naked in the stream near the village? She didn't like the way she was being singled out and left a day early to go back to the Group's headquarters in Laos. She was ready to serve and wanted to get on with it.

Chau did not own a wristwatch but could tell the time by the sky. The sky had just begun to lighten which meant it was now 4 AM. She had downshifted to slow her truck as it headed down a steep slope. Her cargo was ammunition. She didn't know what type but imagined grenades and maybe some mortar or recoilless rifle shells. It was a heavy load. Ammunition was just as important as weapons in her mind. The Viet Cong needed ammunition to win back their country from the fraudulent government in South Vietnam. The VC would also use the ammunition against the Americans. Chau had mixed feelings about that. She knew two Americans and liked them. But she also knew that America had chosen to help the anti-communists and was expected to invade the North at some point. Communists like herself would need to stop them. She might have to take up arms herself leaving the truck driving to someone else. That was okay. She knew how to fire the gun her commander had given her in case the convoy was attacked. She would continue to serve her country. She just hoped that Coyle was not part of the invasion. She would hate to have to kill him. McGoon would not have approved if he wasn't already dead.

As she approached the bottom of the mountain there was a thin valley with a river. As always, she would wait her turn to cross the river on the underwater bridge the engineers had constructed. Unlike many of the drivers, Chau knew how to swim and the river didn't scare her. What did cause her concern was that the river crossing was out in the open and could be seen by the American warplanes that passed overhead. The drivers had been instructed not to bunch up at the crossing and should remain in the cover of the jungle until it was their turn to cross the river. She held her arm out the truck's window and signaled for the driver behind her to stop. The signal would be passed down the convoy until every truck slowed to a stop and waited its turn to cross. As the driver of the lead truck, she would be the first in her convoy to cross the river.

Chau waited until she received a signal from the guards protecting the bridge. She turned off her truck's lights, slipped the truck into gear, and slowly released the clutch. The wheels moved forward across the gravel bank with a crunching sound. The guards guided her with hand signals. Reaching the edge of the river, she could not see the bridge hidden beneath the surface of the river. Instead, she followed the signals of the guard in charge of bridge crossings. The truck's wheels rolled into a foot of flowing water and onto a mix of sand and gravel over a bed of logs bound together with wire and rope. The bed of logs was held to the river floor with long iron stakes driven deep into the riverbed. Everything was secured to ensure nothing popped up at the wrong time revealing the location of the crossing to the American reconnaissance aircraft.

Chau was halfway across the river when one of the logs cracked from the weight of the truck and the left front wheel plunged downward wedging itself between two unbroken logs. This wasn't the first time this had happened. Most of the materials used on the Ho Chi Minh Trail were primitive. Over time they would fail and need to be replaced. Unfazed, Chau shifted the gearbox into its lowest setting and pressed the gas pedal. She used the clutch to rock the wheel back and forth hoping to pop it out of the newly made pothole.

Things were going along fine until she saw the guards on the riverbank looking skyward, some of them pointing. She felt a sick feeling in the pit of her stomach. She could not hear the sound of the aircraft engines above the reeving of her own truck's engine, but she knew the enemy was up there. She rolled down the window and shouted at the guards to push the truck. The guards hesitated. Angry, she called them cowards. Shamed into doing their duty, the guards waded into the river and pushed the truck all the time glancing skyward.

It seemed something was keeping the wheel from being dislodged. She told one of the guards to look at the front wheel below the water. He ran over and reached down to feel between the tire and the logs. He told her the tire had been punctured by the top of an iron stake when it broke through the log. The tire was flat and stuck on the stake. Chau cursed. She kept trying to unwedge the wheel and the guards kept pushing until she saw through the open window two parachute flares ignite in the sky over the crossing. The Americans were here. She did not hear the sound of jet engines and that frightened her even more. The guards abandoned the truck and ran for cover in the jungle. Chau was alone. She had once been told by a commissar that "bravery was not the absence of fear, but acting despite fear." She wouldn't give up. She would do her duty... no matter what happened.

Chau had never seen the American dragon, but she had heard about it from others that had seen it and had lived to tell about it. She didn't believe in mythical creatures, but that didn't mean she didn't fear them. There had to be some other explanation as to what it was. Soldiers had said it was invisible at night until it breathed its fire and then it was too late.

While continuing to rock the flat tire back and forth hoping to free it, she glanced skyward. It was a full moon and she could see the silhouette of a pair of wings and a long body against the clouds. Then, three tongues of fire descended from the heavens and reached down the riverbank in front of her where one of the guards was firing his machine gun skyward. The three columns surrounded the guard, then consumed him. His body disappeared in a dark mist. Her imagination ran wild. She was next. She changed gears into reverse and gunned the engine. Still, the wheel would not budge. The three fiery columns moved toward the river, toward her. She was out of time. She had to choose between duty and life. She chose life. She opened the door and jumped out of the truck's cab into the river. The current caught her and pulled her downstream. Floating on her back she watched as the three columns of fire reached her truck. The gas tank exploded sending a fireball skyward, then the ammunition in the cargo bed ignited creating an even bigger explosion. Fire burst out from the truck toward her. She grabbed for the bottom of the river but found nothing to cling to and pull herself beneath the surface. The fire rolled over her and she felt the water on her face boil blistering her skin. The air was gone, consumed by the inferno. She couldn't breathe. She was going to die. And then... it was over. The fire receded and the air returned. She could breathe again.

She steered herself to the riverbank and pulled herself out of the water. Her face stung from the blisters, but they too would eventually go away, and she would heal. She looked skyward. The fiery columns had disappeared, and the dark silhouette was moving off toward a mountain ridge. Then, after a few moments more, even its shadow against the clouds was gone. It was over. She had survived. Her truck and its precious cargo had not.

Sitting in his pilot's seat in the cockpit of his gunship, Coyle did not know that he had almost killed Chua, one of the women he had promised McGoon to protect. All he knew was that the Viet Cong would not be receiving a shipment of supplies. He had done his job and slowed the enemy. For that, he was satisfied.

Da Nang Air Base, South Vietnam

The war had changed for Lincoln and Turner as they continued to protect the perimeter of Da Nang Air Base. It was now hours or even days of boredom mixed with a minute of terror.

The Viet Cong did not assault the perimeter fence surrounding the airfield. That would have been suicide with the number of U.S. Marines now guarding the base. But that didn't mean that the Viet Cong had given up on destroying the American bombers attacking North Vietnam. The Viet Cong needed the men, weapons, and supplies the northern leaders were sending by way of the Ho Chi Minh Trail. In turn, Le Duan and the politburo wanted the American bombers based at Da Nang destroyed by the Viet Cong. To facilitate the destruction of the base, the North sent mortar shells. Several times a day, hidden Viet Cong mortar emplacements in the nearby houses and buildings would shell the air base hoping to hit a few bombers and terrorize the U.S. Marines protecting them.

The Viet Cong's problem was that the Chinese-made Type 31 and Type 63 mortars they were issued had a maximum range of a little over a mile which made their positions easily identifiable by the U.S. Marines guarding the perimeter of the air base. While the Marines were not permitted to use their mortars or artillery to defend their positions, they could call in air strikes.

To combat the air strikes, the Viet Cong limited their mortar assaults to one minute or less. By the time the American fighters were in the air and had closed in on the Viet Cong's position, the VC had packed up their mortars and disappeared into the city or jungle.

There were South Vietnamese patrols around the air base, but they never seemed to arrive in time to catch the VC mortar and rocket teams. ARVN morale was at an all-time low and few soldiers felt the need to fight for the unstable and unresponsive government. Some South Vietnamese troops that wanted to avoid fighting would cough or step on an old leaf or dried twig to warn the VC that they were coming and give them time to retreat before a firefight could begin.

In addition to the mortars, the Viet Cong were given rockets that had a range of over five miles making them much harder to find. At thirty-two pounds each, the 107 mm rockets were also bigger and more powerful than the mortar shells. The rockets were far more effective at destroying American aircraft on the ground. The VC mostly used single rocket launchers in their daily attacks. Their prized possession was a Type 63 multiple rocket launcher that could fire twelve rockets within twenty seconds. The rockets would explode in a tight pattern. Because they only had one and it used twelve rockets with each salvo, the VC only used their precious multi-rocket launcher when there was a clear target, such as a bomber preparing for takeoff at the beginning of a runway. Otherwise, the single rocket launchers spread throughout the surrounding neighborhoods and jungle were used to pick off U.S. Marine positions and jets parked on the apron or taxing after landing.

When the mortar assaults began, the U.S. Marines kept their heads down below the layers of stacked sandbags. With each attack at least one Marine was pelted with shrapnel and rushed to the base infirmary by corpsmen. Even under the care of veteran doctors and nurses, some Marines died from their wounds. While some death was expected, it was never welcomed.

Lincoln and Turner hated the mortar and rocket attacks. They always came at the most inconvenient time, like after a can of peaches was opened or when they were sitting in the latrine. It didn't matter what they were doing when the shelling started, they hunkered down and said their prayers while the world around them exploded, shaking the earth. The most frustrating part was that they couldn't do anything about it. The Marines were not permitted to leave the air base, not even to hunt down an enemy mortar crew after they had identified its position from the smoke that rose from the tubes after firing several rounds. The Marines were expected to endure the attacks without retaliation. It was a shitty job, but they did it.

Hanoi, South Vietnam

Le Duan had failed to defeat the South Vietnamese and win the war before the Americans had arrived as he had promised. Undeterred, he simply changed strategies. The North Vietnamese and the Viet Cong would be used to wear down the American public as the Viet Minh had done against the French public. By incurring great damage and loss of life against the French military, the Viet Minh had forced the French public to call for their troops to return to France. Now, they would do the same against the Americans that were invading their country. During a speech in the politburo, Le Duan said, "The Americans will see the bloody war and count their losses until they finally demand their troops return home. By contrast, the North will not count the cost. We will fight whatever way the United States wants, and though there may be temporary losses in battle, we will win in the end."

Le Duan's confidence was bolstered, and his political power grew when, seeing the American buildup of forces in the South, the Soviets and Chinese expanded their financial and military aid to North Vietnam.

DAVID LEE CORLEY

A New Strategy

April 20, 1965 – Honolulu, Hawaii

Everyone in the U.S. military's high command agreed, that America's war in Vietnam needed a new strategy. It did little good to hold a key position only to be bombarded by Viet Cong mortars and rockets. The American troops needed to secure the area surrounding their defensive positions and facilities. Ambassador Taylor was the ultimate commander in Vietnam and as such, he came up with a strategy that he proposed at a meeting in Honolulu. Honolulu was a halfway point that allowed those in Washington to get away from their everyday meetings and the commanders in Vietnam to leave behind their day-to-day task of putting out fires while they focused on planning and policy. The meeting was attended by Taylor, McNamara, McNaughton, Bundy, Westmoreland, Wheeler, and Admiral Grant Sharp, along with a series of CIA and military analysts that presented reports and summaries of data.

Having thought long and hard about the current situation in Vietnam, Taylor proposed what he called the "enclave strategy." The concept was to limit U.S. ground operations to within fifty miles of key positions mainly in the coastal area of Vietnam while the ARVN would carry out counter-insurgency operations in the surrounding area beyond the fifty-mile ring. Taylor felt it was vitally important that despite their disorganization and low morale, the ARVN needed to take the fight to the enemy. It was their country and if they didn't fight for it, they would never be able to fully defend themselves against the communists and the American military would be stuck in Southeast Asia forever. With expanded American support from air and artillery power, along with safe havens created by the American firebases and outposts, the ARVN would gain confidence and morale would improve. The enclave strategy was an expansion of the current strategy with more American support. American troops' exposure was limited which is what President Johnson wanted. He dreaded the images of American fathers and sons returning home in coffins.

The group of planners agreed with Taylor's revised strategy and recommended it to President Johnson. Pleased to see what he thought was forward progress, Johnson signed off on the strategy and ordered the Joint Chiefs of Staff to implement it immediately.

Da Nang Air Base, South Vietnam

With the implementation of the enclave strategy, the U.S. Marines protecting Da Nang Air Base were finally allowed to patrol the area around the perimeter and hunt down the Viet Cong mortar and rocket teams. The problem was that the air base was surrounded by civilian neighborhoods and the Viet Cong were masters at hiding their weapons until they were needed and mixing in with the local population. The only time the Marines could be sure they had caught the Viet Cong was if they had caught them firing on the base or during a firefight. Any other time was merely an educated guess as to a person's allegiance and there was no real proof. While the war was not conducted with judges and juries, the American Marines felt it was their duty to make sure a prisoner was Viet Cong before turning them over to the South Vietnamese counter-intelligence teams. The U.S. Marines knew that the counter-intelligence teams could be brutal in the methods of interrogation of prisoners of which many "disappeared" never to be heard from again. Some of the interrogators were even suspected of being agents of the North and would ensure that captured Viet Cong were killed before they could reveal any important information. Nobody seemed to be sure who they could trust and who they couldn't.

The U.S. Marines did not make excuses and carried out their mission even though the conditions were not ideal. The Marines were known for improvising and making do when necessary.

Lincoln and Taylor's company was selected for the first patrol beyond the wire. The Marines had mixed feelings but liked the idea of seeing some of the country beyond the air base. As true Marines, they wanted to get at the enemy. They also wanted to stretch their legs and see more of the beautiful girls that greeted them on Red Beach when they landed.

There was a large patch of jungle to the west of the airfield. Allowing the Viet Cong to view the airfield at all hours, it was an ideal hiding position. The U.S. Marines moved in to clear the area. Lincoln and Turner were surprised at the density of the jungle. Once below the jungle canopy, the air thickened and was more difficult to breathe. It was hot too. The canopy was like an oven trapping the heat. They were both in excellent shape, but their leg and arm muscles struggled to get enough air and they sweated profusely soaking their uniforms to the point that they would need to wring them out to lighten their load.

The jungle floor was uneven and tree roots nicknamed "ankle-breakers" were everywhere. Downed tree trunks covered with green moss and infested with termites were dangerous. The rotting wood could collapse at any moment trapping one's foot or leg. With the foliage so heavy, it was hard to see beyond twenty or thirty yards an easy shot for an enemy rifle. It created an uneasy feeling that the Marines were constantly being watched by an unseen enemy. They could be surrounded and outnumbered and never know it until it was too late. Even the veterans kept a close watch on the broad leaves and hanging vines looking for movement. Being caught off-guard was not an acceptable option for a Marine, especially those that had fought in the jungles during the Pacific War. They knew the dangers and how to minimize them. They would teach the others, but it would take time. The job at hand was keeping everyone alive until they could learn for themselves. It was the way of the U.S. Marines.

The Viet Cong were not expecting the Americans that day. The Marines had always stayed behind the wire at the air base and were nothing to fear. The Viet Cong were the aggressors. They were the hunters, and the Marines and aircrews were their prey. They would soon find that things had changed. The Marines were the point of the U.S. military's spear and fearsome fighters. It was the Viet Cong that would now become the prey as the two sides faced off in the jungle outside the Da Nang air base.

It was a Marine reconnaissance team that first encountered a platoon of Viet Cong sitting in their hidden camp cleaning their weapons and eating the rice with fish sauce. They did not fire at their enemy but withdrew to report back to their company commander while leaving one Marine to keep watch.

The Marines were spread out in a long skirmish line as they searched the jungle. Word came that the enemy had been found and everyone tensed. Lincoln and Turner were excited and chilled by the thought that they were about to have an actual firefight that they had heard so much about from the veterans. The Marines closed ranks and advanced toward the enemy camp. They were well trained and kept spread out so that an unseen enemy machine gun or mortar round could not take out more than a couple of Marines before the others could return fire.

Lincoln and Turner were assigned to the flanking squad that would wait until the enemy was engaged with the rest of the Marine company, then hit them from the side where they were weakest and roll up the enemy line like grandma's biscuit dough. It was an ancient tactic but effective. They took up a firing position behind a large fallen tree. Lincoln was sure the tree was rotten inside and would offer little protection against the enemy's return fire, but it was better than nothing.

Once in position, the Marine assault began with three 60 mm mortar rounds and a volley of fire from the rest of the American company hidden in the jungle. The Viet Cong that survived the volley and mortar rounds hit the dirt and scrambled for their weapons. They returned fire hoping to keep the Americans from charging before they were prepared. More mortar rounds slammed into the VC's campsite severely wounding two more men.

In position on the flank of the enemy's line, Lincoln and Turner were ordered to open fire with the M60. The machine gun ripped into the camp from the side. The other Marines in the flanking squad opened fire pinning the VC down.

The VC's mortar teams finally fired off their first rounds. They were random shots since the mortar crew didn't have a clear idea of their enemy's location. The Marines seemed to be firing from every direction. More Viet Cong went down, wounded or dying.

The Viet Cong commander was hit in the chest by one of Lincoln's bullets and fell backward. Seeing their commander down, the Viet Cong began to break. At first, it was just one or two soldiers, but the feeling of defeat quickly spread as more and more ran for their lives.

The Marine commander, a captain, did not want to let the enemy escape and ordered his men to charge. They did and several Marines were hit by the Viet Cong veterans that continued to hold the line.

Seeing the company charge, the flaking squad Marine sergeant ordered his men to "get up and at 'em."

Being charged from two sides broke the will of the VC veterans. They retreated while continuing to fire their weapons.

Lincoln watch in horror as the Marine sergeant caught a round in the neck and fell. He knelt beside him and put his hand over the wound. The sergeant growled, "Get your fucking gun up, Marine."

Shocked, Lincoln released his hand from the wound and went back to firing at the enemy. Blood poured out of the sergeant's neck. He put his hand over the wound, but it was no use. Blood poured out between his fingers and onto the ground. Knowing what was about to happen, the sergeant closed his eyes and went limp. He was dead.

The Marines chased the Viet Cong through the jungle until the VC had vanished. The company captain thought it uncanny how an entire platoon could just disappear like that. It was frustrating.

The tally for the battle was one Marine dead and three wounded. Seven Viet Cong bodies were recovered, and four wounded prisoners were taken. All and all it was a good day for the U.S. Marines, but they would have to get better at fighting the Viet Cong... a lot better.

While the other Marines celebrated with cold cokes and steaks provided by the battalion commander, Lincoln sat off by himself staring at the ground. Turner walked over and said, "Are you sad about the sergeant dying and all?"

"I guess," said Lincoln.

"People are going to die in this war. Good people. There ain't nothing we can do about it. It's just gonna happen. We gotta move on and stay alive."

"Is that right?"

"That's right."

"Then let me ask you something… if a veteran like the sergeant can get killed, how easy is it gonna be for us to die?"

"Don't jinx us, Linc. Things is bad enough as it."

"Sorry. Go eat your steak."

"You'll be along?"

"Yeah, just a couple more minutes."

Turner left. Lincoln sat staring at the ground for another minute then rose and joined Turner with the rest of the company.

April 22, 1965 – Washington D.C., USA

As President Johnson's Secretary of Defense, McNamara often spoke to the press giving them updates on the Vietnam War and other potential conflicts around the world. Talking about the overall strategy for nuclear weapons, McNamara asked reporters not to use his name when he said, "We are not following a strategy that recognizes any sanctuary or any weapons restriction. But we would use nuclear weapons only after fully applying our non-nuclear arsenal. In other words, if 100 planes couldn't take out a target… we would try 200 planes, and so on. But our 'inhibitions' on using nuclear weapons are not overwhelming. It is 'inconceivable' that nuclear weapons would be used in the present circumstances of the Vietnam War. However, we do not rule out the possibility that circumstances might arise in which nuclear weapons may have to be used."

In response to McNamara's comments, Nikolai Feorenko, the Soviet Ambassador to the United

Nations said, "See the statement made today by Mr. McNamara... The United States is not averse to utilizing — this time perhaps as tactical weapons - nuclear warheads against the people of an Asian country as they have done once before, covering themselves with indelible shame for centuries to come. Mr. McNamara clearly reserved the right to unleash nuclear war in Vietnam."

Leaders around the world flooded President Johnson with cables criticizing McNamara's comments and warned the United States that the use of nuclear weapons was immoral and would not be tolerated under any circumstances except in defense of the American homeland.

Johnson had made clear his position of not using nuclear weapons except in defense but agreed with McNamara and the Pentagon that all options needed to be left on the table as a deterrent to more aggressive action in Vietnam by China or the Soviets. The Joint Chiefs of Staff often reminded the president that the American military had developed smaller, tactical nuclear weapons including a reengineered nuclear version of the MGR-3 Little John missile that could be used on enemy chokepoints without the broad nuclear fallout suffered in Japan.

April 29, 1965 – White House – Washington D.C., USA

FBI Director J. Edgar Hoover met with President Johnson in the White House to explain the implications of a recent U.S. intelligence report that had caused concern among several cabinet members and advisors. In the report, an analysis of American protests against the Vietnam War was part of Chinese and North Vietnamese strategies to support the members of America's "New Left" in their goal to intensify anti-war protests within the United States to the point that they would create a traumatic domestic crisis leading to a complete breakdown in law and order. The only way to restore domestic tranquility was to withdraw U.S. troops from Vietnam and bring them home.

At first, Johnson thought the idea was farfetched, but as Hoover explained how the crisis could realistically evolve, Johnson became less confident in his conviction. Hoover concluded his explanation by revealing that several members of the American media were unknowingly helping the communists achieve their goal and showed Johnson surveillance photographs of anti-war meetings with photojournalists documenting the proceedings. Karen Dickson, holding her camera up to snap a photo, was the first photo in the folder that Johnson reviewed. As he thumbed through the photos, Johnson asked, "So, what are you doing about this?"

"At the moment just surveillance. The protests have been mostly peaceful, and the agitators haven't broken any major laws that would require federal legal action. However, if the protests become violent, we would most likely expand our surveillance to include wiretaps and undercover agents infiltrating anti-war organizations and possibly media organizations in hopes of discovering actual collaboration with the enemy," said Hoover.

"I see. I suppose that is not a bad idea… just in case things get out-of-hand," said Johnson closing the folder. "But be careful, Edward. I don't want any violation of constitutional issues. I've got enough problems."

"Of course, Mr. President."

April 29, 1965 – Canberra, Australia

Speaking before Parliament in Canberra, Australian Prime Minister Robert Menzies informed the ministers that he was sending the 1st Battalion of the Royal Australian Regiment to South Vietnam to fight the war against the communist aggressors.

The day before the announcement, Menzies had sent a cable to South Vietnamese Premier Phan Huy Quat stressing that it was urgent that South Vietnam actually send a request asking Australian troops to enter the war. Quat's cable did not arrive until two and a half hours before Menzies was scheduled to speak to Parliament avoiding an international faux pas.

Johnson and McNamara were pleased by the news that Australia was entering the war. The more countries that joined the war effort, the more American military forces were perceived to be part of a coalition and not an imperialist power bent on taking over Vietnam for themselves.

May 3, 1965 – Saigon, South Vietnam

The Viet Cong had been making major advances in the South almost daily. Heavily armed and well-trained, the U.S. Marines were holding their own, but they couldn't be everywhere at once. Laden down by poor leadership, the demoralized South Vietnamese troops were almost useless and some units would retreat even before putting up any type of resistance against the VC. The situation had clearly turned from really bad to worst.

The head of MACV General Westmoreland was not a quitter. He was determined to save South Vietnam even if the South Vietnamese were not capable of saving it themselves. Westmoreland had already requested and was about to receive the 173rd Airborne brigade to protect the Bien Hoa Air Base and the port of Vung Tau, but he already knew that they alone would not be enough to stem the Viet Cong tide. Realizing that the ARVN military in the South was just weeks away from collapsing, Westmoreland with Ambassador Taylor's approval sent an urgent request to the Pentagon asking for 20,000-30,000 more troops right away.

In turn, the Joint Chiefs of Staff relayed Westmoreland's request to the White House.

White House – Washington D.C., USA

Having read Ambassador Taylor's reports, Johnson had been expecting a request for more troops. McNamara argued that there wasn't much of a choice in the matter if the president wanted to save South Vietnam. Johnson said, "I want to do enough, but not too much. I doubt this will be the last request for more troops. We need to meter things out, so our generals understand it's not an open bank vault where they can get whatever they want, whenever they want. They have to keep their requests within reason."

"I don't think General Westmoreland is crying wolf, Mr. President," said McNamara. "You've read the same reports I have. The South is falling faster than we imagined. If the Viet Cong take over the government, it's over. We will have no choice but to withdraw."

"We could still fight them."

"Mr. President, I don't doubt your sincerity, but how would that look to the world? We have other interests that need international support. I don't think we want to make this our last stand if we can help it."

"I suppose you're right, Bob. This is gonna be a bloody war and a lot of that blood is gonna come from our boys."

"Yes, Mr. President. But it can't be helped. We've got to stand by our ally even if they won't stand for themselves."

"I wanna think about it, Bob. Two full divisions are a really big deal and one Helluva commitment."

"I understand, Mr. President. But there isn't much time if we hope to salvage what's left of the South."

"I know, Bob. Give me until tomorrow morning to think about it."

"Of course, Mr. President."

Johnson did not sleep much that night. He didn't even try. Instead, he sat in his study where his "thinking chair" had been brought from Texas. It was his grandfather's rocking chair made of oak and lubricated with linseed oil every year to keep the wood from cracking over time. As he rocked, he stared off into space. He couldn't believe the situation he was in. It was the opposite of what he wanted. He felt like he was being dragged into Hell while grasping for a rock or a root to halt the devil's progress. It was useless and he knew it.

The next morning, Johnson, with sleepless bags under his eyes and looking pale, called McNamara into the Oval Office and told him to inform the Joint Chiefs of Staff that General Westmoreland's request for more troops would be granted, but not to the full extent of his petition. The American military would send two more battalions of Marines already forward deployed in the Philippines in hopes of showing America's commitment to their ally and stabilizing the situation. The president also changed the mission from base security to active combat. It was the first time U.S. troops were being ordered to take the fight to the enemy in Vietnam. The Marines would no longer be tethered to the American air bases. Johnson ordered that the change in mission be kept secret. By order of the president, the truth would be withheld from the American public. McNamara agreed that it seemed reasonable and carried out Johnson's orders.

Saigon, South Vietnam

Receiving a cable from the Pentagon informing him that two Marine battalions were being sent and should arrive within the week, Westmoreland was disappointed but determined to make do. He figured he could use the Marines and the South Vietnamese troops in joint operations. Hopefully, the U.S. Marines esprit de corps would inspire the ARVN soldiers and boost their morale. He wasn't sure it would work, but he didn't have an alternative but to suggest that the U.S. military pull out of Vietnam immediately before the whole thing came crashing down. But retreat wasn't in Westmoreland's character. He and the troops under his command would fight on and hope for the best. In the meantime, he would continue to request the troops and resources he needed to win but that the president was not yet willing to give him.

UCB - Berkeley, California

The University of California Berkeley campus was the West's lightning rod for anti-war protests. After a noon rally on campus, hundreds of students and professors marched to the city's draft board. Forty male students huddled like a football team, removed their draft cards from their wallets, and pitched them onto a small fire that had been started by one of the organizers. They squatted down to watch their anti-war protest burn. Draft card fires were becoming a popular form of protest as young men across the country showed their commitment not to join the war effort. Some were cowards that feared being killed or severely wounded while fighting in a far-off land. Others were truly committed to stopping the war that in their minds had national interest and was immoral. The anti-war movement was growing rapidly on campuses in the western and northern United States.

Most of the students and professors on campuses in the south and midwest were supportive of the war. The students shouted down anti-war demonstrations whenever they appeared.

Karen had flown out the day before and was there to document the protest with her camera. She moved around the circle snapping photos of the young men watching their cards burn, some making a V with their fingers to signify peace. She took photos of police, some on horses, standing by in case things got out of hand. While most of the citizens living in Berkeley were law-abiding, there was a more liberal attitude toward the demonstrations, and many had expressed their concern that the police should control themselves and not arrest the protestors unless they started destroying property. Berkeley was a nice community with expensive homes and businesses that needed protection. Karen caught the ambivalence of the passersby as they watched the demonstration unfold with a cautious eye.

Across the street, two men in an unmarked sedan took photos of the protest participants and were particularly interested in Karen standing in the middle of the group of draft card burners.

The initial protest was against the U.S. intervention in the Dominican Civil War that had recently erupted, but the students that had protested in front of the draft board said their emphasis was on the Vietnam War. Organizers of demonstrations were frustrated at the students that kidnapped their cause. How was anyone supposed to take them seriously when their student followers seemed to have a problem with anything the U.S. government did anywhere in the world? In the beginning, the Vietnam anti-war movement struggled to find its footing, but matured and found focus as the war drudged on with more and more American teenagers being called up to serve in an unjust war. The organizers saw their efforts as a righteous cause.

White House – Washington D.C., USA

As the bombing of North Vietnam continued and U.S. Marine landed in South Vietnam, world leaders became more concerned that the war in Southeast Asia was escalating and could soon spread to other parts of the world. President Johnson was barraged with phone calls and cables from American allies pleading for restraint on behalf of the United States.

United Nations secretary-general U Thant proposed a three-month ceasefire that garnered no response from North Vietnam or the Viet Cong. Britain's Prime Minister offered to reconvene the Geneva peace talks that had originally created North and South Vietnam. The new proposed goal was to reunite Vietnam. The United States was not a supporter of a neutralization policy it believed was equivalent to surrendering to the communists. The Americans still believed that if an election encompassing all of Vietnam was held, the communist leader Ho Chi Minh would be elected president and the South would fall under the control of the communists. The president felt that as bad as things were at the moment, the loss of Vietnam to the communists would be far worse because it would give the revolution of China and the Soviets a victory and encourage more aggressive action in other countries in Southeast Asia.

Frustrated by the growing descent, Johnson decided to take his argument directly to the American people. During one of Johnson's greatest speeches on the Vietnam War given at John Hopkins University, the president said, "Tonight Americans and Asians are dying for a world where each people may choose its own path to change.

This is the principle for which our ancestors fought in the valleys of Pennsylvania. It is the principle for which our sons fight tonight in the jungles of Vietnam.

Vietnam is far away from this quiet campus. We have no territory there, nor do we seek any. The war is dirty and brutal and difficult. And some 400 young men, born into an America that is bursting with opportunity and promise, have ended their lives on Vietnam's steaming soil.

Why must we take this painful road? Why must this Nation hazard its ease, and its interest, and its power for the sake of a people so far away?

We fight because we must fight if we are to live in a world where every country can shape its own destiny. And only in such a world will our own freedom be finally secure. This kind of world will never be built by bombs or bullets. Yet the infirmities of man are such that force must often precede reason, and the waste of war, the works of peace. We wish that this were not so. But we must deal with the world as it is, if it is ever to be as we wish.

The world as it is in Asia is not a serene or peaceful place. The first reality is that North Vietnam has attacked the independent nation of South Vietnam. Its object is total conquest.

Of course, some of the people of South Vietnam are participating in the attack on their own government. But trained men and supplies, orders and arms, flow in a constant stream from north to south. This support is the heartbeat of the war.

And it is a war of unparalleled brutality. Simple farmers are the targets of assassination and kidnapping. Women and children are strangled in the night because their men are loyal to their government. And helpless villages are ravaged by sneak attacks. Large-scale raids are conducted on towns, and terror strikes in the heart of cities. The confused nature of this conflict cannot mask the fact that it is the new face of an old enemy.

Over this war—and all Asia—is another reality: the deepening shadow of Communist China. The rulers in Hanoi are urged on by Peking. This is a regime which has destroyed freedom in Tibet, which has attacked India, and has been condemned by the United Nations for aggression in Korea. It is a nation which is helping the forces of violence in almost every continent. The contest in Vietnam is part of a wider pattern of aggressive purposes.

Why are these realities our concern? Why are we in South Vietnam?

We are there because we have a promise to keep. Since 1954 every American president has offered support to the people of South Vietnam. We have helped to build, and we have helped to defend. Thus, over many years, we have made a national pledge to help South Vietnam defend its independence. And I intend to keep that promise. To dishonor that pledge, to abandon this small and brave nation to its enemies, and to the terror that must follow, would be an unforgivable wrong.

We are also there to strengthen world order. Around the globe, from Berlin to Thailand, are people whose well-being rests, in part, on the belief that they can count on us if they are attacked. To leave Vietnam to its fate would shake the confidence of all these people in the value of an American commitment and in the value of America's word. The result would be increased unrest and instability, and even wider war.

We are also there because there are great stakes in the balance. Let no one think for a moment that retreat from Vietnam would bring an end to conflict. The battle would be renewed in one country and then another. The central lesson of our time is that the appetite of aggression is never satisfied. To withdraw from one battlefield means only to prepare for the next. We must say in southeast Asia—as we did in Europe—in the words of the Bible: "Hitherto shalt thou come, but no further."

There are those who say that all our effort there will be futile—that China's power is such that it is bound to dominate all southeast Asia. But there is no end to that argument until all of the nations of Asia are swallowed up.

There are those who wonder why we have a responsibility there. Well, we have it there for the same reason that we have a responsibility for the defense of Europe. World War II was fought in both Europe and Asia, and when it ended, we found ourselves with continued responsibility for the defense of freedom.

Our objective is the independence of South Vietnam, and its freedom from attack. We want nothing for ourselves—only that the people of South Vietnam be allowed to guide their own country in their own way. We will do everything necessary to reach that objective. And we will do only what is absolutely necessary.

In recent months attacks on South Vietnam were stepped up. Thus, it became necessary for us to increase our response and to make attacks by air. This is not a change of purpose. It is a change in what we believe that purpose requires. We do this in order to slow down aggression. We do this to increase the confidence of the brave people of South Vietnam who have bravely borne this brutal battle for so many years with so many casualties.

And we do this to convince the leaders of North Vietnam–and all who seek to share their conquest–of a very simple fact: We will not be defeated. We will not grow tired. We will not withdraw, either openly or under the cloak of a meaningless agreement.

We know that air attacks alone will not accomplish all of these purposes. But it is our best and prayerful judgment that they are a necessary part of the surest road to peace. We hope that peace will come swiftly. But that is in the hands of others besides ourselves. And we must be prepared for a long-continued conflict. It will require patience as well as bravery, the will to endure as well as the will to resist.

I wish it were possible to convince others with words of what we now find it necessary to say with guns and planes: Armed hostility is futile. Our resources are equal to any challenge. Because we fight for values and we fight for principles, rather than territory or colonies, our patience and our determination are unending.

Once this is clear, then it should also be clear that the only path for reasonable men is the path of peaceful settlement. Such peace demands an independent South Vietnam—securely guaranteed and able to shape its own relationships to all others, free from outside interference–tied to no alliance–a military base for no other country. These are the essentials of any final settlement."

Johnson went on to offer the Vietnamese people in both the North and South one billion dollars in U.S. development aid if the Northern leaders would lay down their arms and stop supporting the Viet Cong. The development aid would be used to build schools, hospitals, hydroelectric dams along with tools and technology to improve Vietnamese harvests. In addition, the United States would send surplus crops stored in American warehouses to feed both North and South. While the amount seemed exorbitant, it would have been the deal of the century. The Vietnam War would end up costing the American people $168 billion in military expenditure and financial aid. It proved once again that war was futile as well as a great waste of blood and treasure.

Over the weeks following Johnson's speech and offer, the president was not surprised when the North Vietnamese declared that his offer of development aid was a trick and continued their attacks on the South. In their eyes, the North was winning, and it was not prudent to give up what they had fought so hard to gain. The revolution would continue until the final victory was won and the country was united under a communist flag.

After hearing of the North's rejection of his offer, Johnson assembled his cabinet and advisors to discuss how many U.S. troops would be needed to bring the North Vietnamese and Viet Cong to their senses. If the North would not accept his carrot, Johnson would use a stick to force them to the negotiating table.

Hearing wide-ranging council from his cabinet and advisors, Johnson decided on what he felt was the right number of troops. He ordered McNamara and the Joint Chiefs of Staff to send 50,000 combat troops to General Westmoreland immediately and ordered the military to prepare to send another 50,000 before the end of the year. The huge troop commitment was designed to show the North Vietnamese and their allies that America was in it for the long haul. America was in it to win.

May 9, 1965 – Chu Lai, South Vietnam

The American commanders soon realized that the time aircraft took to reach a battlefield had a direct correlation with the effectiveness of air-to-ground support. The Viet Cong preferred to hit fast and hard against the Americans and often retreated before air or artillery could be called in to drive them off. If aircraft were closer to the areas of conflict, the warplanes could play a bigger role and give the American outposts and patrols an advantage against their elusive enemy.

As a result, the 10th U.S. Naval Mobile Construction Battalion began construction of the first combat zone Short Airfield for Tactical Support known as "STAS." The new airfield would utilize a 4,000-foot runway that was quickly cut out of the jungle. The entire installation was built in twenty-three days and immediately went into use. A-4 Skyhawks from VMA-225 and VMA-311 took off and landed on the short runway. Throughout the day and night, pilots would stand by in or next to their armed aircraft waiting for airstrikes to be called in for the troops in the surrounding area. Their jet fighters would usually arrive on target within five minutes of a radio call catching the Viet Cong before they could flee into the jungle. The Americans were learning what worked and what didn't.

Battle of Song Be

May 7-15, 1965 - Song Be, South Vietnam

The South Vietnam military was in desperate need of experienced snipers to fend off the Viet Cong. Before any attack, the VC surveyed the area of operation, especially the ARVN or American defenses. Detailed maps were created to develop a proper plan of attack. An experienced sniper could curtail VC reconnaissance teams. A single bullet could set back a VC assault for several days giving the defenders more time to prepare.

The problem was training, or the lack thereof. The American military had snipers but was reluctant to release them from their current assignments to train the South Vietnamese. The snipers were needed to defend American air bases and facilities.

Granier had trained CIA officers before being recruited for Lansdale's paramilitary teams in South Vietnam. He was also a sniper. One of the best in the country. Although he suspected that something was up, the Saigon embassy's CIA station chief did not know that Granier was on a covert assassination assignment for the director of the CIA.

The CIA Chief of Station in Saigon had received orders that Granier was to be given a thirty-day leave, but gave no reason. Granier didn't want it or need it. In his mind, if nobody in Langley informed him otherwise, Granier was available for assignment.

When asked to train a team of snipers in Song Be, Granier could have refused. He didn't. He saw the need and was tired of waiting around for intelligence to come up with something useful on the location of Colonel Thao his target. Granier was never one to just sit around and relax. Relaxing made him soft which was something he couldn't accept... ever. Besides, it was easy enough to check in by phone or radio with the various intelligence groups collecting data for him. He could do that in the field while being productive.

The Be River started in Cambodia and flowed into South Vietnam on its way to Saigon. The river was often used by the North Vietnamese to transport weapons and supplies to the Viet Cong.

To cut off the enemy boats that mostly traveled at night, the ARVN began construction of a fortified outpost on a hill overlooking the river and a nearby town. The engineers constructing the garrison were protected by the South Vietnamese 34th and 36th Ranger Battalions which would occupy the outpost once completed. A detachment of U.S. Special Forces known as SF B-34 was sent to reinforce the rangers during final construction. Several light tanks operated by local militiamen rounded out the South Vietnamese defenses.

Coyle used a small plane to fly Granier to the airfield just outside of Song Be. Granier brought three new sniper rifles that he had secured from MACV. Before flying back, Coyle helped Granier carry the rifles to the construction site on the hill. "It looks ominous enough," said Coyle.

"I suppose they'll find out soon enough," said Granier.

"They're expecting an attack?"

"Yep. VC don't want their river supply line cut off by a fortress. It's better to hit it before it's completed than after when all the weapon systems are in place."

"So, why in the hell are you here?"

"Because they asked nicely. Besides, I am only staying three days."

"Is that long enough to train snipers?"

"Of course, not. It takes years. But that's as long as the CIA was willing to loan me out. I'll have to make do. If they're smart enough, I can teach 'em the basics."

Reaching the top of the hill, Coyle set down the two rifles he was carrying and said, "I should probably get back before sunset."

"Right. Thanks for the lift."

"No problem. Watch yourself, Granier."

"I always do."

Coyle went back down the hill. Granier asked around for the commanding officer in charge of the Special Forces detachment in hopes of borrowing a translator and finding a place to stow his gear.

The Ranger battalion commanders had each selected four of their best shooters to receive instruction from Granier. Using his Special Forces translator, Granier looked over the candidates' service records and disqualified two of them for being idiots. Three of the students were assigned to be spotters and given rangefinder binoculars. The three remaining soldiers were to become snipers. The group was divided into two-man teams of a spotter and a sniper, and each team was handed a rifle with a scope and a pair of rangefinder binoculars.

As his truncated course began, Granier ordered the two-man teams to field strip their new weapons to ensure proper cleaning and operation. Even though it chewed up valuable time, Granier was a stickler for proper maintenance of a sniper team's weapon. When one of the soldiers complained about the mundane task, Granier said, "My course, my itinerary."

Once the weapons were reassembled, Granier inspected each weapon meticulously and pointed out any flaws he saw. "Details are what will keep you and those you protect alive," said Granier. "Once I am gone, I want each team to practice with blindfolds until they can field strip their weapons in the dark. Each of you must train to become a perfectionist when it comes to maintaining your team's weapon. I guarantee you, your lives will depend on it."

Granier spent little time observing them shoot. He knew they were good or they would not have been chosen. Besides, while essential, shooting was only a fraction of what they needed to learn to become a sniper team. He would tell them to practice shooting on their own. In time, they should be able to hit a large coin three consecutive times at 100 yards. They were to keep practicing until both team members could do it. If the shooter was ever wounded or killed, the spotter would need to complete the team's mission.

The lives of others would depend on the sniper team succeeding. The team members were to become redundant, each knowing how to correctly perform the other's job. They were told that once they mastered the 100-yard shot, they would continue to perfect their skill at 200-yards and so on until they can hit a coin at 800-yards. He told them to keep in mind that the effects of wind and gravity would increase as they increased their range. And that they should always try to use bullets from the same batch by checking the lot number. They needed consistent gunpowder to hit a target at 800-yards. If possible, they should just take an entire box of bullets from the armory and hide it for their personal use.

For three days Granier taught them the basics of being a sniper. He also taught them the tips and tricks he had learned over the years. Things that only a veteran sniper would know. He imparted his knowledge freely so they would succeed. So, they would stay alive. "Never stay in a fixed position. It's sure death. A sniper is a nomad that pops up where the enemy least expects, then moves quickly once his shot is fired and the enemy is eliminated," said Granier. "You must be rigorous about gathering intelligence. Talk to the soldiers nearby and find out where the enemy thinks there are weak points in your outpost's defenses. Work slowly, cautiously, and methodically. A successful sniper will calculate and re-calculate before firing one shot. You should only need one shot if you do your job right. Motion is what kills you. Learn to lie like a stone, completely invisible to the enemy. Nerves, concentration, and endurance will carry the day. Do not fire until you are certain of a kill. It's a discipline you must master if you are going to be victorious. Impatience is your death."

At the end of the third day, it was time for Granier to go. His closing remark to his students was a Chinese proverb, "Kill one man, terrorize a thousand."

He left them and went to the Special Forces area of the outpost to gather his gear. He found the Special Forces commander, a captain listening to a radio report. He looked concerned which was rare for anyone in Special Forces. "Are you heading out?" said the commander.

"Yeah. Just wrapped up. What's up?" said Granier.

"The VC are coming. Two regiments – the 761st and 763rd."

"Twenty-five hundred?"

"Something like that."

"How many do you have?"

"All-in? Just under one thousand. How did your students do? I have a feeling we're gonna need them."

"Honestly, I think they'll do their best, but they're new."

"Well, we'll take what we can get. Sorry, I can't chat. Things to do."

"Where do you want me?"

"I appreciate the offer, but one man ain't gonna make a difference."

"Depends on the man."

The commander considered for a moment, then said, "If we could take out their platoon commanders and political officers, it could make a big difference."

"I could do that."

"Really?"

"Really. But I'm gonna need a box of ammo."

The commander laughed and said, "You can have as much ammo as you need, Granier."

"Do I have time for some chow?"

"Yeah. They won't attack until after sunset. Probably closer to midnight."

"Do you mind if I take charge of the guys I just trained? I think I can still teach them a thing or two."

"You seem pretty sure we're gonna live through this thing, aren't you?"

"It's just another battle, Captain. Ain't nothing I haven't seen before," said Granier as he turned and walked off.

The captain felt better like he might survive the night. He knew he needed to portray confidence like Granier. He owed it to his men.

The Be River firebase was built in the shape of a rough triangle that covered the loped-off top of a hill. All trees and foliage had been cleared away creating a clear line of sight around the entire camp. Three 50-Cal Machine guns were positioned inside entrenched circles topped with three-layer sandbags at the three points of the triangle allowing them to support one another during an attack. There were also 20 mm recoilless rifles and 30-Cal machine guns placed inside blockhouses and along the trenches that encircled the base. The heavy mortar pits were dug in the center of the base and surrounded with more sandbags.

Granier placed his three sniper students in between the three points of the firebase near the top of the hill where they would have clear shots at the enemy. He would roam between them, checking up on them and giving little pointers on how to acquire and kill their targets. He knew it would be difficult to identify the

VC platoon commanders and political officers. They all wore the same black pajama uniforms. The only way to tell them apart was by their actions. Commanders and political officers often stood as they ordered an attack in order to give confidence to the men under their command. They also motioned with their arms and hands. It seemed silly but it was true. They acted as one would expect a leader to act and that gave them away. While the snipers' goal was to decapitate the leadership at the platoon level, they were not above shooting anybody that looked like an officer. Granier warned them to be patient and make sure they would kill their target before squeezing the trigger. He could tell they were anxious to try their newly learned skills. He supposed that would be good but hoped they would quickly settle down as the battle commenced. He needed them confident, but calm. Being a successful sniper required patience and thoughtfulness, skills hard to practice when bullets and mortar shells are flying in every direction. He would teach through example during the battle and hopefully, it would rub off on the trainees.

Not all of the ARVN Rangers were stationed at the firebase on the hill. About half were in the town below by the river and out on patrols in the surrounding jungle. The firebase's heavy mortars supported the rangers in the town and on patrol. Two of the 50-Cal machine guns could also support the town if the angle of the enemy's attack was within reach. The rangers in the town were protected by fortified firing positions and some hastily dug trenches. They had their own 60 mm mortars, light machine guns, and recoilless rifles but were far less protected than the rangers on the hill fortress. The rangers were experienced in battle and knew it was important to eat and sleep if they could before the attack began. They weren't sure when or if they would have the chance again. Nobody wanted to die with an empty stomach, and they would need their energy once the fighting was at hand.

Two of the light tanks were in their dug-in positions on the hill, while the other two were at both ends of the town's main street behind emplacements with three layers of sandbags. They would have clear shots at any approaching enemy, but the reverse was true also. They were considered rich targets by the Viet Cong recoilless rifle teams that were sure to accompany the troops.

Construction on the firebase stopped. They would fight with the defenses that were already completed. It was more important that everyone had something to eat and a little rest before the battle. The Rangers were in an unusually good mood encouraged by the U.S. Special Forces detachment cracking jokes like everything was going to be okay. Morale was up for a change.

At 1:45 AM the Viet Cong, shrouded by a heavy mist, attacked the town of Song Be from three sides. Pre-targeted VC mortar rounds and recoilless rifle shells pummeled the Ranger positions. Unseen heavy machine guns sprayed the town from multiple angles. The residents hid in their homes stacking up furniture or whatever else they could find for protection against shrapnel and bullets that penetrated their walls. The rangers held their ground and fought bravely which was unusual for local ranger units which tended to flee their defensive positions when heavy fighting broke out. The light tanks within the town used their machine guns to strafe the mist in front of them while their cannons remained silent.

The rangers and Special Forces on the hill were unable to see the Viet Cong attacking the town. The mist was too heavy. They could see the location of explosions which lit up like light bulbs through the mist and then quickly dissipated. Granier and his sniper unit could do nothing. They watched and waited for a break in the mist. The mortars within the hill fortress launched parachute flares, but they did little to illuminate the VC troops advancing on the ARVN Ranger positions.

Coyle and his aircrew arrived with the CIA gunship hoping to drive the enemy back, but they couldn't see the enemy's lines through the mist. The gunship turned into a flare ship launching powerful parachute flares as it circled above the town. Igniting high above, the flares floated down and disappeared in the mist.

The parachute flares did help the rangers in the town see the advancing VC as the mist turned into a vivid fog with a pulsating glow. Everything and everyone were soft, and shadows played havoc. It was an eerie scene. A nightmare for both sides.

Coyle was frustrated that he and his crew couldn't weigh into the battle. He looked to the jungle west of the town and saw dimmed flashes beneath the mist. *Mortars*, he thought and repositioned his aircraft over the jungle. The gun crew readied the miniguns. Coyle waited patiently until he saw a dim glow that was only visible for a second. He repositioned his sight over where he thought the mortar was located and opened fire with a two-second burst before releasing the trigger. Sometimes he would see a series of explosions beneath the mist which he imagined were mortar rounds hit by the burning tracer rounds and exploded. When he didn't see an explosion, he fired another burst. After two attempts and no explosions, he moved on.

After a while, the VC mortar crews stopped firing and the gunship went back to dropping flares over the town. He would return later when he saw more dim flashes from the enemy mortars firing. The trips back and forth between the jungle and the town went on all night. Coyle doubted he would be able to silence all the enemy mortars, but he hoped he and his crew were making a difference for the rangers and townspeople.

The VC had a dozen flamethrowers which they used to good effect against the ranger defensive positions. As more Viet Cong poured into the battle, the ARVN Rangers were forced back into the streets of the town using buildings and homes for cover. The heat from the flamethrowers burned off patches of mist hovering over the town.

Granier and his snipers were able to take some shots at the enemy below. Granier targeted a VC with a flamethrower barely visible through the mist when he squeezed off a round. Granier's bullet hit the soldier in the chest, then passed through and pierced the flamethrower's hose. The compressed fuel ignited and sprayed fire in all directions as the hose wiggled back and forth. The VC soldier was consumed and finally died when the tank on his back exploded. The area lit up the area around the fallen soldier for a couple of minutes until the fuel was exhausted. Granier and his snipers were able to take out several more VC advancing into the town. The heavy machine guns on the hill were finally able to join the battle and had some effect, driving the VC to cover. But the ranger machine guns were silenced once the blaze dimmed and then went out. There was too much risk of hitting friendly forces or civilians when firing into the mist indiscriminately.

The battle for the town continued through the night. Attacks and counterattacks pushed the battle lines back and forth. Pockets of resistance were assaulted by the VC, some rangers held their positions, while others were overwhelmed. It was a bloody battle that at times turned into hand-to-hand fighting with small swords and bayonets. Some rangers found it easier to pounce on the enemy as the VC passed their positions hidden by the mist. A swift stroke from a blade was more effective than a bullet and ensured that the enemy was fully dispatched. No wounded were allowed to rise again.

Hearing the pleas of their fellow rangers in the town over the radio, the rangers on the hill wanted to flak the enemy and relieve the pressure on the besieged rangers. The American advisors were against it. The town could not be secured by the Viet Cong unless the hill fortress was taken. It was far better to let the Viet Cong attack the firebase which would cost them a heavy price than to attack them in the town where the odds were more even. It was disheartening for the rangers to stand by and do nothing, but it was the smart move.

As the morning approached, the mist thickened and turned into a heavy fog until nobody in the town could see anything beyond a few feet. The incidents of friendly fire and civilian collateral damage increased dramatically as soldiers shot at whatever moved in front of them.

The fog surrounding the hill fortress rose until the ranger's trenches were engulfed. With the rangers and special forces on the hill unable to see their outer perimeter, the Viet Cong sent in their sappers to cut the wire and breach the perimeter. Everyone on the hill stopped talking and listened. The slight sound of wire being cut was mixed with the battle raging below. It was all the rangers needed. They ignited the few fougasse canisters they had already placed around the perimeter at potential breach points. The results were fried VC sappers. The rangers couldn't see them, but they could hear the enemy's screams as the inferno consumed them.

By the morning, the Viet Cong had taken three-quarters of the town and were pushing hard against the rangers that remained. Many on both sides had been wounded or killed. It had been a fierce battle and it wasn't over. One of the two tanks had been destroyed when a VC recoilless rifle team had moved up until they could see the faint silhouette of the armored vehicle through the fog. They assembled their weapon and fired into the side of the tank until its machine gun went silent. It took them three shots to kill the steel beast. Victorious, they disassembled their weapon and moved to the back of the town where the second tank and the majority of the rangers were located. They were unable to find the tank in the fog and were killed when an ARVN light machine gun heard their approach and fired waist-high through the fog.

As the sun broke the horizon, Coyle and his crew were tired. The gunship was now visible from the ground and anti-aircraft guns hidden in the jungle opened fire. With fuel running low and a team of helicopter gunships on their way into the battle, Coyle broke off his attack and headed back to base. He knew it was best not to mix a fixed-wing gunship with helicopter gunships. There was too much risk of hitting a friendly aircraft as they moved below the circling fixed-wing gunship.

The helicopter gunship crews faced the same problem with the fog as Coyle did. They were flying lower which gave them a clearer view, but it was still a thick soup of white fog. They did what they could, but it wasn't much. They took turns flying back to the closest airfield to refuel and rearm. Two gunships were always on site and ready to attack as soon as the fog lifted.

Just past noon, the fog finally dissipated, and the gunships were finally able to target the enemy, not in the town. They also made several passes over the hill fortress and strafed the enemy trying to breach the defensive perimeter with machine guns and rockets.

But the Viet Cong did not want to give up their hard-earned prize and fought back as best they could. They fired small arms at the helicopters as they roared past their positions. This caused many of the American helicopter pilots to circle back and attack the VC brave enough to fire at them.

As the fog lifted from the hill fortress, Granier could see VC entangled in the wire around the perimeter. He ordered his students to kill them, hopefully with one bullet each as he had taught them. Snipers did not waste ammunition if it could be helped. It was a point of pride. Granier found a position overlooking the town and calmly waited as the fog lifted more and more. His mission was to eliminate the field and platoon commanders. He watched for signs.

He did not shoot at regular troops. He did not want to warn the commanders that a sniper was watching until it was too late.

His first shot came when a soldier waved to the men in his squad to flank a ranger position in a building. Granier studied the wind for a moment by tossing some dirt into the air and watching which way and how fast it blew. It was as he imagined. No wind. If there had been wind, the fog would have moved off sooner. He placed his sight on the man's head, took a breath, then slowly let out half. He squeezed the trigger until his rifle lurched. He watched through the sight as the man's head jerked, then his body slumped over. Dead. Granier moved on.

His second target looked like a big fish, maybe a company commander. A radio operator handed him a handset. Granier killed him in mid-sentence.

It didn't take long for word to travel through the Viet Cong ranks – an enemy sniper was nearby and taking shots. It struck fear in their hearts… the idea of being killed by the invisible. It was the same principle as the fixed gunship circling high above taking its time before reaching down and snatching lives. Fear paralyzed the rank and file. The commanders grew cautious and kept their heads down.

Granier's opportunity dried up after five kills. Now, he would need to wait until someone made a mistake. He knew it would happen, but it required a lot of patience which was something he practiced. Patience, calm, and staying alert.

As the last of the fog lifted on the battlefield, a squadron of F-4 Phantoms carrying napalm canisters and cluster bombs under their wings roared across the sky. The rangers on the hill radioed the position of the enemy's heavy machine guns that had pinned down the rangers in the town. The fighter pilots used their cluster bombs with contact fuses to take out the enemy machine gun emplacements. Over one hundred bomblets were released from each cluster bomb as it approached the ground. Much like napalm, the bomblets would explode over a large area killing anyone in their path. Few survived a cluster bomb attack.

The Viet Cong commander could see that as the fog lifted his men were taking more fire from all sides and the American aircraft were taking their toll. In his mind, he had won a great victory against the ARVN rangers who were considered some of South Vietnam's finest soldiers. He didn't want his victory turned into a defeat. He gave the order to pull back. The Viet Cong withdrew from the town and their positions around the hill fortress then disappeared back into the jungle.

The American helicopter gunships attempted to chase the retreating enemy, but the VC were experts in disappearing and there were no targets available.

The Battle of Song Be was over. Eighty-five Viet Cong had been killed. Forty-nine ARN Rangers and five American advisors had also been killed. Both sides claimed victory.

Granier stayed for another day to ensure that the enemy was truly gone and not just hiding in the jungle regrouping for another attack. He critiqued each of his student's performances. Overall, they did well. He caught a ride on an ambulance heading back to Saigon. He slept the entire way.

May 13, 1965 – White House, Washington DC, USA

President Johnson was unsettled by the vast troop commitment headed for Vietnam. He knew many of the young men would return in coffins. While Johnson publicly ignored the growing number of anti-war protests, privately he contemplated the demonstrators' message and actions. He disagreed with them less than most thought. He wondered if as a younger man he might have joined them. Johnson did not want American troops in Vietnam, but he saw no other way to stop the communists. It was a horrible and bloody strategy and would chew up America's treasure until nothing was left for the people. It bothered him that the protestors didn't understand his rationale. Surely, they understood that if Vietnam fell so would the rest of Southeast Asia. And soon the communists would be at the doorstep of the United States. What he was doing was saving America for future generations. Their generation.

Johnson questioned whether he had done enough to seek peace before committing more American troops. Was it too late? He was the president, and it was his responsibility to what was best to protect the country and its citizens. The communists in Hanoi had said that Johnson's olive leaf of development aid was insincere, a trick to pause a war they were winning. While Johnson knew that he would have kept his promise if the leaders in Hanoi had agreed, he also understood why they might feel the way they did. He wondered if he could find a way to convince them.

Johnson called in Secretary of Defense McNamara and Secretary of State Rusk into the oval office and presented a plan that he knew would be controversial, especially to the Pentagon and Ambassador Taylor in

DAVID LEE CORLEY

Saigon. Johnson told McNamara that he wanted to stop all bombing of the North. After a few days, Rusk was to reach out through diplomatic channels in hopes that the communist leaders would accept his original offer of one billion dollars in development aid for Vietnam. McNamara was naturally hesitant and doubted that they would accept, but he understood Johnson's reservations about troop commitments. Rusk had always felt that the bombing would be ineffective, so stopping it for a time would not be much of a risk. After hearing their counsel, Johnson ordered a stop to the bombing for an unspecified amount of time. He wanted to give peace the best possible chance and this last-ditch effort at diplomacy was his only alternative without surrendering and bringing everyone home.

The pause in bombing only lasted five days when the leaders in Hanoi responded that it "was an effort to camouflage American intensification of the war."

Johnson was naturally disappointed and wondered if he gave the bombing halt more time would the communists see his attempt at peace as sincere? It was McNamara that convinced him that his plan was not going to work. The communists needed to feel pain before they would be willing to negotiate peace. American bombing and the deployment of ground troops would create the necessary pain. Johnson conceded and ordered the bombing of the North to resume.

Johnson felt that the halt was not a waste of time even though it didn't work. He had tried and failed. There was no dishonor in attempting peace. He felt better about doing what was needed from that point forward including the deployment of more troops. The echoes of the protestors were silenced in his mind. He had done what he could. The war would continue and even intensify as the communists had suggested. It was a self-fulfilling prophecy.

May 16, 1965 – Peking, China

Once again, Ho Chi Minh flew to China to meet with Mao. Ho, who was struggling with his age, was exhausted by the time he arrived. The meeting was postponed one day to allow Ho to recover. When they met, Mao asked Ho what more China could do to help its little brother, meaning Vietnam. Ho already knew he was not going to ask for combat troops from Mao. He knew Mao would refuse, not wanting to broaden the war by infuriating the United States. Instead, Ho said, "We, the Vietnamese, will take the burden of fighting the war by ourselves. However, we would ask our Chinese comrades to increase their economic and military support."

Mao agreed to Ho's request. How could he not? Ho Chi Minh was a hero in China and the rest of the communist world. Ho was a legend for being the leader of the only communist army to solely defeat a western army by expelling France from Vietnamese soil. Mao and Ho decided on the rules of China's involvement: North Vietnamese would fight the South Vietnamese and the Americans. The Chinese would provide financial and logistical support but would not interfere militarily unless the United States invaded North Vietnam with ground troops. China would supply engineers and laborers to build and maintain defense works, airfields, and roads. In addition, China would provide trained anti-aircraft personnel to defend North Vietnam against air attacks such as the American bombing campaigns. Finally, China would supply construction equipment, weapons, ammunition, and supplies. Mao agreed to dedicate 160,000 men and women to the tasks at hand. The first tranche would arrive before the end of May.

It was a big commitment from China. Ho and his traveling associates were grateful. Relieved, Ho uncharacteristically slept the entire flight back to Hanoi.

Battle of Ba Gia

May 28, 1965 – Ba Gia, Quang Ngai Province,
South Vietnam

On the south-central coast of South Vietnam, Quang
Ngai Province was located 520 miles North of Saigon.
Seven miles northwest of the provincial capital of
Quang Ngai town, Ba Gia was a small village chosen
as the center point of the VC crusade. The area had a
series of hills and mounts that made the area
particularly attractive to the Viet Cong. The hills were
key firing positions similar to the French garrison of
Dien Bien Phu.

It was the beginning of the Viet Cong's Summer
Offensive called the "Le Do Campaign." The VC
commanders wanted to make a major impact on the
South Vietnam military that it knew was wavering.
Their feeling was that with the right blow, the ARVN
would finally crumble, the South Vietnam government

would surrender, and the Americans would go home. They were overly confident in the situation and their abilities, but not by much. The situation in the South was indeed dire, but the American forces were gaining steam and numbers. If the Viet Cong wanted to have an effect, they needed to strike big right now.

Quang Ngai Province was a hotbed of Viet Cong activity and a frequent target of U.S. fighter aircraft called in for air support by local ARVN forces and their American advisors. But the Viet Cong had been unable to secure any significant territory beyond a few days after which they were forced to retreat. The VC commanders were determined to change that.

The province was home to ARVN 1st Brigade, I Corps, commanded by Major General Nguyen Chanh Thi. Also stationed within the province, were the 51st Infantry Regiment, 25th Infantry Division, 3rd Marine Battalions, the 37th, and 39th Ranger Battalion, and two artillery battalions equipped with 105mm artillery guns. Twenty-five hundred men in total, the ARVN forces were substantial with a dozen of American advisors. The air bases at Hue and Pleiku were nearby and could be called upon for major air support. Helicopter support and gunships were based at Camp Holloway and could reach the province within an hour. American and South Vietnamese military forces knew that the Viet Cong wanted Quang Ngai and they were determined to deny them the province.

In preparation for the campaign, the Viet Cong had been transporting troops and supplies to the area of operation since the beginning of the year. VC Reconnaissance units had been observing the ARVN forces moving in and out of the province and had studied the ARVN fortifications extensively creating a clear picture for their commanders. As the launch date neared, PAVN Major General Chu Huy Man traveled South to take overall charge of the operation.

At the beginning of May, the VC 1st Regiment, 2nd Division moved into the neighboring Quang Nam Province. Under the command of Le Huu Tru, the 1st Regiment had three VC battalions, the 40th, the 60th, and the 90th. The 1st Regiment was joined by the 45th Independent Battalion and the 48th Local Force Battalion in the North of Quang Ngai Province, along with the 83rd Local Force Battalion in the South. It was a major commitment of 2,000 troops for the Viet Cong. They ensured their success with dozens of anti-aircraft and heavy mortar units.

Consulting with Major General Thi, PAVN Major General Man knew that the ARVN forces would attempt to take the hills in the area in addition to securing the villages and towns. This would be their downfall. The Viet Cong would set up ambushes and pounce on the ARVN troops when they least expected it. They wanted to inflict as much damage to the ARVN as possible early in the battle. The idea was to demoralize their enemy in hopes that they would break. The Viet Cong could then pursue and destroy them.

At night on the 28th of May, the Viet Cong marched into their designated ambush positions around Ba Gia. The 90th Battalion was stationed at Minh Thanh while the 60th Battalion took up their hidden position at Vinh Loc. The 40th Battalion moved to positions at Duyen Phuoc and the 45th Battalion occupied their ambush positions at Vinh Khanh. The 1st Regiment Headquarters were set up on Mount Hoc Khoai. The 83rd Local Force Battalion encircled Nghia Hanh, the South Vietnamese administration center.

As the troops moved into position, everyone knew this would be a battle to remember. A battle they must win to push the revolution forward and once again reunite their country under the communist flag. It was why they joined the Viet Cong and were willing to sacrifice their lives if need be. The political commissars tried to reassure them, but in the end, it was each individual soldier that had to reach deep inside and find courage.

At 5:45 am on May 29th, the VC 1st Regiment executed a surprise attack on Loc Thou, a small village just south of Ba Gia. After just ten minutes of fighting, the two ARVN platoons defending the village were overwhelmed and withdrew after heavy losses. The Viet Cong consolidated their forces and took up defensive positions around the village preparing for the counter-attack they knew would come. It didn't take long.

At 6:00 am, the ARVN 1st Battalion under the command of Captain Nguyen Van Ngoc led his men from Go Cao to counterattack the VC 1st Regiment. It took them over three hours to reach the village and the ARVN soldiers were tired by the time they arrived. The delay allowed the VC to further strengthen their defensive positions at Loc Thou.

At 9:50 am, the ARVN 1st Battalion entered Loc Tho which seemed peaceful as they marched down the main street. Then, all hell broke loose as the VC 90th Battalion waiting in ambush surrounded the ARVN battalion and opened fire. The VC had occupied nearby Mount Khi where their recoilless rifles and machine guns could fire down on the ARVN within the village. Surprised by the VC, the ARVN could not mount their counter-attack and were soon in deep trouble. Within one hour of fierce fighting, the ARVN battalion was annihilated with 270 soldiers killed or wounded and another 217 captured. Sixty-five ARVN soldiers and three American advisors were able to escape and rejoin the government forces stationed nearby. It was a terrible loss for South Vietnam and further demoralized the ARVN troops as word spread of the defeat.

At the same time, the VC 83rd Battalion advanced to Tra Khuc River and attacked the ARVN forces station there. The Battle of Ba Gia was quickly becoming lopsided in the Viet Cong's favor. The battle raged the rest of the day with the ARVN forces getting the worst of it. By the end of the day, the VC controlled Ba Gia and the surrounding area.

In response, Major General Thi, the commander of the South Vietnamese I Corps Tactical Zone, organized a task force to retake Ba Gia. He planned to attack the Viet Cong from multiple positions using American air support and artillery.

As dawn broke on May 30th, American fighter-bombers and ARVN artillery units pounded Ba Gia with little regard for any civilians that might still be in the village. The Viet Cong had no choice but to stay in the trenches they had dug during the night as the explosions from bombs, rockets, and artillery shells sent shrapnel in all directions.

At noon on May 30th, the 3rd Marine Battalion and ARVN 2nd Battalion advanced from the west toward Ba Gia with the help of a squadron of M113 armored personnel carriers. While the M113s could not fit everyone inside, they did give the ARVN troops confidence as they took the lead. At the same time, ARVN 39th Ranger Battalion advanced from the north to secure Mount Chop Non where they could fire on any VC reinforcement units.

Viet Cong reconnaissance teams on Mount Khi spotted the approaching ARVN columns and sent word to the commander in the village. As shelling and bombing continued the Viet Cong rose from the trenches and created ambushes for the ARVN forces.

The VC 45th Battalion was called in to set up ambush positions in and around the village of Vinh Khanh.

The VC 60th Battalion was deployed to Mount Ma To where they set up ambush positions for the ARVN forces they knew would come to take the hill. When ARVN forces arrived, the hidden Viet Cong let the enemy troops pass by before springing their traps and attacking their flanks.

It seemed like all hell broke loose at the same moment for the ARVN forces. The Viet Cong sprung their ambushes in synchronization pinning down the ARVN so they could not reinforce one another. The Viet Cong had grabbed their enemy by the belt negating artillery and air support. Only the American helicopter gunships were accurate enough to attack the enemy with rockets and machine guns without endangering friendly forces and civilians. But it was too little too late.

On Mount Ma To, the ARVN troops in the 2nd Battalion were in a fight for their lives against the VC 60th Battalion that had attacked them from the rear in a well-executed ambush. Having had much success lately, the Viet Cong were in good spirits and wanted to get at the enemy, while the ARVN troops seemed demoralized as soon as the fighting began. The American advisors did what they could to boost morale and led by example, but they were too few to make a real difference. Unable to call in artillery or air support, the ARVN forces knew they were at a disadvantage. The 3rd Marine Battalion in nearby Phuoc Loc was called in to relieve the 2nd Battalion. Within an hour, the South Vietnamese marines were surrounded by VC from the 60th Battalion that had prepared ambushes for ARVN reinforcements. The Marines too were in a fight for their lives as VC heavy mortars pounded their positions at the base of Mount Ma To.

As the sun set, the fighting diminished. Both sides had suffered heavy losses. The 2nd Battalion and 3rd Marine were forced to fall back with four M113s covering their retreat back to Phuoc Loc.

During the night, the VC commanders ordered their troops to wipe out the remains of the South Vietnamese task force in Phuoc Loc. The 40th Battalion resumed their attack against the South Vietnamese in the village. The 3rd Marine Battalion and the ARVN 2nd Battalion put up a vicious resistance, giving as good as they got. But in the end, the Viet Cong forces overpowered them, and the South Vietnamese and their American advisors were again forced to retreat leaving Phuoc Loc in control of the communists. When the VC entered the village, they found the bodies of 94 South Vietnamese soldiers.

The villagers in Ba Gia sided with the Viet Cong and helped them round up South Vietnamese soldiers to be taken captive.

On Mount Chop Non, the ARVN 39th Ranger Battalion was dug in and waiting for an attack. The VC 45th Battalion encircled the Rangers and was able to advance within 100 yards of the ARVN perimeter without being noticed. Before sunrise the next morning, the Viet Cong began their attack by hammering the ARVN positions on Chop Non with heavy mortars followed by an all-out ground assault. The fighting was fierce and often hand-to-hand as the Viet Cong jumped into the ARVN trenches and grappled with their enemy. As the sun rose the next morning, the Rangers with over one hundred dead were forced to retreat leaving the Viet Cong to control Mount Chop Non.

The South Vietnamese forces had been decimated in what amounted to a huge loss. The VC claimed to have killed 915 South Vietnamese soldiers with another 270 captured. Two full South Vietnamese battalions were gone and a regimental-size ARVN Task Force had been defeated in battle for the first time. The Viet Cong had lost a total of 556 soldiers killed. It was a massive victory for the Viet Cong. By early June, the Viet Cong would control five districts in northern Quang Ngai Province, home to 10,000 civilians.

June 7, 1965 – Pentagon, Arlington, Virginia USA

Although he hated the idea of leaving South Vietnam during a time of crisis, General Westmoreland felt it was imperative that he deliver the report he had prepared in person to the Joint Chiefs of Staff. The news was far from good and he wanted to be there to answer their question of which he thought there would be many. He was right.

The JCS were not pleased with Westmoreland's report, but they weren't surprised either. Each general or admiral had his own people on the ground in South

Vietnam and was receiving his own intelligence. Still, there was something about seeing it in writing that made the truth more real.

The Viet Cong were stronger than ever and their numbers were growing by the day. The ARVN forces were taking losses equivalent to one entire battalion per week. There were also a high number of desertions and a general unwillingness to take the offensive. It was a devastating report. Westmoreland concluded when he said, "I see no course of action open to us except to reinforce our efforts in South Vietnam with additional U.S. and third country forces as rapidly as is practical." He identified U.S. units that could be assigned to South Vietnam. He planned to bring U.S. military strength in country to forty-four combat battalions which would be joined by third-country forces. The Joint Chiefs knew better than to ask if that would be enough to win the war. They knew it wouldn't be and certainly, Westmoreland didn't have a realistic answer no matter what he said. They agreed to talk with McNamara and the President about Westmoreland's request.

White House – Washington DC, USA

The South Vietnamese losses at the Battle of Ba Gia and Westmoreland's report hitting his desk at the same time were like a nightmare from which President Johnson could not awake. Even McNamara that was normally so logical and took bad news in stride was in a funk. The president knew that the situation in South Vietnam was not McNamara's fault... at least not all of it. The South Vietnamese military government with the constant squabbling among generals and the threat of another coup had bitten them in the ass and demoralized the men under their command. The American forces were doing their best to keep the country afloat, but it wasn't enough and both Johnson and McNamara knew it. "As I see, Mr. President, you have three options none of which is optimal," said McNamara on a couch across from Johnson in the oval office sitting area.

"Go on, Bob. It's safe. I ain't in a biting mode," said Johnson downcast.

"Option 1 – You could pull out all Americans from Vietnam and Laos to minimize our losses. South Vietnam would fall within months, maybe weeks, and the communists would take over. There would be little leverage to negotiate peace terms and I doubt the Viet Cong would show much compassion. America would take a hit from our allies and the international community, but we would survive. The world still needs America to anchor the western alliances and everyone knows it.

Option 2 – You could continue America's commitment at our present level of about 75,000 men. It would be questionable how long South Vietnam would survive, but I imagine the South Vietnamese forces could hold out until the end of the year with our help. If you choose that path we should be prepared to evacuate all American personnel at a moment's notice. Because we showed some resolve, America would fair slightly better on the international level, but let's face it... nobody likes a loser.

Option 3 – You could substantially expand the U.S. military presence in Vietnam as Westmoreland is suggesting by increasing our troop levels to 125,000 men drawn from our U.S. Army regulars and U.S. Marine Corps. We would also call on our ally nations to increase their troop commitments. But, Mr. President, that will most likely not be the end of it. We will need even more troops if South Vietnam is to survive."

"Aren't you just a bundle of good news, Bob?"

"Like I said the options are far from optimal."

"What do you think I should do?"

"Honestly, Mr. President, I am a bit torn. Like you, I don't see a light at the end of the tunnel. Just more darkness and misery. Yet, I don't think we can lose this war without losing the rest of Southeast Asia, almost 400 million people under communist control. And that thought is just too much to bear. It would give the communists incredible power and a well of nations from which to draw troops for further expansion of their revolution."

"I know you have reservations, Bob. We all do. But I am the one left holding the bag when it comes to making decisions, and I need your help."

"Yes, Mr. President. Option 3 seems to be the most prudent."

Johnson thought for a long moment, then said, "I agree. Make it so."

"Yes, Mr. President," said McNamara as he rose and left the Oval Office.

Hanoi, North Vietnam

Hearing intelligence reports that America was once again increasing its troop levels, Le Duan and the other politburo members were undeterred. They increased the number of civilians to be called into active duty in the military. They would match the commitment of the United States which they considered their main advisory from that point on. The South Vietnam military was all but useless. It was the Americans that North Vietnam and the Viet Cong must defeat.

The news of overwhelming victories like Ba Gia softened the blow to the public. Many North Vietnamese wanted to share in the glory and volunteered. The people did not fear the South Vietnamese troops and the Americans. Like the French before them, the Americans would be driven from their country. Only then could the people enjoy the peace that they felt they deserved.

June 12, 1965 – Saigon, South Vietnam

After receiving news that his request for more troops had once again been granted, General Westmoreland tested his luck even further, by asking the U.S. Department of Defense to increase his authority which would allow him to undertake offensive operations when he saw fit. Although he didn't say it directly, it was implied that if he was expected to win the war, or at least not lose it, he should be allowed to fight the men under his command how he wished. Westmoreland said, "We have reached the point in Vietnam where we cannot avoid commitment to combat of U.S. ground troops."

After consultation with the White House, the Pentagon gave Westmoreland what he requested but they made clear that by taking off of the general's leash he was expected to produce positive results. It was what Westy wanted... to fight and win with enough rope to hang himself if need be. Even after all that had happened during his command of MACV in Vietnam,

Westmoreland was fearless and confident... as all generals should be.

June 17, 1965 – North and South Vietnam

Everything was going smoothly for Lieutenant Jack David Batson sitting in the pilot's seat and Lieutenant Robert Doremus sitting behind him in the navigator's position of their F-4 Phantom. They were flying MiGCAP with four other F-4s for a flight of A-4 Skyhawks headed north on a bombing mission. At a speed of 300 knots to conserve fuel, their altitude was 10,000 feet which allowed their radar look-up at the skies ahead. This was Batson's 30th combat mission.

On the way in, the Phantom's radar picked up multiple enemy aircraft flying over Hanoi some fifty miles away. It didn't concern Batson and Doremus. Hanoi was not the target. Doremus kept an eye on the enemy aircraft anyway.

Once the bombing mission was completed by the Skyhawks and the strike group leader called "feet wet," the aircraft headed for home and that's when things got interesting...

As the Skyhawk strikers approached the border, two of the Phantoms broke off and turned around for one more "look-see" for anything following them. They found two enemy targets thirty-seven miles out and went into fighter mode increasing their speed to 500 knots.

The incoming enemy aircraft were MiG-17s flying at 400 knots. The distance between the fighters and bandits closed quickly at more than one mile every four seconds.

Doremus continued in his radar's search mode as Batson turned on the CW illuminator for the AIM-7 Sparrow air-to-air missiles carried on the underwing hardpoints. The Sparrows were twelve-foot homing missiles armed with eighty-eight pounds of high explosive blast-fragmentation warheads. They had a range of fourteen miles and flew at Mach 2.5. For several years, the Phantom pilots had been trained to use their missiles instead of their 20 mm cannons. Although it was less exciting to kill an enemy aircraft with missiles than guns, it was a lot safer.

As the American aircraft closed, their radar changed from two to four enemy aircraft. They were outnumbered. Two of the MiG-17s broke off and the Americans followed them. The lead Phantom flown by Commander Lou Page - pilot and Lieutenant JC Smith – RIO fired at the lead MiG-17 and scored a hit that tore off the enemy aircraft's wing.

Seeing the lead MiG-17 dispatched, Batson switched his targeting radar to the follow-on MiG-17. At three miles out when his targeting circle was at its widest circumference, Batson fired a Sparrow. The missile swiftly closed the gap and exploded when it hit the enemy aircraft head-on. Both enemy aircraft were destroyed in less than a minute of aerial combat. Smith spotted one parachute as it descended to the ground. Low on fuel, the American aircrews turned for home. The two remaining MiG-17s would be left for another day.

When Batson and Doremus landed on the USS Midway aircraft carrier, they were given a hero's welcome. But the celebration was short-lived when the aircrews were ordered back into their aircraft where they would fly to Saigon for a press briefing. The four

Navy aviators were credited with the first confirmed air-to-air kills of two MiG-17s in the Vietnam War. The US Navy was on the scoreboard.

June 18, 1965 – Andersen Air Force Base - Guam, USA

Covered in palm trees and ferns, Guam was a tiny island and an unincorporated U.S. territory of enormous strategic importance. Part of the Mariana Island chain and home to Andersen Air Force Base on the northern end of the island, Guam was only 2,600 miles from Hanoi making it the ideal location for long-range bombers.

Operation Arc Light used Boeing B-52 Stratofortress heavy bombers for the first time in the Vietnam War. Subsonic jets nicknamed "BUFFs," the B-52s carried a massive bomb load of 70,000 pounds and could fly 8,800 miles without refueling making them within easy reach to Hanoi from Guam and back in one round trip.

The first B-52 strike was made up of twenty-seven B-52s delivering almost two thousand 750 and 1,000 bombs. The target was a Viet Cong stronghold. While the bombing showed little evidence of Viet Cong casualties, it did make a big impression on the VC troops and the civilians in the area. Barely able to see the American aircraft flying at 70,000 feet, the ground shook violently during the bombing and many thought it was the end of the world. Even the American and South Vietnamese troops stationed many miles away from the bombing site, were suitably impressed with the power of Operation Arc Light. Surely such devastation against the enemy would tip the war in their favor.

On their way back to Guam with the aircrews fatigued from battle, two of the 52s collided in mid-air killing everyone onboard. Even with the significant losses, the mission was deemed a success and would become the pattern for future missions. After a twenty-hour roundtrip flight, the exhausted American bomber crews returned to hot showers and roast beef dinners before sleeping in their own beds.

My Canh Café

June 25, 1965 – Saigon, South Vietnam

The Viet Cong could not let the American bombing raid go unpunished. Within a week they struck back and once again showed the South Vietnamese in a brutal way that the Americans could not protect them. The Viet Cong had a list of hotels, restaurants, sports facilities, and entertainment venues that they had targeted and preplanned for terrorist-style attacks. They had also hidden bomb-making material at various points around the city to give them quick access to create terrorist weapons.

Because of the size of the American bombing raid which the Viet Cong believed used a major amount of U.S. resources, they wanted to create a spectacle the aftermath of which would be on all the front pages of the foreign newspapers, especially the American newspapers. They chose one of Saigon's favorite restaurants – My Canh Café floating restaurant.

The massive barge on which the restaurant had been built was tied to a pier on the Saigon River at the doorstep of Tu Do Street's entertainment district. While it was capable of sailing down the river, it never left its pilings allowing customers to board and deboard anytime they wished. The restaurant had several hundred tables on two decks and an open-air rooftop patio. The window tables overlooking the river were the most popular and needed to be booked well in advance. While its food was considered good, it wasn't great when compared to some of the other famous Saigon restaurants. Customers didn't care. They came for the ambiance and beautiful views.

Huynh Phi Long and Le Van Ray were members of Saigon's 67th Commando Unit. They had staked out the restaurant and watched as Saigon's elite boarded the vessel night after night. They took particular note of the ARVN generals and high-ranking officers that frequented the restaurant on Friday nights. Celebrating the news of a new baby or a recent promotion brought groups of American advisors and servicemen to dine with the crowds.

Security was extremely tight. Three armed policemen stood as guards next to the gangplank leading into the restaurant's entrance. Plainclothes officers watched from an open platform opposite the barge. In addition, armored vehicles and squads of soldiers were stationed nearby and Navy vessels patrolled the river around the floating restaurant. The sappers noted which vendors and customers were allowed into the restaurant with a minimum of scrutiny.

On the night of the attack, the two VC sappers rode bicycles, one of which was motorized and carried a hidden bomb on a timer, to the restaurant. Long drove the bicycle bomb, while Ray's bicycle carried a stack of newspapers in which he had hidden a mine. They had chosen the most crowded of nights— Friday. They weaved their bicycles through the crowd on the pier and moved toward the restaurant's entrance.

The tensest moment came when they passed through the main checkpoint using a crowd of Vietnamese party-goers as cover. Long parked his motorized bicycle next to a stand selling cigarettes. He pulled out some pocket change and purchased a pack of Vietnamese cigarettes before walking a short distance to a motorcycle that he had parked nearby earlier that day.

In the meantime, Ray set his Claymore-style mine hidden within the stack of newspapers on a nearby table. After ensuring the direction of the blast would cover a wide area of the restaurant, Ray moved off and joined Long on the motorcycle. They escaped undetected.

On their way back to their base, the two sappers were stopped by police at the Nguyen Hue traffic circle. They were asked to produce their IDs which they did. At that moment, Ray's bomb went off spraying the restaurant's patrons walking up the gangplank and seated at tables along the edge of the vessel with flying steel ball bearings that tore their flesh into shreds. People screamed and rushed to get off the vessel, some trampling the wounded lying on the decks and gangplank. It was mayhem. The police tossed back the sapper's IDs and ran to the bomb site. Long and Ray drove off.

Within minutes, emergency response teams arrived and began tending to the wounded by carrying them down the gangplank and setting them on the piers. It was then that Long's bicycle bomb exploded sending shrapnel in all directions causing more death and destruction.

The Viet Cong terrorist attack on the My Canh Café was the most sensational of the entire Vietnam War and became a model for further Viet Cong terrorist attacks. In all, 123 casualties of which forty-eight were dead. The bodies included twelve Americans along with another sixteen seriously wounded. There were also French, German, Swiss, and Filipinos among the dead.

As predicted, worldwide the morning's newspapers showed photos of the unforgettable carnage and told the story of the bombing of the My Canh Café floating restaurant that was now a smoldering ruin.

Long and Ray were heroes among the Viet Cong and were even smuggled north to Hanoi to meet First Secretary Le Duan and the legendary Ho Chi Minh who presented them with certificates of honor. It was a mighty blow against the Americans and their air force.

June 28, 1965 – War Zone D, South Vietnam

A battalion of the 173rd Airborne Brigade was ordered to carry out the first U.S. led search and destroy mission of the Vietnam War. With them were ARVN and Australian units.

Their area of operation known as War Zone D was located seven miles north of Bien Hoa with a northern boundary of Route 14, a southern boundary of Route

13, and an eastern boundary of the Dong Nai River. Unlike most other PAVN/VC bases War Zone D was located away from the Cambodian border which made it difficult for the PAVN in the zone to supply their troops. They also lacked the ability to hop across the border for protection if things got too intense. For these reasons and its proximity to Saigon, the area was chosen for search and destroy operations.

The PAVN main supply route was named the Adams Trail. It began on the Cambodian side of Phuoc Long Province, then twisted its way through a triple canopy rainforest, passed through the western half of War Zone D, then terminated in northern Bien Hoa Province at a base named The Catcher's Mitt by the Americans. Between the American bombing and multiple clearing operations, The Adams Trail was a risky supply chain that was often disrupted.

When the units participating in the search and destroy mission gathered up and prepared to enter the area of operation, the Americans led the way by calling in a massive artillery strike. The Australians did not carry out a strike using their own artillery to prepare their advance. Instead, they just stood back and watched. The Australians were veteran jungle fighters having fought in the Malaysian Emergency several years earlier. When the American commander asked the Australian commander why he was not using his artillery to soften up the enemy, the Australian commander replied, "Well, how many Viet Cong do you think you've killed with your arti strike?"

"A few," said the American commander. "But I guarantee you we scared the bejesus out of them."

"Yeah, you probably did. But you also let them know your location and from which direction you will be advancing. So, good luck with leading the way. We're happy to follow."

The American commander had no response.

The goal of the search and destroy missions was not to take territory. It was to flush out and destroy the enemy, then harass the surviving enemy troops by denying them food and medical supplies. Villages collaborating with the enemy were burned and the animals killed. Any stores of rice or supplies were burned with M34 white phosphorous grenades called Willie Petes. All weapons, ammunition, and medical supplies were confiscated. Nothing of use was left for the enemy or the villagers. It was seen as a warning to other villages in the area that were considering collaborating with the enemy. Once the job was done, the troops would pull out of the village lighting the thatched roofs with Zippo lighters as they left. Search and destroy missions quickly gained the nickname of Zippo missions.

As the artillery strike subsided, the allied troops were shuttled into the area of operation by helicopters. Much to the Americans consternation, the more experienced Australians followed them into the jungle. There was no resistance, the Viet Cong were gone. The VC would choose the ground on which they would fight and, in most cases, create effective ambushes to spring on their enemy when the time was right. The search and destroy team had lost the element of surprise just as the Australians had suggested.

The team fanned out in smaller units that stayed close enough to their flaking units that they could call for help if needed. As they moved through the countryside they came across all types of terrain – rice fields surrounded by earthen berms, dense jungle, hills covered with elephant grass, orchards, corn fields, swamps covered in reeds, termite hills by the dozens, and streams with high banks. The enemy could be anywhere and was often where they least expected it. The mist would come and go without warning making their job even more dangerous. In as heavy mist patrols from both sides could pass each other a dozen yards away and never even notice each other. It was unnerving knowing that the enemy was out there but you couldn't see it.

Once engaged, the Americans had the advantage with their ability to call in artillery and air strikes. They even had helicopter gunships if they needed them. As usual, the Viet Cong would try to close the distance to the front line and grab the enemy by the belt so the Americans could not use their artillery or air power without hurting their own troops.

Unlike the VC, the wounded Americans, Australians, and ARVN troops could be quickly airlifted to a nearby combat surgical hospital. The ability to get seriously wounded soldiers to a forward surgical team quickly made a huge difference in the survival rate.

Wounded VC were dragged underground into hidden tunnels where medics had carved out aid stations. Power for lights was generated by a soldier on a bicycle. The crude facilities were far from ideal operating conditions and many Viet Cong died from infections. Amputations were often used to reduce fatalities.

After several weeks of combing the area and destroying two dozen villages, the mission was ended and the allies were once again carried out by helicopters and trucks. No units were left to protect captured territory. The entire operation produced fifty VC killed and was branded a success. Within a week, the Viet Cong were back in control of the area. Learning of the final results, the Australians just shook their heads in disgust. The Americans had a lot to learn.

July 3-16, 1965 – Saigon, South Vietnam

Frustrated, Granier sat in front of several piles of intelligence reports. Most were sightings of Colonel Thao. None of them had panned out. Granier supposed that should have been expected. Because of Thao's long history as a sleeper agent for the communists, there was little doubt North Vietnamese intelligence had trained him well. Still, nobody was perfect. Granier knew that Thao would eventually slip up and reveal his whereabouts. He just had to make sure he recognized the signs when they happened.

Thao was a Catholic and as such was protected by the Catholic community which encompassed seven percent of the South Vietnamese population. Considered a celebrity for his defense of the church, there were hundreds of Catholic villages spread all across South Vietnam that would give Thao refuge. Many of the Catholic villages had their own militias usually under the control of the local priest.

Granier poured through Thao's military record and the dossier prepared by the CIA. There were holes in both. There were periods when Thao just disappeared from existence. It was possible that Thao had slipped back across the border to meet with his superiors in North Vietnam or maybe he was just out on a joy ride on the motorcycle he loved so much.

Thao had worked on motorcycles since he was a teenager. He liked them fast and stripped down to the bare essentials. There were over a quarter million motorcycles in Saigon alone. Most were well-worn Asian brands and used to drive supply or food carts. Some families used them like a station wagon piling everyone on one motorcycle including babies, grandparents, and several cartons of eggs to be sold at a weekly market. Many motorcycles had been handed down from one generation to the next. Some were so old that parts for repairs could no longer be found in which case, the motorcycle was scraped for metal, or a new part was manufactured by a talented metal worker.

When the Americans arrived in country and began delivering military aid, Thao immediately bought a Military Police Harley Davidson on the black market. He imagined the motorcycle still in its shipping crate had fallen off the boat when the freighter entered the port of Saigon. Ten percent of all equipment delivered to the South Vietnamese military was subject to Madame Nhu's secret tax and fell off the boat. To avoid any questions, Thao stripped the Harley of its faring, crash bars, saddle bags, and the police-style flashing blue and red lights on the front handlebars. He gave the entire bike a fresh coat of black paint. When asked where he got it, he said he had it shipped from America.

Motorcycles were not reliable because of the rough terrain in South Vietnam. Like cars, they needed constant maintenance and spare parts. Granier wondered where Thao was getting his parts. There were hundreds of black markets throughout Vietnam. Thao only needed to ask a motorcycle parts vendor and the part he needed would be produced within a week or two… for the right price. There were times when a brand-new motorcycle was worth more in parts than whole and would be disassembled to be sold off in pieces. The Vietnamese were very good at getting the highest value of anything they sold.

The Harley-Davidson motorcycles used by the U.S. Military Police were heavy monsters with big engines. This made them fast if all the extra gear was stripped away. But they still had problems. The clutch wore out rapidly. Head gaskets leaked oil if the engine was not given enough time to warm up before riding. The heavy motorcycle burned through brake pads and drums like butter.

Since Thao had a Harley-Davidson motorcycle it was inevitable that it would be subject to these same problems and would need parts. It was also probable that those parts came from Saigon where the military's Harley's were delivered. Thirdly, it was probable that Thao was not hiding in a city where he might be recognized by ARVN soldiers. Instead, he would seek to hide in a village or small town. Furthermore, it would have a strong Catholic population that could protect him.

Granier was tired of sitting on his ass and decided to investigate for himself. He made a list of all the black-market dealers in Saigon that sold motorcycle parts. There were dozens, but only four had large inventories of parts that they would ship around the country at the request of a customer. Granier paid each a visit. Naturally, the vendors were anxious to sell the American whatever he wanted. He had American dollars which were far more stable than South Vietnamese currency and could be used as a hedge against the constant inflation everyone faced. Granier told the vendors that he wanted Harley-Davidson parts for his motorcycle. Each said they could get whatever he wanted in a few days, except one which showed him a warehouse full of motorcycle parts stored on shelves. He determined that that warehouse was most likely where Thao, who had years of experience working on motorbikes, was getting the parts for his motorcycle. Granier bought a headlight and left. He would return later that night after they were closed for the day.

When Granier returned, he brought a South Vietnamese intelligence agent with him. They had worked together when Colonel Lansdale was in charge of paramilitary operations. Since he could not read Vietnamese, Granier needed someone to find and translate the shipping documents.

After slipping the guard dog an opium-laced meatball, Granier and his translator broke into the warehouse by picking the lock in the fence surrounding the building. Once inside the fence, they relocked the lock, so nothing appeared out of place. Moving inside the building, they found the office.

Granier told the translator what he was looking for in the way of shipping invoices. Granier shuffled through folders and envelopes trying to help but quickly realized that he was doing more harm than good. Leaving the translator to perform the search on his own, Granier moved back into the warehouse and kept watch. This wasn't the kind of operation where he would kill anyone if discovered, but he didn't want South Vietnamese intelligence learning what he was searching for. He needed to find Thao first and dispose of him before the South Vietnamese intelligence officers.

While watching, Granier saw a guard patrolling the warehouses in the area approach the fence. He told his translator to extinguish his flashlight. The guard was surprised that the dog was nowhere in sight. He checked the lock on the fence and saw that it was secure, then moved on. Granier gave his translator the okay to continue his search.

After another twenty minutes, the translator indicated that he had found the handful of documents that Granier was seeking and had placed them in a large envelope. They wrapped up and moved back out of the building and fence, picking the lock, and once again relocking it. Hopefully, the office workers would not notice the missing documents for a week or two when customers called to complain about not receiving the parts they had ordered.

Granier reviewed the shipping documents and found three villages that he thought were good candidates for the hiding place of Thao. The closer he got to Thao, the more careful Granier was to not spook his prey. If Thao even got a hint that someone was watching him, Granier was sure Thao would bolt and his search would need to start over. Granier decided he needed to investigate each village himself and he needed to perform the surveillance in such a way as to not tip off Thao or South Vietnamese intelligence operatives hunting for him.

Granier knew he needed to be quick about finding Thao before he escaped once again. An American walking through a village was unusual and would set off warnings that would eventually scare off Thao. Granier decided to spend one day of surveillance at a distance for each village, then, if he didn't find anything, he would move in closer under the cover of darkness.

The first village was a nothing-burger. Even so, Granier stuck to his plan by observing the village during the day and moving in for closer observation at night. The one good thing that came out of his surveillance was that he eliminated the village as a potential hiding place for Thao.

Early the next morning, he moved on to the second village. Again, nothing. The highlight of the day was Catholic mass where almost the entire village filed into the small church. Upon exiting, Granier got a good look at almost everyone living in the village. It was possible that Thao would avoid meetings like mass, knowing that it was an obvious event that anyone searching for him would use. Once again, Granier went into the village after dark and looked around. There was nothing of interest.

The final village also looked like a washout, but it didn't sound like one. While Granier was surveying at a distance, he heard a familiar sound – a motorcycle starting. When the engine finally kicked in, Granier heard the throaty muffler that Harley-Davidson was known for. Someone in the village had a Harley-Davidson motorcycle. He watched closely for signs of the motorcycle and rider. He saw nothing, but the throbbing noise continued as if a mechanic was turning the engine. Granier wanted a closer look, but dared not reveal himself until he saw something strange…

On the far end of the village, three men were working on a small construction project – a well. Two of the men were Vietnamese, but the third was an American or at least a light-skinned foreigner. He was in his early twenties and wore a white shirt and khaki pants. It looked like they were almost done with their project. They seemed to be building the inner stone casing that protected the well from collapse.

Granier had an idea and pulled a surveillance camera from his rucksack. He pulled out a spare khaki shirt and put it on. He hid his rifle and rucksack, then walked to the edge of the village and approached the construction team building the well. "Hi," said Granier. "Is that the well we've heard so much about?"

Peter Hunting, twenty-two years of age and a member of a humanitarian NGO group called International Voluntary Services or IVS, looked up from the well and saw Granier with a camera around his neck. "I don't know. Who are we?" said Hunting with an easygoing smile.

"Daryl Singer with AP," said Granier offering a handshake.

"Pete Hunting, International Voluntary Services," said Pete cleaning the mud off his hand with a rag, then shaking. "So, what are you doing in these parts?"

"Looking for you. My boss wanted some shots of your project. Sent me. Do you mind?"

"I don't see the harm. It's all God's work. I didn't know anyone even knew about the well."

"Guys in the office keep track of this kind of humanitarian stuff going on around the country. Makes for a good public information story on slow news days."

Granier removed the camera from around his neck and started snapping shots. He could hear the motorcycle engine cut out and he wondered if he was too late. He glanced down the village's main street and saw nothing beyond pigs and chickens. He figured most of the villagers would be out tending their fields during the day. He continued snapping photos of Hunting and his construction crew. "So, is this a locally-generated project?" said Granier reloading his camera.

"Of sorts. I guess. The local priest asked IVS for an engineer. I was the closest thing they had in the area."

"You build a lot of wells?"

"No. This is my first. But I borrowed a good book on how to make a well from the library at our headquarters. I think I'm doing it right."

"What types of things do you normally build?"

"Anything the villagers need. Last week, it was a fish pond. The week before I finished work on a school."

"A school?"

"Yeah. We got a grant from an American religious foundation. The whole village pitched in and helped me build it. It was really something. Normally, I build a lot of windmills for farmers needing irrigation which is great. But that school…"

"Your parents must be proud. Where are you from?"

"Oklahoma City."

"And school?"

"Graduated from Wesley before coming out here. I figured it was a good place to get some experience. But it kinda grows on you, ya know?"

"Yeah. I know. When did you arrive in-country?"

"'63"

"Miss home much?"

"Sure, but this work… it's important. It can change lives for the better. So, here I am."

"Pete the engineer from Oklahoma City."

"Yep. Rain or shine."

Granier took another look down the main road. No motorcycle. The engine noise was gone. He had lost his prey. Then, he saw something he hadn't noticed before. It wasn't a whole motorcycle, but it was part of a wheel stick out from the side of a hut. The wheel looked heavy like it could support a lot of weight. It was hard to tell if it was from a Harley-Davidson. Granier desperately wanted to walk down the road and look at the motorcycle beside the hut, but he knew it was sure to cause attention and spook Thao if he saw him. The evidence was still thin, but he decided to wait in hopes of getting a better look later. The sun was low in the sky and it would be dark in a couple of hours. "Oh, I almost forgot. I built a smokehouse too. That was a village favorite," said Hunting.

"I bet. So, Pete… I think I've got what I need. It's getting late. I appreciate you talking to me."

"Sure, Daryl. Anytime."

Granier turned and walked back the way he came.

Once out of sight, Granier went back to the location he had hidden his rucksack and sniper rifle. He checked his rifle and chambered a round. He may only get one opportunity at Thao and he wanted to be ready. He heard a truck engine and looked down the road leading into the village. It was an ARVN jeep and troop truck heading toward the village. Granier thought it would have been too much of a coincidence to be a regular patrol. He used his rifle's scope for a closer look. A Vietnamese man in a suit was riding in the passenger seat of the jeep. He looked like he was in charge. Granier knew the look. He was South Vietnamese intelligence. Somehow, he had found

Thao. Seconds now mattered as the convoy came closer to the village.

Slinging his rifle, Granier took off at a run through a field just outside the village. He knew he would reach the village first but only by a minute. As the sun began to set, the shadows were long making it more difficult to see. Granier entered the village and advanced down the road to where he had seen the wheel. It was gone. He looked around and saw nothing. He unslung his rifle. He heard a door opening and turned to see Hunting standing in the doorway of a hut with a towel in his hands. Hunting stared at Granier and seemed disappointed. "You're not a photojournalist, are you, Daryl?" said Hunting.

"No, Pete. I'm not. You should go inside where it's safe," said Granier.

"Are you CIA?"

"Go inside, Pete."

As the truck engine drew close, another man from another hut emerged and looked down the road.

The sun was directly in Granier's eyes. He squinted to get a better look. He only saw the man's face for a brief moment, but he was sure of his identity - it was Thao. Granier raised his rifle and aimed. For a strange reason, Granier did not want Hunting to see him kill Thao. Hunting was innocent and somewhat naïve. But more than anything, he was an optimist. There were few optimists left in a cynical world. It seemed wrong to shatter his idealized world. "Go inside, Pete."

Hunting looked down the road and saw Thao. He realized Granier was going to kill him. "He's just a man like you and me, Daryl," said Hunting.

"Pete, I promise you. He's more than that. Far more."

"And for that, he has to die?"

"Yes."

Hunting rushed forward and grabbed the barrel of Granier's rifle. Hunting was bigger than Granier and strong like a country mule. "Get your fucking hands off my rifle," said Granier struggling.

"It's not right."

"What the hell do you know?"

Fed up, Granier kicked Hunting in the crotch. Hunting went down to his knees. Granier swung his rifle around. Thao was gone. "What have you done, Pete?" said Granier as the jeep's headlights flashed across him.

"I saved a life, you son of a bitch," said Pete in a painful voice.

"No. You didn't," said Granier as he watched the jeep and the truck pull to a stop.

Granier slipped into the shadows. Troops piled out and advanced into the village going door-to-door, searching for Thao. Granier watched as he kept moving through the shadows, keeping out of sight whenever possible. Granier finally ended up next to the village church where he caught a glimpse of Thao hiding inside. He watched as the village priest seemed to be leading the troops away, then turned to the man in the suit and pointed at the church. The troops returned and quickly surrounded the church. Moments later, Thao was brought out and forced to kneel in the town square as he was placed in shackles and kept under heavy guard.

In yet another coup attempt in early 1965, Colonel Thao and a core group of fifty loyal Catholic soldiers had attempted to kill Prime Minister Quat and kidnap Generals Thi and Ky. When the coup failed, General

Thi, the co-head of the military junta, wanted to kill Thao himself. He had offered a reward of $30,000 U.S. to anyone who was instrumental in the capture of Thao. The local priest needed funds to rebuild his dilapidated church and had turned Thao into the government. Once again, betrayal was the willful slaughter of hope for Thao. Thao did not fight. He desired to survive so that he might escape as he had done so many times before.

Thao had been in the village for several weeks and the villagers had grown close to him. They were unhappy with the priest that had betrayed him but did nothing. It was out of their hands at that point. Even the village militia stood down and just watched. The government forces were far better armed and well-trained.

Hunting appeared in the square and saw Thao kneeling on the hard stones. He felt compassion for Thao but knew better than to interfere with the South Vietnamese troops.

The troops waited all night with Thao as their prisoner, kneeling in public. They did not fear the villagers or their militia. A radio call had been sent to Saigon. The commander of the troops had been ordered not to move Thao at night when their vehicles could be ambushed. It was too risky. Thao was too valuable. A light mist settled in over the village. Everything was still. Nobody spoke.

At first light, the sound of helicopter blades approached. Granier knew what was about to happen. They would take Thao to Saigon by helicopter. Granier moved off into a field just outside of the village. The mist hung low covering the ground. He stopped when he reached an earthen berm. He readied himself and his rifle. He would only have one shot. It would most likely be a fast-moving shot and the sun would be in his eyes. There was nothing he could do about that. There was no time. The only advantage he had was that there was no wind. Not even a light breeze. He adjusted his rifle's sight as best he thought imagining the distance from where the helicopter might emerge. It was nothing more than a wild guess. He stood in the rice field with his head and arms just above the layer of mist. He hoped his rifle sight would not fog.

The helicopter arrived and landed on the main road at the edge of the village. It was two hundred yards away from Granier's position. A very long shot for a moving target in bad light. It took several minutes to escort Thao up the road to the helicopter.

Granier thought for a moment, then made one last tweak to his rifle's sight as Thao was loaded into the aircraft flanked by two guards on either side. It made Granier's job even more difficult. The guard between him and Thao could lean into his shot at any moment and he would be helpless to stop him.

As the helicopter engine whined and the blades accelerated, Granier readied himself wrapping the rifle's strap tight around his wrist. He held the rifle firmly, but not so tight that he might quiver. He aimed and waited. It was a bad angle. One of the guards was blocking the shot. Granier didn't panic. He was too experienced for that. He waited.

The helicopter kicked up a brown cloud of dust as it lifted off into the morning sunlight. Everything was in silhouette. Impossible to identify. And still, Granier waited, unmoving as a mountain. The helicopter turned toward the East. "Shit," whispered Granier to himself.

But still, he waited, keeping his sight on the passenger area. Then, the helicopter turned for a slight moment. Thao was exposed for no longer than one second. Granier didn't hesitate and squeezed his trigger. The rifle bucked. He knew the results before they happened. He smiled a little.

The bullet entered through the doorway and passed under the guard's chin, no less than an inch. It hit Thao in the throat just below his jaw and severed one of his carotid arteries. Thao seemed confused like he didn't understand what had just happened. The two guards didn't even notice as large amounts of blood ran down and pooled in Thao's shirt turning it a beautiful deep red in the morning light. After a moment, Thao, his eyes still open, slumped over. Colonel Thao, the North Vietnamese sleeper agent, was dead and his secret was safe… thanks to Granier.

A few days later, Pete Hunting was driving an IVS jeep along the road back to the village where he had dug the well. He was still troubled by Thao's betrayal and death. He felt that Granier's lie was almost as bad as the priest's betrayal of Thao. The priest may have sold out Thao for pieces of silver, but it was Granier that had killed Thao. Even as bad as he felt, life went on and there was still good to be done. He was studying how to repair the generators that many villages used to create power for streetlights. Nights were safer with lights. The Viet Cong didn't like lights, especially flood lights.

As Hunting neared the village, a convoy of South Vietnamese troops heading in the opposite direction rambled toward him. He pulled over to let them pass. He could see that the troops on the transports had recently been in a battle. Many were bandaged and blood was seeping through the gauze. War was not kind to humans no matter which side you were on.

As the last truck passed his jeep, Hunting pulled back onto the road and proceeded toward the village. Hunting went another mile when he was flagged down by three Vietnamese rebels in black pajamas. Hunting had a Thompson submachine gun under the backseat and for a brief moment, he considered retrieving it. Hunting didn't want to kill another human being, but he didn't want to die either. He decided to have faith in humanity. Surely, these men could see that he was not the enemy. He stopped the jeep and put his hands in the air. The Viet Cong motioned for him to pull off the road. He didn't like that idea but complied when one of the men pointed his rifle directly at his face.

He pulled the jeep into a field and the three men once again surrounded him. They began searching his jeep. Hunting knew they would find the submachine gun and when they did, they would probably kill him. He decided to offer it to them as a gift along with the two extra magazines of bullets. When they found the weapon, Hunting made hand motions like he wanted them to have it. One of the soldiers knew the weapon from the Indochina War and chambered the first round. Hunting smiled as if somehow a friendly gesture would save him. It didn't.

The next morning Peter Hunting was found dead, still in his jeep. He had fifteen bullets in his corpse – five in his head and ten in his body. He was the first humanitarian aid worker to die in the Vietnam War. There would be more... many more.

As his friends and family would say upon hearing of his death, he was a good man with a good heart that

died too soon. He loved all the Vietnamese people…
even the one that shot him. He died doing what he
loved – serving.

Granier read about Peter Hunting's death in an English
newspaper, and it affected him deeply. It was rare for
Granier to feel anything about anyone or anything. But
he too had become an optimist for a brief moment as
he had watched Hunting build a well for people he
hardly knew. Granier swore to himself that he would
never be an optimist again.

July 4, 1965 – Gulf of Tonkin, South Vietnam

A new aircraft appeared in Vietnam on the flight deck
of the USS Enterprise aircraft carrier – the Grumman
A-6 Intruder, nicknamed the "Iron Tadpole" for its
blunt nose and slender tail. Doubling the payload of
the A-1 Skyraider which it was designed to replace, the
dual jet engine Intruder packed a powerful punch. As
an attack aircraft, its ability to fly both close air support
and long-range bombing missions in all-weather, made
the A-6 perfect for Vietnam where the weather could
change dramatically with little warning. Even with
eighteen 1,000-pound bombs on its five hardpoints,
the Intruder was capable of short takeoff and landing
(STOL) for Marine close air support. It was a
welcomed brute in America's arsenal.

Unlike previous attack aircraft, the Intruder used a
side-by-side pilot and navigator seating configuration
in the cockpit. This allowed the navigator who also
served as co-pilot and bombardier to share the pilot's
workload when necessary or even take over if the pilot
was wounded. Since air support was one of the main

advantages the Americans had over their enemy, the Intruder's ability to fly in all conditions day or night made it a useful instrument of death to both the Navy and the Marines. For ground commanders, the Intruder was seen as a sort of Holy Grail. The Intruder, which was originally introduced in 1963, had gone through extensive testing and development before entering service in Vietnam. The additional development had greatly improved the aircraft's performance and serviceability. It would remain in America's arsenal for over thirty years.

Using an advanced design, the Intruder had sophisticated avionics with a high degree of integration. It was so advanced, that many were skeptical that the aircrew would be able to use the complex gadgets during actual combat. But their objections were quickly put aside when the Intruder first started flying missions in Vietnam. The Intruder was designed to fly low even during attack or bombing. It hugged the contours of the earth. Unfortunately, this also made it vulnerable to enemy anti-aircraft fire. The good news was the Intruder with its twin turbojet engines could take a beating and remain air-worthy.

July 8, 1965 – Saigon, South Vietnam

Ambassador Taylor packed a box of personal items from his U.S. Embassy office. After serving only one year, he had resigned. Henry Cabot Lodge was coming back to Vietnam for a second term as U.S. Ambassador to replace him. President Johnson needed a strong-willed ambassador to deal with the constant coups and rotating South Vietnamese military leaders. Few were stronger than Lodge who many considered too rigid and conservative.

Taylor had opposed the use of American ground troops in Vietnam and supported intensified bombing in the North. The bombing strategy was clearly failing to make much of a dent in Hanoi's thinking and attitude toward peace talks. As far as troop deployments, it was too early to tell, but clearly, Johnson had chosen that route. Taylor felt that Johnson needed an ambassador that supported his strategy. It was obvious that he needed to go. Taylor knew Johnson would be secretly grateful when he resigned no matter what he said in public. It was better this way. Vietnam was his third war and he was tired. He wondered if he had become too rigid in his thinking. Too much experience could stifle new ideas labeling them as unworkable. He would find other ways to serve his country.

It took a lot of convincing for the president to get Lodge to come back to Vietnam. Lodge had served both Kennedy and Johnson as ambassador in previous years. He had been U.S. Ambassador to South Vietnam during the coup that overthrew and instigated the death of President Diem and his brother. Lodge had supported the coup leaders and kept them on track when others in Washington had wavered.

Lodge had resigned as ambassador when he decided to run against Johnson for president. Lodge lost the Republican Primary to Goldwater and was available to serve as an ambassador once again. Johnson was killing two birds with one stone when Lodge agreed to be ambassador once again – he had eliminated a potential political opponent and had a competent ambassador that knew the situation in Vietnam well and could hit the ground running. It was a shrewd move on Johnson's part.

One thing was for sure, Lodge didn't pull punches. He thought out his decisions and said what he believed. Johnson did not envy the South Vietnamese military leaders that would face Lodge. Toes would be stepped on and crushed in some cases. Lodge was a force to be reconned with and if anyone could straighten out South Vietnam, it was Lodge. Johnson liked the idea of releasing the reins to Lodge. It would give him time to concentrate on the Great Society and other key issues that had been neglected for too long. Even though he did not always agree with him, Johnson trusted Lodge.

July 16-20, 1965 – Saigon, South Vietnam

Shortly after Lodge arrived back in South Vietnam, Secretary of Defense McNamara visited General Westmoreland to get an update on the situation for President Johnson. It wasn't that Johnson didn't trust the Joint Chiefs of Staff. It was that he understood that the Pentagon was a political organization with its own strange culture whether the Joint Chiefs admitted it or not. At times, Johnson wanted the straight scoop on what was happening in the war. McNamara gave him the straight, unfiltered truth. He could trust McNamara's observations and reports as reliable and use them to form his own opinions.

McNamara liked Westmoreland. They both had straightforward personalities that allowed them to cut through the niceties and get at the meat of the conversation within a short time. McNamara found Westmoreland's candid attitude refreshing. It wasn't that Westmoreland could not be diplomatic when necessary, he just didn't feel the need to be diplomatic around McNamara who was always an analytical guy that loved facts and figures. Westmoreland knew how to produce the data that McNamara loved, and he had gained the secretary's trust.

Westmoreland's briefing on Laos was less than encouraging. The bombing of the Ho Chi Minh Trail had failed miserably at stopping the flow of arms and supplies into South Vietnam. The Viet Cong were better equipped than ever and the situation was getting worse with new advanced weaponry from the Soviets and Chinese making its way in country. McNamara had miscalculated the effect of the bombing campaigns from the very beginning. He had only made matters worse by trying to bomb the enemy back into the stone age. It wasn't happening and now the Viet Cong and PAVN were even more dangerous. Just because McNamara's mechanical heart was in the right place, it didn't make him an effective leader.

As Westmoreland, an experienced combat leader, knew from the start, the ARVN and the Americans would need to win on the ground if they ever planned on defeating the North Vietnamese and Viet Cong. But Westmoreland also knew that sometimes Washington needed to have its way before it was willing to hear the hard truth. Now was the time. It would be another big ask… a really big ask.

Westmoreland unveiled his plan to win the war along with a timetable, something McNamara and Johnson both wanted. The ask and the timetable would work in tandem. The ask was another fourteen battalions supported by additional squadrons of helicopters. The helicopters had been the shining light in the darkness. They worked well in combat situations and stifled the enemy at every turn. More was better when it came to helicopters. They were a true force multiplier and would be a key part of all American forces from that point forward. Westmoreland wanted a lot of them.

Westmoreland's timetable was to reverse the deteriorating military situation in South Vietnam for the remainder of 1965. Once the country was stable, the military would take the offensive in 1966, then destroy the Viet Cong and capture their strongholds by the end of 1967. Once the Viet Cong were defeated, there would be another time of stabilization before the American troops could be brought back home in victory. Westmoreland had a plan and, after asking a plethora of questions which were promptly answered, McNamara liked it.

Surprisingly upbeat, McNamara returned to report to Johnson. He knew that Johnson would be upset by the additional troop request so soon after Westmoreland's last request. But McNamara didn't care. He had something that Johnson craved, a realistic timetable to get out of Vietnam. It even had benchmarks to measure the plan's progress. McNamara was right. Johnson received the additional troop request with little resistance once he had been presented with a plan and timetable. He was onboard and so was McNamara.

McNamara recommended that Johnson increase the number of U.S. troops in Vietnam to 175,000. In addition, he recommended that 235,000 soldiers in the Reserve and National Guard be activated and that the overall military personnel should be increased to 375,000. An additional 2,500 to 4,000 air strikes would be used to hold the enemy in place until the new troops could arrive in-country and be deployed to where they were needed.

Feeling like they were finally getting someplace, Johnson swallowed it all in stride and immediately called a meeting of the fifteen-member National Security Council to go over the request and help him decide the direction of the war. If Johnson thought that everyone would be on board, he was wrong. U.S. Under Secretary of State George Ball strongly disagreed with McNamara's request and Westmoreland's plan. Ball urged the president to cut America's losses and allow the South Vietnamese government to do what seemed natural and let it fall apart from its internal squabbling. He closed his argument with a prophetic statement saying that South Vietnam would ultimately lose to the Viet Cong guerrillas, regardless of McNamara's additional troops. The United States would not get out with the victory that everyone wanted. Instead, "We'll double our bet and get lost in the rice paddies of Southeast Asia." They were solemn words that were hard to ignore. Feeling like it may be the last station to jump off the Vietnam War train, Ball had been passionate.

Listening to Ball, General Greene estimated that to win the war, the United States would need five years and 500,000 troops. He said that the American people would back such a commitment if told the truth.

All of the other advisors in the council were against Ball and for McNamara's plan. Listening to each of the men he trusted, Johnson took it all in before making his decision.

Johnson was not a timid leader, but he insisted on being well-informed on important matters before deciding on a course of action. He just wanted to understand when and where he was going before actually going there. McNamara had given him the information he needed, and he was content. But he had also listened to Ball and Greene. He didn't agree with them, but he did believe they were giving him their honest opinions.

In the end, Johnson gave Westmoreland what he wanted. He just did it more gradually than what Westy had requested. It would be a buildup of troop levels and equipment over time. Johnson was hedging his bets, willing to pull back if things didn't go as planned. Unlike General Greene, Johnson did not believe that the American people were ready to support such a high troop commitment. Like frogs swimming in a cool pot of water, he would slowly turn up the heat until the water was boiling, and the unknowing frogs were dinner. It wasn't evil or even misleading in Johnson's mind. It was what was required to defeat communism which is what the American people wanted. Johnson would do what was necessary to win… for the good of the country and its people. It was the only way he knew that would get America out of Vietnam.

The Hunt

July 24, 1965 – Hanoi, North Vietnam

Hanoi had been deluged with SAM-2 emplacements making it the most dangerous area for bombing targets in all of Vietnam. Because most of the SAM sites were positioned to protect the majority of the population and its leaders, they still gave the American aviators plenty of targets on the outskirts of the city where there were far fewer SAM sites. Fuel depots were popular targets because they not only slowed down troop movements in and out of the area, but they also slowed down manufacturing. The machines within the factories needed oil and gasoline to grind out bullets and bicycles.

USAF Captain Richard Keirn and his bombardier/navigator Captain Roscoe Fobair were part of the 47th Tactical Fighter Squadron stationed at Ubon Royal Thai Air Force Base, Thailand. They had taken off in their F-4C Phantom earlier that morning and were closing in on their target, an oil refinery ten miles northeast of Hanoi. It had been an uneventful flight up until Fobair's radar display lit up. It was a SAM on its way. There wasn't much time for evasive maneuvers, but Keirn did his best trying to break the missile's lock. It didn't work. The missile hit the engine and exploded. The aircraft shuttered violently as it quickly lost altitude. They were going down. "Eject, eject, eject," said Keirn in his helmet's microphone. As the backseater, Fobair was supposed to eject first. Keirn called Fobair but got no response. He waited as long as he could and repeated the eject order. Still no response. Keirn wondered if shrapnel from the missile's explosions might have reached Fobair. With no time left, Keirn punched out.

As he floated down, he watched his burning aircraft smash into the ground. If Fobair wasn't already dead, there was little doubt the crash would have killed him.

Landing, Keirn was confronted by a farmer with a rice harvesting knife. He thought about pulling out his pistol, but the farmer was close enough to use his knife, and frightened. He didn't want to give him a reason to attack. It wouldn't have made much of a difference anyway. The local militia arrived a few minutes later and took Keirn captive. He would remain a prisoner for eight brutal years until he was finally released as part of Operation Homecoming. Captain Fobair's remains would not be recovered until 2001.

The downing of F-4C Phantom #63-7599 was the first American aircraft to be lost by a North Vietnamese SAM-2 missile. Three days later, the Airmen would seek revenge.

July 27, 1965 – Suoi Hia, North Vietnam

To say that the American airmen were angry about the downed Phantom aircrew was a gross understatement. They were seething and wanted their pound of flesh from the North Vietnamese. Their vengeance came in the form of Operation Spring High. Using current aerial intelligence, the Air Force identified two SAM sites near each other, site 6 and site 7 in Suoi Hai, Ha Tay Province, North Vietnam.

Forty-six F-105 fighter-bombers took off with fifty-eight support aircraft. Six planes were lost while bombing the two sites. One of the two targets was destroyed with a direct hit, Site 6, although there were no secondary explosions. Even with their losses, the airmen returned to base feeling triumphant.

Days later, bomb damage assessment photos revealed that Site 6 had been a dummy missile and that Site 7 was empty. The airmen had fallen into a North Vietnamese trap and had accomplished nothing. Many of the American aviators were demoralized.

Saigon, South Vietnam

Granier had been ordered to report to MACV at the American embassy in Saigon. He thought it strange. He was CIA and while the agencies cooperated regularly, his orders usually came through the CIA, not MACV. He supposed it didn't matter.

When he arrived, he was escorted into an office reception area where Captain David Mendez, leader of an elite reconnaissance unit, was sitting as if waiting to be called into an office. Granier noticed the captain's 101st Airborne shoulder patch with its screaming eagle. Granier didn't care too much for most of the Airborne guys. They were obnoxious. Besides, he had been a

Marine and didn't need to prove himself to anyone. He sat quietly and waited saying nothing to the captain.

Granier was called into an office first. The captain watched him like a tiger watches its prey. Airborne were like that… always looking for a fight. That's what made them good warriors and the tip of the Army's spear, naked aggression. Granier may not have liked Airborne but that didn't mean that he didn't respect them.

Granier entered the office of Colonel Spitz, one of Westmoreland's commanders. Granier had seen him before around the embassy and Saigon. Spitz was experienced. Granier liked soldiers that knew their shit. He knew his shit.

The colonel got right to the point, something else that Granier liked, and explained that MACV had requested that the CIA assign Granier to accompany a 101st Airborne long-range reconnaissance team (LRRP) in crossing the border into North Vietnam and hunting down SAM-2 missile emplacements in and around Hanoi. The U.S. Air Force didn't want to lose any more aircraft on wild goose chases. They wanted confirmed targets before sending a sortie to take them out. "Why me?" said Granier. "I am sure an Airborne team is more than capable of pulling off a reconnaissance mission."

"The 101st Airborne just arrived in country a few weeks ago. Although they are mission ready, they do not have experience with the terrain which I am sure you can attest to is sometimes challenging," said the colonel. "Besides, you know the North better than anyone. Your help in finding the sites could prove invaluable. Morale is suffering. The Air Force needs a win and it needs it now. You're our best bet."

"Okay. But why Airborne? I could use my own team."

"Probably and you might even have better luck. But there is something to be said about handing down tradecraft. Your experience could give these boys a jump start."

"I see."

"Can I count that as a 'Yes'?"

"I didn't know I had an option."

"You don't. I was just being congenial."

"Well, in that case, I'm in."

Spitz pressed the intercom on his desk and invited Mendez into his office. The captain snapped to attention before being asked to sit. Niceties were exchanged and Granier was introduced. Granier didn't like that part… being introduced. He liked his anonymity. He was a spy for Christ's sake. The older he got, the more obstinate he became. He liked working alone and wasn't looking forward to the mission. Too many team members meant the chances of someone fucking up were increased even if they were Airborne.

The tension between Granier and Mendez was palatable. The meeting was civil enough and laid out the mission. The team would be working in an area that Granier knew well between the border and Hanoi. Even in the preliminary stages, Granier was already suggesting locations where they might look for the missiles. Mendez's stiffness softened slightly as he realized that Granier might be a valuable asset to the team, but he still didn't like the former Jarhead.

It took another week of pouring over maps and deciding on a route before the team was ready. Coyle flew them as far North as practicable without getting into SAM territory. The team secured ground transportation the rest of the way to the border. Granier knew where to cross safely. He had done it dozens of times and had it down to an art — waiting for the PAVN patrols to pass, skirting the line of sight of the watchtowers, avoiding the tripwires that set off flares, and most importantly knowing the path through both the PAVN and ARVN minefields.

It took all night, but the team made it across the border without incident. Once they had penetrated North Vietnam, the team moved off a couple of miles and rested. Granier could fall asleep within seconds when he wanted. Unlike most of his missions across the border, he was with a team of soldiers that would keep watch and protect him while he dozed. Although he wouldn't admit it… it was nice. The rest of the team slept in shifts. They would wait until nightfall before moving again. There was too much of a chance of being spotted during the day.

Hiking across the country at night, the team reached the area of operations within three days. They checked out a half dozen of Granier's suggestions on where the missiles might be located and came up empty-handed. Mendez had a VHF/FM AN/PRC-25 radio that he used sparingly to report to command. There was nothing to report except that they hadn't found the missiles yet and were continuing the search. There was little sense in breaking radio silence and risking exposure of the team. During one of the calls, the team learned that two more American aircraft had been shot down by SAMs. The team's failure meant capture or even death to the American airmen. The bad news weighed heavy on the team.

It took another week to search all the areas that Granier had suggested, and they still came up with nothing. Everyone was frustrated, except Granier. He knew these types of missions took time. The team was young and gung-ho. When one of the team members suggested that Granier might be too old to keep up with the team, Granier said, "There were two bulls, one young and one old, standing on a hillside overlooking a pasture filled with heifers. The youngest bull said, 'Let's run down there and fuck one of them heifers.' To which, the old bull replied, 'Let's walk down and fuck 'em all.'"

The team laughed. Granier had made his point.

Early the next evening, Granier called Mendez over to look at the map he was studying and said, "This area has a series of caves and an abandoned hut I stayed in a few times."

"Why haven't we checked it out?" said Mendez.

"Too obvious. The North Vietnamese are too smart for that."

"So, why now?"

"We're running out of options. Besides, I may give the enemy too much credit."

"Let's hope that's the case."

"It's always a bad strategy to underestimate your enemy."

"Yeah, but it's just as bad to overestimate them."

Granier grunted in response.

It was during their search of the new area that the team almost stumbled over the SAM site and its crew. Granier had been right. The North Vietnamese were using the hut as their quarters and had placed the SAM site nearby. Granier had also suggested that they might be using the caves to store additional missiles to reload the launcher quickly.

The recon team spent several hours surveying the site to ensure that the missiles were indeed real. They were. Satisfied, Mendez radioed for an airstrike.

While the news was well received by the Air Force commanders, they were cautious and took their time planning out the mission. It would be the next day before the air strike was executed.

The team waited impatiently. They were concerned that they might be discovered, and the missiles moved before the fighter-bombers could get to them. They would have to start over to reacquire the missiles. In the meantime, Granier decided to take a closer look at the caves by himself. Too many soldiers were not covert, but an invasion.

At the third cave he examined, he found what he was looking for. Two PAVN guards were standing watch at the mouth of the cave. Granier knew instinctively that he had found their supply depot which most likely contained the extra missiles. He needed a closer look. He removed a pair of grenades from his rucksack and taped them together. He pocketed a small spool of thin wire. Leaving his rifle behind, he moved into the jungle thirty yards away from the cave's entrance. There was a downhill slope. He used his knife to carve a small stick from a fallen tree branch. He pried up a small boulder from the soil and propped the stick under to prevent it from falling back down. He carefully placed several smaller rocks on the uphill side of the boulder. It was a simple diversion that seemed more natural in some ways. He pulled his canteen from his rucksack and poured water at the base of the stick. He figured he had about a minute before the stick failed and slipped from underneath the rock pile. He moved off to his previous hidden position overlooking the cave.

After three minutes of nothing happening, he began to wonder if the diversion had sprung but didn't cause enough noise. Then he heard it and so did the guards. Rocks clacked together as they rolled. A little late, but perfect in results. The guards moved off to investigate. Granier slipped into the cave. As he expected, there was a tripwire stretching across the mouth of the cave. He carefully stepped across it.

Twenty feet into the cave Granier found the missiles. There were more than he suspected, and he wondered if there might be a second SAM site nearby. He tied the wire from his pocket to one of the grenade's safety pins, the placed the two grenades next to the back of one of the missiles. His hope was not to detonate the warhead but to ignite the missile's propellant and let nature take its course. He led out the wire as he moved back to the mouth of the cave. His plan was to detonate the grenades after the air strike on the SAM site.

He slipped the spool of wire under the tripwire and walked out of the entrance. The two guards returned just as he appeared. Bad timing. They leveled their submachine guns. Granier had little choice but to surrender. He grabbed the spool of wire tight in his hand and raised his hands to signal his surrender. The wire tightened.

As the safety ring wire's slack decreased with the raising of Granier's hands in surrender, the wire caught on the tripwire and pulled the pin free from the grenade.

Granier felt the release of tension on the wire in his hand. Keeping his hands in the air, Granier moved toward the side of the cave and away from the mouth. The guards yelled at him. Granier kept moving. The guards ran forward to punish him and bind him. Just as Granier reached the side of the cave, the grenades exploded setting off the propellant. The missile flew unguided and slammed into the wall of the cave. It was the explosion of the propellent that set off the warhead which exploded detonating the other missiles in a chain reaction.

Granier dove out of the way and one of the guards fired his submachine gun just missing him. The stream of fire that belched from the cave entrance was similar to the fiery blast from a jet's afterburner, a long horizontal column. The two guards were instantly incinerated. Granier rolled away from the flames. He was safe but had mucked up the mission. He grabbed his rifle and headed back to the team's position overlooking the SAM site. Moving through the jungle he heard machine gun fire, a mix of AK-47s and the team's M60. A firefight had broken out. The team was better armed and trained but outnumbered by the SAM site security force.

Granier changed course and headed for higher ground where his sniper rifle might do some good. He emerged uphill from the firefight and immediately engaged the enemy with well-placed sniper shots killing four soldiers and wounding another. Granier's accurate shots tipped the balance of the battle back in the Airborne team's favor. A few minutes later, the PAVN soldiers had been driven inside the hut they had been using for barracks. It was a stupid mistake as the thin walls provided little real cover.

As the recon team surrounded the hut, a radio call notified the team that the US Navy strike force was inbound. Mendez ordered his team to back away and seek cover behind a grouping of boulders. Granier found his own cover up the hill but kept sending the occasional bullet down range to keep the PAVN pinned inside the hut.

Two minutes later, four U.S. Navy A-4 Skyhawks screamed over the SAM site dropping their Mk-20 Rockeye cluster bombs, 247 bomblets were released from each of the Rockeyes. Each aircraft carried six Rockeyes. The entire area went up in hundreds of small explosions. The SAMs were destroyed and a bomb that fell short even hit the hut the PAVN troops were hiding in and destroyed it killing everyone inside.

Granier thought it strange the USAF would allow the Navy to draw first blood in the war against the SAM sites. He didn't understand military politics and didn't have a desire to learn. All he cared about was that the mission had been accomplished aside from his mistake. That's just the way it was sometimes. If fate smiled on you, you took it with grace.

When the smoke finally cleared, Granier went back to the cave where the spare missiles had been stored. He looked around for signs of the second SAM site. There were none. As he was heading back, he came upon a road. There were tire tracks from a truck and a lighter trailer that it was towing. As Granier studied the tracks, he noticed that the tire tracks from the trailer had grown deeper as if the weight had increased. And then it hit him… the SAM launchers had gone mobile. The tire tracks showed that the trailer's weight had increased when the replacement missiles from the cave had been loaded onto its mobile launcher.

The mobile missile revelation was a game-changer for the U.S. military. No longer fixed emplacements, the SAM sites could be positioned anywhere and after firing their missiles they could move to an entirely new location. It would be impossible to track them. The danger for American and South Vietnamese aircrews had increased exponentially.

When he returned to the team, Granier told Mendez what he had discovered. Realizing the importance of the discovery, Mendez radioed his commander and gave him the bad news. Granier didn't care about credit for the discovery. What he did care about was that it meant that more Americans would die.

It would take a week for the team to travel back across the border. The North Vietnamese knew that a recon team was operating in the area of the SAM site and they sent several companies to find them. The Airborne team had to be even more careful as they traveled. As long-range recon, their job was to avoid conflict if possible. The information they carried was more important than the damage they could inflict on the enemy.

After a long debriefing on the operation and the discovery of mobile missile launchers, Granier was happy that the mission was over. Even Granier needed a couple of days rest. Mendez didn't thank Granier. He had too much respect for him… besides, he was still a Jarhead.

Pleiku, South Vietnam

It had been four months since Mr. Dung had given Coyle the name of the village where Nguyet and her daughter were living. Coyle was not a coward, but he wasn't a big fan of conflict and avoided awkward situations whenever possible. Seeing Nguyet after ten years had the potential of being a very awkward situation. What had taken him so long to find her? He had hired a detective but didn't go beyond that when things didn't pan out. The North and the South had divided and over a million Vietnamese had traveled South. How was he supposed to find her in that mess? He hadn't really tried. He felt guilty and his promise to McGoon haunted him, especially his dreams. There was no good excuse for not searching for her and he would need to fess up when he found Nguyet... assuming she could even understand what he was saying. The last time he saw her, she spoke very little English.

And then there was the matter of her daughter... that would be a very awkward conversation. If Nguyet claimed her daughter was his, Coyle could ask for a blood test. He wasn't sure Nguyet would understand and might feel insulted. Coyle didn't want to hurt her or her daughter but taking on the responsibility of a child was big deal for anyone. A child? She was ten. He imagined she was no longer a child, but... a young girl. He didn't like that thought. It brought too many possibilities that he couldn't deal with at the moment. He decided she was still a child. It was less overwhelming.

He also didn't know what to do with Nguyet and her daughter. He had promised McGoon he would watch over Nguyet. He couldn't very well do that with her living in a village in the Mekong Delta where the

Viet Cong had a stronghold. He wondered if making contact was the best idea. Nguyet could be perceived as a collaborator if she was seen with an American. The last thing he wanted to do was to put her in danger. He decided that if she and her daughter lived in a city it would be safer. He could arrange that and even pay their rent. But who was to say that was even what they wanted?

There were too many variables and the only way to eliminate them was to find and talk with Nguyet. He decided he had procrastinated long enough, and it was time to discover the truth. He would face whatever consequences he was dealt. He was a man after all, and men solved problems... usually...

Coyle volunteered for a supply run to a CIA listening outpost near the Cambodian border. The team's radio monitoring device had conked out and needed replacement parts. Coyle had decided to take a translator with him so he could speak with Nguyet. He would pick up the translator in Can Tho after he dropped off the supplies. He didn't want to use anyone in the military or CIA. This was a personnel matter.

Nguyet's village was actually a reinforced hamlet which made Coyle feel a bit more comfortable about her current living situation. While the hamlets were targets for the Viet Cong, they were also protected by ARVN forces and local militias. It was far better than an open village that the Viet Cong could march in without resistance.

It didn't take long after he picked up the translator to fly to an airfield near Nguyet's hamlet. When they landed, Coyle hired a motorbike taxi to take him and the translator to the hamlet. The driver, the translator, and Coyle all crammed onto the motorbike's seat for the twenty-minute trip.

When they arrived, Coyle paid the driver to wait. Coyle didn't know how long it would take or even if Nguyet would see him. She might be angry with him. He just didn't know what was going to happen. The translator asked a villager where Nguyet lived and was pointed toward a hut near the center of the hamlet.

As Coyle and the translator approached the hut, a girl appeared in the doorway. She was gathering wooden branches for the cooking fire. She was tall and her skin was light in color. Her shoulders were broad far beyond most Vietnamese. Hearing their footsteps she turned to face the two strangers. Coyle could see her face and he knew instantly she was McGoon's daughter. He couldn't help but smile. She smiled back. "Hello," she said.

"You speak English," said Coyle surprised.

"Little."

"Mom teach you?"

She shook her head and said, "Priest."

Coyle nodded approvingly and said, "That's good. You speak good."

She grinned, happy with the compliment, and said, "Thank you."

"You're welcome," said Coyle, then pointed to himself. "Coyle."

"Coyle," she said back.

"You?" said Coyle pointing to her.

"Tuyet," she said pointing to herself.

"Nice to meet you, Tuyet."

She grinned. Coyle laughed and said, "Shit, you even smile like McGoon."

"Shit?" said Tuyet not understanding the new word.

"No. No shit. Bad word."

"Shit," said Tuyet.

"Ah, crap," said Coyle realizing he was corrupting the girl.

"Crap?"

"No. No crap. No shit."

"Crap-shit?"

Coyle gave up and said, "Is your mother here?"

Tuyet looked confused like she didn't understand the question. Coyle panicked. He had pushed her too far. "It's okay. It's okay."

The translator jumped in and asked if her mother was home. The girl nodded and went back inside the hut. After a moment, Nguyet appeared in the doorway with Tuyet. She was wearing a simple Ao Dai and looked beautiful. She seemed shocked at seeing Coyle and said in a quivering voice, "Coyle?"

"Yeah, it's me. Coyle. You look great, Nguyet."

A tear rolled down her cheek as Nguyet walked over to Coyle, wrapped her arms around him, and hugged him like she would never let go. Coyle smiled as his eyes teared up. "I'm sorry I'm late."

The interpreter translated their conversation, waiting until each had finished their thought. "I'm sorry I'm old," said Nguyet.

"Old? You haven't aged even a little. You look the same as when I met you."

"You got fat."

"Well, I may have gained a few pounds, but..."

"I like fat."

"Good. I'm glad. You have a daughter."

"Yes. McGoon was her father. She looks like him, no?"

"Yeah. Spitting image."

"She eats like him too."

"I bet. The man liked his food."

"I miss him."

"Me too."

She invited them in for tea and the conversation continued with Tuyet occasionally jumping in to practice her English. When Coyle talked with her, he made his sentences as simple as possible. After an hour, Nguyet sent Tuyet to fetch some water. When she left, Nguyet asked, "Why are you here, Coyle?"

"I promised McGoon that I would look after you and Chau. I tried to find you, but the war ended and the country was divided. I didn't know where you had gone."

"But you did find me."

"Yeah, better late than never, I guess. Do you know where Chau went?"

"No. I think she stayed in the North. Her family was there."

"That's what the detective said. I'm going to find her too. I promise. I'm going to make sure you're both okay from here on out."

"I'm okay, Coyle. So is Tuyet."

"That's good, but if you want to move to the city where it's safer, I could help."

"I've lived in a city. This is our home."

"But the Viet Cong?"

"They don't bother us now that we've moved into a hamlet. The militia protects us."

"Yeah, but that's not always enough."

"We'll be okay. We're happy here."

"Happy is good. Look, you don't have to decide now. I'm always going to be here to help you if need anything. Anything at all. I'll give the phone number of the air base where I live. You just tell them you want to talk to me and they'll find me. Or you can send a cable if you like that better. Just tell me what you need."

"You're a good man, Tom Coyle."

"Not really. But I'm going to get better."

Tuyet returned with the water and Nguyet made some more tea. They visited for another hour as the sun began to set. Coyle knew better than to travel in the countryside after dark. The Viet Cong owned the night. They said their goodbyes, then Coyle and the interpreter left.

As he traveled back to the airfield on the back of the motorcycle, Coyle grew melancholy. Tuyet was McGoon's daughter and that was good. But she wasn't his daughter. He thought he would be grateful for dodging that bullet, but he wasn't. McGoon was a lucky man even in death. He would be remembered.

August 1, 1965 – Peking, China

Two men sat in a radio broadcast room, one interviewing the other. General Lo Jui-ching was a firebrand. He was also the Chief of Joint Staff of the armed forces of the People's Republic of China. He never failed to disappoint when it came to interviews on the radio. He always said something to inflame the Chinese masses. He saw it as his calling. Politicians calmed and reassured the people. He didn't. "China has fully recovered from the Korean War and is ready once again to face the United States if that is what is required," he said.

"And will it… be required?" said the interviewer.

"It is hard to say. Time will tell the truth of the matter. What I can tell you is that we will be ready if it does happen. Morale is high. Ammunition is plentiful. Our weapons are the best they've ever been. We've learned the lessons that the Americans taught us in Korea. Vietnam could be our proving grounds if the Americans chose to invade North Vietnam."

"Why would President Johnson be so careless when he knows he will lose?"

"Humph. Why did Adolf Hitler invade Russia? Lust for power. Hitler could not stand the thought of being at the mercy of the Russians. He had lost the battle for North Africa to the British and the Americans. He needed the oil locked away in the Siberian tundra. He tried to take it and in so doing lost his army and the war. Johnson is no different. It is his desire for power that will eventually overcome him and he will underestimate China's strength and the determination of its people, just as Hitler underestimated the Russian winter and the blades of the Cossacks on the western plains. I hope he does impose war upon us and compels us to accept the challenge. It is the only way to put the matter to rest once and for all. The Chinese People's Liberation Army has long prepared for this moment and is standing in battle array as we speak. It would be a shame to disappoint our troops. I invite the Americans to come in large numbers, the more the better."

As usual, General Jui-ching did not disappoint his listening audience.

The Burning of Cam Ne

August 3, 1965 - Cam Ne, South Vietnam

CBS Correspondent Morley Safer and his film crew were granted access to U.S. 1st Battalion, 3rd Marine Division, as they went on patrol near Da Nang. The battalion commander's orders were to search four villages for caches of rice and arms meant for the Viet Cong. If found, the village was to be burned.

As the Marine company that Safer and his crew approached the village of Cam Ne, a Viet Cong sniper opened fire wounding one of the Marines and driving the rest of the company to cover. Within minutes the angry Marines were in the village searching for the sniper. None of the villagers knew of his whereabouts. While they didn't find any weapons or large stocks of rice, the Marines felt justified in the actions that followed. Using their Zippo lighters and flamethrowers they set the entire village ablaze. Safer's crew recorded it all on film as it unfolded.

When the deed was done and the peasants' huts were burned to the ground, Safer interviewed several of the Marines and asked their thoughts on what they had done. Did they have remorse? A young corporal responded on camera, "I feel no remorse. I don't imagine anybody else does. You can't be expected to do your job and have pity for these people."

The operation burned down 150 huts, wounded three women, and killed one baby. The Marines had captured four prisoners.

Two days later, American families sitting down for their evening meal viewed Safer's CBS report. They watched while eating their roast beef and potatoes as Vietnamese villagers, the people America was supposed to protect, stood back and watched the young Marines set fire to everything they had worked a lifetime of back-breaking labor to accumulate. As their homes burned many peasants ran inside to retrieve what they could.

Americans were in shock. For most, it was the first time they had seen anything like this. It all seemed so un-American. Nobody knew how to react. Anger was the go-to response. Thousands called their local station to complain. If it was true, it shouldn't have been shown at dinner time. Others threatened to boycott CBS sponsors. The White House switchboard lit up like a Christmas tree.

The next morning, President Johnson called his friend, Frank Stanton, the head of CBS, and said, "Hello,

Frank, this is your president. Are you trying to fuck me?"

Johnson went on to insist that CBS fire Safer. He had defaced the American flag. Intelligence had suggested that Safer was probably a communist agent hired by the Kremlin. The Marines claimed that Safer had provided the Zippo lighter that was used to ignite the hut's roof that they filmed. The Marines went on to claim it was Safer that had asked them to burn the hut for the camera.

Safer denied the accusations and used the film from the Marines' interviews to prove his innocence.

A Marine major at the Da Nang press office called CBS the "Communist Broadcasting System."

It was early in the war, but things were already becoming unhinged in a way nobody could have expected. The media had always been on the side of the American soldier during World War II and even the Korean War. But a new type of journalist was emerging that was more interested in revealing the truth rather than propaganda. The truth was far from comfortable for most Americans. It all seemed so unpatriotic.

When Westmoreland was confronted about the burning of Cam Ne, he said, "We have a genuine problem which will be with us as long as we are in Vietnam. Commanders must exercise restraint unnatural to war and judgment not often required of young men."

American soldiers had come to South Vietnam expecting to be cheered as saviors as American soldiers had been welcomed in Europe. But the Vietnamese people that they were supposed to be saving from the communist, saw the Americans as they had seen the French, soldiers coming to enslave them once again. It was all they knew. It was a different time and a different war.

It was a rude awakening for the American public and an even ruder awakening for the American soldiers. Nobody understood how things got so crazy, so quick.

Sutherland, Nebraska, USA

Jenny's Diner in Sutherland, Nebraska was an institution by local standards. It had survived the Highway 80 bypass because of its gravy. That's right… gravy… on its chicken fried steak. Nothing like it anywhere else. It was a bigger recipe secret than Coca Cola and Earl, the diner's owner, wasn't about to give it up. He loved his diner and its customers, many of which he had watched grow up over the years.

It was a typical crowd that morning. Yes, the townsfolk ate his chicken fried steak in the morning too. But it was his strawberry waffles that were the thing for breakfast. They came with a side of eggs and a biscuit covered in… you guessed it, gravy. The farmers and ranchers sitting at the counter had been up since before dawn. Families sat in the booths. There were lots of those.

Most travelers didn't stop in Sutherland unless they had heard about Earl's gravy. But on that morning, Peter and Hazel Davis were sitting in a booth with their two young children, Sarah and David. The television in the corner blared the latest cereal commercials in between the local news. A story on a unit fighting in Vietnam appeared. A soldier with an M60 rattled off rounds at an unseen enemy. Peasants cried. A Viet Cong prisoner was bound and blindfolded. Seeing the report, Earl quietly left his grill and walked over to the counter where Sid Johnson was sitting and said, "Sid, you want me to change the channel?"

Sid didn't look but simply shook his head and said, "No. It wouldn't be right. I should remember."

"Okay," said Earl moving off.

"I'd like you to change it. It's upsetting my kids," said Peter, sitting at his booth next to the television. "They don't need to see this crap."

Earl grabbed a half-filled coffee pot and walked over to the booth and refilled Hazel and Peter's cups while he spoke in a low voice, "I know you folks aren't from around here. So, it's understandable that you don't know that Sid lost his son, Gerry, last week over in Vietnam. Someplace called the Mekong Delta."

"I'm sorry to hear that, but the sign on the highway said this was a family restaurant."

"And it is. Sid is family."

Peter leaned over to look past Earl and said, "I'm sorry for your loss, Mister."

Sid said nothing. He was lost in grief. "Maybe you folks would be happier at the Sambo's in North Platte. It's only a ten-minute drive," said Earl.

"Maybe we would," said Hazel.

"No," said Peter. "We've already ordered, and the kids are hungry. We'll eat, then go. Vietnam ain't ruining our waffles."

"Suit yourselves. But the television stays on as long as Sid wants it on," said Earl and walked off.

"I don't see what all the fuss is about. It's a war. People die," said Peter in a voice a little too loud. "We never should have gotten involved in the first place.

Vietnam ain't America. We got no business telling those people how they should live their lives."

Earl stood at his grill listening as he flipped some bacon. The light on his waffle maker came on signaling that the waffles inside had finally reached golden brown. Earl stared at the light and did nothing.

A few minutes later, Earl walked over to the booth where the Davises were sitting and placed a charred waffle with strawberries and whipped cream in front of Peter. "I ain't paying for that," said Peter.

"No. I suppose you ain't, said Earl. "But you are leaving."

Peter thought for a moment, then took a look around at the locals sitting in the diner and decided it wasn't worth it. "Come on, kids. We'll get you coloring books at Sambos," said Peter escorting his family out of the diner.

Earl walked past the counter to his grill. "Thanks, Earl," said Sid, tears welling up in his eyes.

"Don't mention it, Sid," said Earl his own eyes filling with tears.

War was pain. Unbearable pain.

August 3-17, 1965 – Duc Co Camp, South Vietnam

The ARVN 5th Special Forces Group Detachment and a Civilian Irregular Defense Group (CIDG) had been defending Duc Co Camp for several weeks against a besieging PAVN force. The base which monitored communist infiltration of the Ho Chi Minh Trail was located just nine miles from the Cambodian border and approximately forty miles west of Pleiku. Even with air and artillery support, the ARVN and CIDG had heavy

DAVID LEE CORLEY

losses and it didn't look like the South Vietnamese could hold out much longer.

Major Norman Schwarzkopf was the senior military advisor for the ARVN Paratroopers sent to relieve the camp and break the siege. When the paratroopers arrived, they immediately came under heaving enemy fire and before long they too were in trouble. They had taken heavy casualties but continued to fight relentlessly for several days.

On 8 August, the Republic of Vietnam Marine Division's Task Force Alpha and an ARVN armored task force departed Pleiku to relieve Schwarzkopf's group and break the siege. When the larger force arrived, they too made heavy contact with a PAVN battalion dug in on along Route 19. Soon the Marine and ARVN relief force was overwhelmed by the enemy and in need of saving. No help was available. In an all-out effort, the South Vietnamese attacked and dislodged the PAVN battalion on Route 19, only to have another reinforced PAVN battalion attack them from behind. Again, the South Vietnamese forces took heavy casualties.

After two weeks of fighting to save the camp, the ARVN were at the end of their rope and running low on ammunition. Everyone was wounded at least once and many had multiple wounds that would have immobilized most soldiers. As the PAVN prepared for their final assault on the camp, two battalions from the 173rd Airborne Brigade arrived and took up the fight. It was too much for the PAVN and the siege was finally broken on August 17th.

Over 400 PAVN had been killed and seventy-one weapons had been captured. The South Vietnamese had lost twenty-eight Marines with three missing during the conflict. It would not be the last time that North and South would fight over Duc Co Camp. More blood would be shed.

Da Nang Air Base, South Vietnam

Antwan Lincoln lay on his bunk in the Marine barracks on the air base. He used a pencil that he had sharpened with his knife to write a letter to his father in which he said, "Hi, Pops. I hope you are doing well and staying away from the wrong end of Mr. Wilk's mule. Yep, I got your last letter, and it was good to hear that your hip is doing better after you got kicked. I worry about you sometimes like I am sure you worry about me.

I am safe at the moment and in our barracks. We continue to go out on patrol for days at a time and usually end up sleeping in the jungle even when it rains. But I never sleep much when on patrol. It's my M60 machine gun that gives our squad a fighting chance if we encounter the enemy. I always have to be ready. But I am used to it now. I get my sleep when we return to the barracks like now.

I also have time to read the American newspapers when I am in the barracks. We get them all. Even some of the local ones if we ask ahead for them. The Marine Corps takes good care of us. I've never eaten so much in my life. Good food too. Lots of ham and roast beef with taters. I wonder if that recruiter knew what he was getting into when I signed my enlistment contract. Lugging my M60 around makes me powerful hungry most of the time.

There is something I want to talk to you about and I hope you don't think that I am being unpatriotic. I've been seeing lots of photos in the newspapers of anti-war protests in America. I don't understand what they are protesting. We are over here protecting America from communism. It's not like we want to be here. Most of the guys get kinda angry when they hear about the anti-war demonstrations back home, especially the ones at the universities where smart people should know better. Like me, they don't understand why the people are not supporting us. We are fighting for them. I hope you can shed some light on what is happening in the United States and why. Love – Antwan."

A week later, Antwan Lincoln received a reply. He opened the letter with anticipation. His father may not have been educated or even book smart, but he was a wise man, nonetheless. As he read, Lincoln realized that his father didn't have the answers. He was confused and conflicted about the protests. Like any father, he wanted his son to return safely and soon, but the war dragged on and so did the protests against it. He felt that the demonstrators had a right to say what they wished even if it was unpatriotic at times. It was one of the reasons America was fighting overseas, to preserve our freedom of speech. The communists didn't believe in freedom of speech.

His father concluded by telling his son to focus on his mission and to do his duty to the best of his ability. God and time would take care of the rest – "after all, we are all Americans." Lincoln loved his father but found little comfort in his words.

September 7, 1965 - Saigon, South Vietnam

As more American troops arrived in Vietnam, so did journalists from around the world. They made their headquarters in some of Saigon's swankiest hotels and camped out at bars while they waited for the military to assign them a unit in which they could imbed. Unlike World War II, the press was not subject to military censorship. To work with the military, the reporters only needed to agree not to compromise ongoing military operations. Most of American journalists considered themselves patriots and supported America's mission in Vietnam. Their stories were upbeat and indicated that South Vietnam was winning against the communist insurrection.

Joseph Galloway, a UPI journalist, arrived in Saigon. But unlike the other reporters adjusting to the heat and humidity, Galloway picked up his press pass and headed for Da Nang where he had heard the fighting was the fiercest. Galloway had been following the U.S. Army's Air-Mobile 1st Cavalry Division since its inception in the States. It was an experimental unit that used hundreds of helicopters to transport its troops, artillery, and even vehicles, jumping ahead of the enemy and often attacking them from multiple fronts. Air-Mobile could set up a firebase one day and move it the next. As a fighting force, it was fluid, flexible, and fast. And with 16,000 soldiers in its ranks, it was powerful. It was everywhere and nowhere. It completely frustrated the Viet Cong and PAVN forces who had never encountered anything like the 1st Cavalry Division. They were feared. Observing preliminary results, it seemed Air-Mobile would change the way Americans fought their wars from that point forward.

Operation Highland was a series of clearing missions around An Khe performed by the 1st Brigade, 101st Airborne. They were very thorough and ended up killing 692 PAVN and Viet Cong in the area. Only twenty-one U.S. soldiers were killed. That was the kind of kill ratio that the Airborne commanders came to expect from their troops. It was the 101st's way of welcoming the experimental helicopter unit.

When the 1st Cavalry arrived, they set up camp at the An Khe Airbase. The heliport at An Khe was so large it was nicknamed the "Golf Course." From An Khe, Air-Mobile could reinforce and resupply any of its operations in Central Vietnam within a few hours. The Air-Mobile commanders would often send out a small force and if the enemy took the bait, the U.S. forces would quickly ramp up and overwhelm the enemy.

The North Vietnamese could not reinforce and resupply their troops anything like the Americans with their helicopters. It made their encounters lopsided with the Americans having the upper hand. The morale of the North Vietnamese troops was crushed when they heard the heavy thrum of the American chopper blades approaching from the distance. But the North Vietnamese commanders were determined to learn how to fight against Air-Mobile. When necessary, they would sacrifice their troops for knowledge. It was a price they were willing to pay for ultimate victory.

And while the Americans were holding their own and even winning against the Viet Cong and PAVN forces, the North Vietnamese were still destroying the equivalent of one ARVN battalion per week. It was an unacceptable rate of loss by anyone's standards. If the Americans could not turn around the South Vietnamese losses, there would be no military left to defend South Vietnam when the American forces were finally withdrawn at some point in the future.

Westmoreland knew that even if the U.S. military had claimed victory, it would take years to train a new fighting force in South Vietnam. The light at the end of the tunnel was moving farther away.

October 15, 1965 – New York, New York, USA

Karen was frustrated as she sat on a park bench waiting for a group of protestors to show up. She had been taking photos of the anti-war movement for several years and nothing seemed to change. She could foresee what would happen at each event. While continuing to sell well, her photos were becoming redundant. It was not the exciting life she had been hoping to lead. She was bored and restless.

She even recognized the undercover FBI agents waiting in cars at the edge of the park. They were taking photos with expensive telegraphic lenses of anyone that looked remotely suspicious including Karen. They thought they were being covert. They weren't.

After another fifteen minutes and another cup of hot coffee, Karen watched as a small group of protestors gathered in the center of the park. Karen rose and started snapping shots. She moved closer watching the world through her viewfinder. Searching for the composition that would encapsulate the moment.

David Miller was a Catholic pacifist that had come to the park expecting to burn his draft card to protest the killing of the Vietnamese. Fewer protestors had volunteered to burn their draft cards since President Johnson had signed a new federal law that made defacement of a selective service information card illegal. For Miller, it didn't matter. As he saw it, his protest was God's will. He stood over a metal trashcan and lit his card on fire. He held it as long as he could before the fire grew too intense forcing him to drop it into the can.

Five FBI agents supported by local police moved in and arrested Miller placing him in handcuffs before leading him to one of the unmarked cars. Karen caught every moment of Miller's arrest on film. It was dramatic stuff. A man fighting for what he believed was right and the police taking him away to who knows where. A police officer saw Karen and approached her. "You can't do that," said the police officer pointing his baton at her camera.

"Do what?" said Karen continuing to take photos.

"This is an illegal protest. You can't take photos."

"Since when?"

"Since now. Put the camera away."

"Fuck you."

The police officer slammed his baton down on top of Karen's camera, forcing it from her hands. It dropped to the hard pavement and broke open exposing the film inside. "Goddammit. You can't do that," said Karen.

"Do what?" said the cop as he walked away with a satisfied grin on his face.

Karen felt strangely guilty as she held the ruined film in her hand. It was history and now it was gone. David Miller's sacrifice would not be seen.

David Miller was sentenced to twenty-two months in prison for burning his draft card. He served it in prayer and contemplation. He hoped he would be able to protest more once he had completed his sentence. He was that kind of guy.

October 16, 1965

Protests in every major city across the planet were organized by the National Coordinating Committee to End the War in Vietnam. It was a day like no other. When the world got together and expressed their dismay at the violence unfolding in Southeast Asia. The media coverage was massive and impossible to ignore.

In the spirit of inclusion, the organizers of the events had accepted members of other organizations that had similar goals of ending the war. But the members also had other grievances and were intent on expressing them. What resulted was a diluted message that at times seemed like a laundry list of complaints. People with good intentions hogged the microphones and soon many of the protestors became confused about what they were protesting against.

For the most part, the protests were peaceful, and the police kept their distance. But there were hotspots where tempers flared and riots broke out. This was especially true in Europe where protestors were determined to be heard and felt the only way to catch the world's attention was by breaking windows and setting cars on fire. It wasn't what the organizers had envisioned, but they didn't completely disagree with the rioter's sentiments.

In the end, the coverage was mostly positive and the message of ending the war in Vietnam was received. Knowing that it would be a hard-fought uphill battle, the anti-war movement was determined to inform and in some cases change the minds of the people. When there were enough of them, it was the people that force their governments to abandon violence and demand peace for all of the Vietnamese in both the North and the South. They were hell-bent on changing the world no matter the cost.

Battle of Plei Me

October 19-25, 1965 – Plei Me, South Vietnam

Like many outposts in the Central Highlands, Camp Plei Me was created by U.S. Special Forces to train and support the Montagnard tribesmen in their fight against the North Vietnamese and Viet Cong. Less than twenty miles from the Cambodian border, it also allowed the Army to keep tabs on the infiltration of weapons and soldiers into South Vietnam from the Ho Chi Minh Trail.

The outpost was manned by 400 local Montagnard, mostly members of the Jarai ethnic group. Many of the families of the warriors lived just outside the camp's perimeter. Twelve Americans from the 5th Special Forces Group and fourteen ARVN Special Forces assisted and advised the Montagnard. They helped the

Montagnard set up listening posts to monitor enemy troop movements in the area. The Special Forces also patrolled the surrounding area with the tribesmen. Survival in the Central Highlands was all about discovering the enemy before he discovered you.

The Special Forces outposts also protected Pleiku, the headquarters of the ARVN in the II Corps region. The air base at Pleiku had 4,500 ARVN soldiers to protect it. And Pleiku protected Route 19, the main supply road that led to the coast of South Vietnam. The U.S. military had stationed the 1st Cavalry Division at Camp Radcliff near An Khe so it could respond quickly against any enemy offensive. Air-Mobile had eight battalions within three brigades. Everything was interconnected. It was a tempting target for the North Vietnamese PAVN and Viet Cong.

The 1st Cavalry was itching for a fight to prove the effectiveness of their Air-Mobile strategy. They knew that the PAVN were massing their forces near the Chu Pong massif on the South Vietnam-Cambodian border. Once the PAVN engaged, MACV planned to use B-52 airstrikes to destroy the three PAVN regiments during the coming offensive.

Under the command of Brigadier General Chu Huy Man, the 32nd, 33rd, and 66th PAVN regiments were tasked with destroying the Special Forces outposts as a prelude to attacking Pleiku and taking control of Route 19. Man knew that the 1st Cavalry was still ramping up their operations and not ready to face the PAVN with full force. Time was short. He decided to attack Plei Me earlier than planned and before his entire force had been assembled. The 66th Regiment was still en route to the staging area. He felt he had more than enough men in the two regiments already in place to crush the

Special Forces outpost before 1st Cavalry and their helicopters could come into play. It was a calculated, but risky move.

Man's strategy consisted of three phases. First, the 33rd Regiment would surround Plie Me and harass but not overrun the Special Forces outpost. By exerting enough pressure and laying siege to the outpost, the American and ARVN commanders would be forced to respond and would send a reaction force to break the siege. The second phase involved the 32nd Regiment ambushing the reaction force and destroying it. The final phase would see the two PAVN regiments unite and overrun the Special Forces at Plie Me destroying them. Once his plan was completed successfully, the two PAVN Regiments would unite with the 66th Regiment and attack Pleiku.

Knowing that the PAVN regiments had not been completely assembled, MAVC decided to hold off on the B-52 airstrikes until the third PAVN regiment had arrived. The MAVC generals wanted all the rats accounted for before they sprung their trap. The American and ARVN forces were commanded to repulse but not destroy the two attacking PAVN regiments in hopes that the arriving third regiment would be used to support their comrades.

It was early in the evening of October 19th when a Montagnard patrol came under attack near Plei Me. The Montagnard were able to retreat from the battle in good order and returned to the outpost.

Three hours later, a PAVN Company assaulted and overran a small outpost southwest of the camp. The Montagnard were again able to escape and rejoin the forces in Plei Me Camp.

Captain Moore (not to be confused with Lt. Colonel Moore of the 1st Cavalry) was the American commander at Plei Me. Shortly after midnight, the PAVN using small arms, mortars, and recoilless rifles attacked the camp from north, west, and east. Some of the PAVN commandos reached the camp's outer perimeter. Moore called in airstrikes to drive the PAVN back. At 04:00 on October 20th, American and South Vietnamese warplanes joined the fight using napalm canisters and bombs on the PAVN front lines. The airstrikes continued through the day and into the night until there was no more cover anywhere near the camp's perimeter for the PAVN commandos.

ARVN and U.S. commanders agreed that Plei Me Camp needed to be reinforced as soon as possible to prevent the outpost from falling. A convoy of ARVN soldiers was put together and sent overland to reach Plei Me. The commanders realized it was too late. The outpost would be wiped out before the reinforcement convoy could reach them. They decided to airlift 175 ARVN Rangers into Plei Me as a holding force until the larger convoy of troops could arrive. Major Charles Beckwith was the commander of the relief group transported by helicopter to a landing zone three miles to the northeast of Plei Me. Hunkering down during the night, the relief column made its way to Plei Me the next morning. Beckwith took charge of the camp. He was ordered to attack the PAVN outside the perimeter to break the siege. During the assault, his two companies of Rangers came under intense enemy fire and immediately suffered fourteen killed in just a matter of minutes. Unable to break the siege, the Rangers retreated inside the camp.

During the battle of Plei Me, American aircraft pounded the PAVN commandos attempting to breach the camp's perimeter. Captain Melvin Elliot's A-1E Skyraider was shot down by an enemy anti-aircraft emplacement hidden in the surrounding jungle. Plunging his warplane into a rice field covered in muddy water, Elliot was able to escape capture. He evaded the PAVN patrols searching for him for thirty-six hours by covering himself with mud and submerging himself in the rice fields as the PAVN patrols passed by. Elliot was finally rescued by an American helicopter crew that risked their lives to land near the downed pilot scooping him up before the PAVN patrol could return. It was a close call and a risky strategy that paid off. Elliot would be back in the pilot's seat within a few weeks.

Although they were surrounded by PAVN commandos and regular troops, the U.S. Special Forces and the Montagnard were able to receive supplies and ammunition through Caribou parachute drops and helicopters. It was on one of the supply helicopters that UPI reporter Joseph Galloway was able to reach Plei Me Camp.

Short on supplies and soldiers, Beckwith was not happy to see Galloway. He immediately taught Galloway how to operate a 30 Cal machine gun. When Galloway complained that he was a reporter and therefore a civilian non-combatant, Beckwith simply stated that there was no such thing in the Central Highlands and that if Galloway wanted to live, he should learn how to clear a jam in the light machine gun. Galloway learned to load the weapon and clear a jam. He manned the gun during the enemy assaults that followed. He would report and fight at the same time.

Did he lose his objectivity? Absolutely, but he also survived.

The PAVN commandos assaulted Plei Me Camp, again and again, each time whittling away at the defenders. Beckwith and his team of twelve Green Berets suffered seventy-five percent causalities but hung in there and continued to fight for several days. The PAVN plan was not to destroy Plei Me Camp but to lure out II Corps's main force from Pleiku and destroy it in an ambush.

General Vinh Loc, the II Corps Commander, seemingly took the bait when he ordered an armored relief column to advance to Plei Me Camp. The armored column was ambushed on Provincial Road 6C. During the first assault, the armored convoy responded effectively and beat off the PAVN attack. But the PAVN regrouped and attacked again, this time with effective results. The ARVN forces took heavy casualties in the rear of the convoy. Digging in, the ARVN commander called in air and artillery strikes. The ARVN once again repelled the PAVN assault and hostilities broke off with the PAVN forces withdrawing to the west. As the ARVN armored convoy entered Plei Me Camp the siege was effectively broken.

But the ARVN and the Americans were not through with the PAVN troops. Taking advantage of the situation, elements of the 1st Cavalry pursued the PAVN keeping up the air and artillery strikes as they nipped at the enemy's heels. General Westmoreland flew in to observe the new operation.

The 1st Cavalry commanders directed their air-mobile forces to fly ahead of the PAVN and set up ambushes to harass the enemy as they tried to escape.

While 1st Cavalry units pinned the approaching enemy, air and artillery strikes pounded the PAVN forces in the rear causing them to bunch up and take heavy casualties. The U.S. estimated that 850 PAVN soldiers were killed during the siege and the subsequent pursuit. Sixteen ARVN, fourteen Montagnard, and three Americans were also killed.

President Johnson phoned Major Beckwith directly and congratulated him on his defense of Plei Me. It was a big win for the Americans. But it wouldn't last. The surviving PAVN forces had escaped back into the Chu Pongs Mastiff where the North Vietnamese regulars were preparing to confront a new threat in the Ia Dang Valley – the 1st Battalion, 7th Cavalry Regiment under the command of Lieutenant Colonel Harold Moore.

October 27, 1965 – Marble Mountain Air Facility, South Vietnam

American aircraft, especially helicopters, were a thorn in the side of the Viet Cong and PAVN. They were driving them crazy. It seemed like everything was gauged by the air power used during a battle. There was a very short window for the Viet Cong and PAVN to assault an enemy location before fighters, bombers, and helicopters arrived. If the communists did not engage their enemy in hand-to-hand close combat, they would be at the mercy of the American napalm canisters, bombs, rockets, and air cannons. Within just a few minutes, dozens of men could be swallowed up by a series of airstrikes.

The Viet Cong and PAVN commanders would not give up. It just wasn't an option in their minds. They would continue to struggle to find ways to defeat the

American aircraft. More anti-aircraft guns were crossing the border to enter South Vietnam where they could protect communist troops as they engaged their enemy. While the anti-aircraft guns were not as effective against the fast-moving jets, they did buy time forcing their enemy to reconsider their plans of attack.

The most effective way to combat the American aircraft was to destroy them on the ground before they could take off. The Viet Cong knew where the American squadrons were located and they knew the defenses that protected them. They were developing better explosive devices to completely destroy the aircraft rather than just damaging them. Sapper teams were constantly being trained and reinforced. They learned new ways to penetrate their enemy's perimeters. Even though their losses were often numerous, the sapper teams had become quite effective at assaulting the air bases. One forty-man team of sappers could take out a dozen American aircraft during a raid. The lost aircraft saved the lives of hundreds or even thousands of communist soldiers. It was a costly strategy, but it worked. Being selected to become a sapper was considered one of the highest honors for a Viet Cong or PAVN soldier.

As the Battle of Plei Me and the subsequent pursuit continued to unfold, the North Vietnamese were preparing for a much larger offensive in the Central Highlands. They understood that the more aircraft that could be destroyed before the main offensive began, the more soldiers' lives would be saved and the better the chances of achieving their objectives. They targeted several air bases, including the newly completed

Marble Mountain Air Facility near the main Da Nang Air Base.

With more and more Army and Marine units arriving each month, Da Nang Air Base was becoming incredibly crowded. The newly arriving soldiers were badly needed in the field, but that didn't mean that MACV was ready to receive them. It took time to figure out where to place a unit, and where it could be most effective. While the individual soldiers were anxious to get at the enemy, they also appreciated the time at Da Nang to acclimate and catch up on letters to their families, wives, and sweethearts. Everything had happened so fast during their deployment, they hardly had time to say goodbye. But soldiers were climbing all over one another in the struggle to find room for their tents and gear. While the soldiers milled around the air base, the Viet Cong watched.

With overcrowding beyond reasonable, Da Nang was a tempting target. But the air base had been attacked before and was better protected than ever. The Viet Cong sapper teams would be lucky to reach their targets once they breached the outer defensive perimeter.

Instead, the Viet Cong and PAVN commanders concentrated their efforts on the American helicopter air bases around Da Nang. The helicopter bases were not as well protected, and the target area was still rich. The helicopter bases were a more practical bite at the enemy. It was the helicopters the PAVN and Viet Cong troops feared most. The sound of helicopters meant that American troops were coming and they never knew where they would land. Destroying American helicopters greatly increased troop morale.

The Viet Cong sappers had been planning their attack for over a month and had created practice fields with similar defenses to the American air bases. The sapper commanders had decided to use some new techniques to breach the defenses quickly and prevent the American soldiers and aircrews from reaching their helicopters before they could be destroyed or worse, used against the attacking sappers. The Chinese had given the North Vietnamese Bangalore torpedoes leftover from World War II.

The Bangalore torpedo was a pole-type mine containing high explosive charges within several connected tubes. Used by combat engineers, the Bangalore torpedoes could be assembled under cover, then pushed forward underneath obstacles. Set off with either a plunge detonator or a fuse, the resulting explosion would cut a deep three-yard wide path through even the thickest tangles of barbed wire. Using the Bangalores, the Viet Cong sappers didn't need to expose themselves when they cut holes in the wire with cutters. It also took a lot less time. The only disadvantage was the loss of the element of surprise. When a set of Bangalores went off, there was little doubt the base was under attack. Everyone needed to be in place and ready to assault the base as soon as the Bangalores exploded and the perimeter was breached.

On the evening of the 27-28 of October, the Viet Cong had divided their sappers into four teams each carrying a set of Bangalore torpedoes. The Viet Cong commandos that followed the sapper teams would coordinate their assaults using the explosions to signal their attack. It was a simple technique and simple was best during a battle. There was less that could go wrong. The sappers also carried the explosive charges that would be used to destroy the helicopters. The commandos would act as a security assault force drawing away enemy fire while the sappers placed and detonated their explosives.

Advancing silently to the air base's outer perimeter just after dark, the sappers placed the Bangalores beneath the layered stacks of razor wire, some of which were over twenty feet tall. All four of the sapper teams detonated their Bangalores at the same time breaching the outer perimeter in four different locations. A barrage of well-placed VC mortar rounds covered the assault. The Viet Cong commandos rushed forward through the breaches and opened fire.

The Americans grabbed their weapons and flooded out of their barracks and tents to meet the enemy. Emplacements of dual 50 Cal machine guns firing in unison laid down a solid stream of suppressing fire. The Americans knew that the Viet Cong attacking the airfield would be targeting their helicopters and they were determined not to let the enemy destroy their aircraft.

The VC commandos kept the Americans occupied with fierce barrages of gunfire. The Viet Cong sappers were focused and did not engage the American fire teams. They advanced toward the center of the air base where the helicopters were parked. Satchel charges were lit, then thrown beneath each of the targeted helicopters. While any helicopter destroyed was considered a big win for the sappers, it was the newer Huey UH-1E helicopters that they most wanted to destroy.

The VC sappers were able to reach the helicopter ramps and began blowing up the aircraft as the American aircrew tried to drive them off. But the sappers were determined often sacrificing themselves to take out a helicopter. In all nineteen helicopters were completely destroyed and another thirty-five were heavily damaged. Two Marines and one Navy Corpsman were killed during the assault. Seventeen Viet Cong were killed with another four seriously wounded and taken prisoners. Only four aircraft in the American VMO-2 remained in flying condition when the assault had ended, and the VC had withdrawn. It was a serve blow to the American forces and would without a doubt affect upcoming operations in Central Vietnam. Even with their heavy losses, it was a good day for the Viet Cong.

October 30, 1965 – New York, New York, USA

Karen had been covering so many anti-war protests over the years, she found it strange when she was asked by organizers to photograph a large rally in support of the war and the Johnson administration. She had to think about it for a moment before accepting. She had promised herself to always seek the truth in her photos. It seemed like a betrayal of her pledge to not cover the pro-war rally. She, of course, had feelings about the war and the Johnson administration's handling of the war, but she never let those feeling interfere with her work. In some ways, it was like living in two different worlds – one for her personal life and one for work. She imagined that a lot of people felt the same as her. She was a patriot but did not want to see young men sacrificed for a country that few even knew how to locate on a globe. The New York march was sponsored by the New York City Council, the American Legion, and the Veterans of Foreign Wars.

When the day come, she left her hotel room early in the morning. She would give it her all in trying to capture the historic moments during the rally. She wasn't going to cut either side of the argument a break. That wasn't her job. The truth was her job.

As she headed downtown, she wondered how many people would show up. If she was lucky it would be in the hundreds and she would get a variety of photographs. She imagined the rally would be fairly unorganized like the anti-war rallies often were. There would be interlopers protesting for their individual causes and confusing the rally's intended message to show support for American troops fighting overseas in Vietnam and to encourage the Johnson administration to stay the course in their fight against communist expansion.

Karen was stunned when she entered Times Square where the rally was taking place. Twenty-five thousand demonstrators were crammed into several blocks. She had to push and shove her way into the center where the speakers were pontificating their arguments. It was all far better organized than the rowdy anti-war rallies she had attended. One of the organizers spotted her and gave her a press pass that allowed her to go wherever she wanted.

She snapped roll after roll of film. The crowd was diverse, young and old, of all races, and all genders. Some wore dresses and suits while others were in faded jeans and t-shirts. There was no visible opposition, and the rally was peaceful. The police stood back and watched. Some listened.

Late in the afternoon, when the rally was breaking up and the demonstrators were heading for home or back to the hotel room, Karen was loading another roll of film, just in case. She looked up and saw a man standing over her. She recognized his face. He was one of the organizers of the anti-war movement. He had come to watch, looking for ideas to defeat the Johnson supporters' arguments. "Karen," he said. "What are you doing here?"

"My job. I'm covering the rally," said Karen feeling like she was being judged.

"We trusted you."

"You trusted me to show the truth."

"You call this the truth? Have you listened to this bullshit?"

"I listen to all the bullshit from both sides and nothing ever changes. You just shout at each other and in the meantime, while you're arguing, men die."

"That's not our fault. We don't support the war and we don't want any more of our young men to be killed for no good reason."

"See? More bullshit."

Karen rose with her camera and snapped a photo of the man. "Stop that," he said putting his hand up in front of her lens.

"Afraid of the truth?"

"My people won't understand why I am here and neither will yours."

"I don't have people. It's just me," she said snapping another photo of him.

He grabbed her camera and tried to pull it away from her. She kicked him in the shins. He let go and said, "You bitch. You're a traitor."

"To you, maybe," she said. "Ya know, my brother's over there fighting for what he believes in. I admire him far more than I do you and your followers. He's true to himself and that takes uncommon courage."

"He's another one of Johnson's puppets. Killing Vietnamese to show American resolve against the communists."

"Fuck you."

"He's the one that's fucked. You should convince him to lay down his arms and come home."

"You obviously don't know my brother."

"He's just another cog in the wheel. He doesn't matter."

"He does to me. Ya know, sometimes, I wonder if both sides need the war and secretly, they want it to continue so they can continue to sound important and come up with witty sayings."

"That's nonsense."

"Is it?" she said walking off.

November 2, 1965 – Arlington, Virginia, USA

The Quakers were one of the most active religious groups demanding that the United States stop the killing of innocent Vietnamese civilians and pull out of Vietnam. They saw the conflict as a Civil War and that the Vietnamese people should decide on their own what kind of government they wanted – democratic or communist. The members believed that there was no justifiable reason that the American military should intervene in Vietnam. Many Quakers became active in the anti-war movement during one of the most turbulent and controversial times in American history. Many were willing to make great sacrifices to stop the needless killing in a confusing and destructive war being fought halfway around the world.

On the morning of November 2, Karen received a cable informing her that there would be a protest in front of the Pentagon later that afternoon. It was strange. She didn't normally receive cables tipping her off. Her photos had become popular, and editors would often call her about the information they had received through their overabundance of contacts. The sender of the telegram was unanimous.

She considered not going but decided that any protest with the Pentagon in the background would sell and would be considered part of the history of the anti-war movement. She took the next flight out to Arlington, grabbed a cab, and headed for the Pentagon. She could feel her body being weighed down as she traveled. She didn't know what it was but imagined it was the shitty way she had been eating lately. Candy bars and potato chips had become her main staple. She decided to eat healthier as soon as returned to New York where she now lived. Chicken soup with lots of vegetables she thought. That's what I need. New York was chock full of delicatessens, and all served Chicken soup in one form or another. Money was no longer a problem for her. While she wasn't rich, she made enough from selling her photos to sustain a comfortable lifestyle even in New York. She had even been invited to have an expedition of her work at a major art gallery where her framed photos would sell for hundreds and even thousands of dollars. She wasn't sure how she felt about profiting from the anti-war movement but decided it was no different than selling to newspapers and magazines. It was just a different audience... a wealthy audience.

She arrived at the Pentagon a little after 3 PM. She looked around and nothing that looked even remotely like a group of protestors. She wondered if she had missed it and wasted the cost of the plane flight. She asked one of the guards at the main gate if anything like a protest had happened that afternoon. Nothing had happened out of the ordinary. She thought about using her press credentials to go inside the well-guarded perimeter fence made of vertical iron pickets. She decided against it figuring if they showed up, the protestors would not be able to enter, and therefore the best location to photograph the demonstration would be outside the fence.

She had purchased an apple at the airport in an attempt to improve her eating habits. She had wanted a Baby Ruth bar but was determined to show some willpower. Besides, apples tasted good. Maybe not as good as a Baby Ruth bar, but good nonetheless. She chowed down on the apple as she waited. Then she saw something strange…

A man in a car drove along the road paralleling the perimeter fence. He was studying a drawing of the pentagon as if he was looking for a certain area. The car parked along the curb and the man got out. He stared at the building on the opposite side of the iron picket fence. He checked his drawing one last time. Satisfied, he bowed his head as if praying, then moved to the trunk of the car. He opened the trunk and retrieved a can of gasoline.

Karen had a sinking feeling in the pit of her stomach as she watched the man approach the fence and set down the can. She would learn later that his name was Norman Morrison from Baltimore.

Morrison walked back to his car and opened the door to the backseat where he retrieved his infant daughter, Emily Morrison. Smiling down at her as he walked back to the fence, Morrison seemed at peace with what he was about to do. He looked over at Karen, her camera around her neck, and nodded as if inviting her to take a photo of the father and daughter.

After Alice Herz's death, Karen realized she had become part of the story. She suspected it was Morrison that had sent the cable. He wanted his sacrifice and the sacrifice of his daughter to be splashed across the front pages of newspapers and magazines across the world. That could only happen if Karen snapped her shutter. History was repeating itself and she was part of it. She felt physically sick.

The Pentagon guards were also watching and moved closer to Morrison and his daughter. Seeing them, Morrison laid Emily down next to him as he sat cross-legged on the grass. He opened the can of gasoline and poured it over his head until it was empty. The fluid stung his eyes, but he could still see enough to pick up Emily and cradle her in his arms. He looked over once again to Karen, now in tears, and nodded as if everything was okay. Everything was the way it should be. Karen looked at Morrison than at Emily. She looked down at her camera, then back at Morrison. She shook her head to say no. Morrison got the message and seemed disappointed. Karen's unwillingness to photograph his protest would not stop him. He pulled a Zippo lighter from his pocket and held it at arm's length. He flipped the wheel with his thumb and the flame appeared. The fumes from the gasoline on his arm ignited. Karen gasped and said, "For God's sake, put the baby down."

Morrison looked confused by Karen's request. He watched as the fire traveled up his arm, toward him, toward Emily. Major Richard Lundquist, the commander in charge of perimeter security moved forward and repeated Karen's request, "Put the baby down. She doesn't need to die."

Emily began to cry. Something in Morrison changed at that moment. Lundquist was right. His daughter need not be sacrificed. He set Emily down next to him as the flames grew setting his head on fire. Lundquist rushed forward, scooped the infant into his arms, and ran back to ensure the flames did not consume her.

Sitting in his office with his back to the window, Secretary of Defense, Robert McNamara heard Emily's crying. It was a strange sound, not normally heard within the walls of the Pentagon. He turned to the window and looked out. Morrison sat thirty feet away on the opposite side of the perimeter wall. A crowd had gathered and was shouting. Morrison was burning. McNamara watched. How could he not?

Karen realized that this was a moment in history and part of her wanted to capture it. But she knew if she did, more protestors like Morrison and Herz would self-immolate themselves to draw attention to their cause. Instead, she simply let the moment pass without taking even one photo. It was her contribution to ending the madness.

When McNamara went home that night, his wife asked him about the self-immolation at the Pentagon that she had heard about on the evening news. McNamara said

DAVID LEE CORLEY

nothing as he walked up the stairs to his bedroom and closed the door. He wouldn't talk about what had happened until years later when he would admit that Norman Morrison's sacrifice to protest the war had affected him deeply. And from that point on, McNamara would encourage negotiations to end the war whenever possible. "We thought we were acting in the interests of mankind, but the cost in lives was far greater than we or others had predicted," said McNamara.

Later that evening, Karen was at the hospital where Morrison had been taken after the guards had put out the flames that had consumed him. She took no photos even though other photojournalists had arrived and were recording events. Morrison's wife had been called and came to pick up Emily at the hospital. Knowing that her husband had almost killed their daughter, she watched Morrison struggle to breathe. His charred skin cracked with every heave for air. Enclosed in an oxygen tent he would die alone not knowing his wife and his daughter were there beside him.

November 14, 1965 – New York, New York

It took over a week for Karen to recover from Norman Morrison's death and to get back to work. She had committed a professional sin by not photographing Herz's and Morrison's deaths. She also admitted to herself that she was human and she had limits on how far she would go to get the story or in her case... the photograph. She realized that Morrison had raised the stakes by bringing his little girl. Her death would have been sensational and brought far more attention to the

296

anti-war cause than his own death. She wondered what the next martyr would do to catch the media's eye. How far would they go? Even if she wouldn't take the photographs, she knew they would find a photographer that would.

In time, she would forgive herself. She considered quitting her freelance gig and going to work for some faceless media corporation. She certainly had a resume that would attract multiple editors and knew many on a personal level. She imagined it would be nice to be told what to photograph and what not to photograph. She could allow someone else to be her conscious and that would certainly remove a lot of stress from her life. She would give it some more thought before making such a change. That was the smart thing to do.

That evening while she was sitting down to chicken salad with a white wine chaser, she turned on the television and watched the evening news. It was the normal stuff. A liquor store robbery, and a rape at a local community college. And, of course, Vietnam. There were two stories about Vietnam. The first was a humanitarian mission carried out by U.S. Army engineers in a recently occupied reinforced hamlet. The engineers had constructed a small aqueduct from a nearby spring that brought fresh drinking water to the villagers.

The second story was far more personal... photojournalist Dickey Chapelle had been killed by a Viet Cong booby-trap while on patrol with the Marines in Operation Black Ferret. Karen felt a pain in her chest from a huge sense of loss. Chapelle was a hero for many photojournalists, especially women. She was brave beyond measure and set an example of how far to go to get a truly meaningful photograph that captured the moment. She was the first female war correspondent to be killed in Vietnam. Georgette Louise Meyer, later known as Dickey Chapelle, was born in Milwaukee, Wisconsin. By age sixteen, she was studying aeronautical design at MIT. She was a genius but grew restless. She left MIT and went home to work at a local airfield. She wanted to learn how to fly aircraft, not design them. She craved adventure. She also took weekly photography classes from Tony Chapelle, who she eventually married. She became a war correspondent for National Geographic during World War II when she covered the Battle of Iwo Jima and the Battle of Okinawa with the U.S. Marines.

After the war, Chapelle learned to jump with paratroopers and was known for going to great lengths to cover a war. This earned her many awards in addition to the respect of the military and journalistic communities. Known for her refusal to kowtow to anyone even though she was tiny in stature. Her signature uniform was fatigues with an Australian bush hat, Harlequin glasses, and pearl earrings. She was an outspoken anti-communist and loudly expressed her views at the beginning of the Vietnam War. In the early 60s, her stories focused on the American military advisors that were already fighting and dying in South Vietnam. She was one hell of a human being.

Chapelle had been killed twelve miles south of Chu Lai in Quang Ngai Province. Far from a shrinking violet, Chapelle wore a bullet-proof vest and carried an M16, which she knew how to use and maintain properly, in addition to her cameras. While on patrol, the young lieutenant in front of her stumbled over a tripwire boobytrap which was a mortar shell with a grenade wired to the top. The explosion sent a piece of shrapnel into Chapelle's neck just above her body armor and severed her carotid artery. Even as the platoon medic tried to save her, she didn't last long as her life's blood soaked her fatigues and flowed onto the ground.

Tears flowed down Karen's face. It was all too much. She wanted to crawl into bed and never leave. The world was not a kind place and she was fed up.

Over the few days that followed Chapelle's death, Karen considered her place in the world and began to wonder if she really mattered. Chapelle would be missed by the people that Karen most respected… her fellow journalists and editors. Chapelle had left a huge hole and Karen was determined to fill it as best she could. In doing so, she hoped to give her own life meaning. Dicky Chappelle would not be the last female journalist to die in Vietnam, but she certainly was one of the best and most courageous. Karen couldn't help but wonder what kind of legacy she would make for herself and if she would survive.

November 27, 1965 – Washington D.C., USA

While making preparations to go to Vietnam, Karen decided to photograph her last demonstration. It was called the March on Washington for Peace in Vietnam and was organized by the Committee for a SANE Nuclear Policy. McNamara had not ruled out the use of nuclear weapons in Vietnam should there be an all-out attack on the South. That made the Vietnam War part of SANE's platform. The organizers were concerned with the public's perception of the antiwar movement and SANE's role in it. They asked the protestors to only use placards and signs with

DAVID LEE CORLEY

authorized slogans. They warned speakers not to
demand immediate withdrawal and not to burn the
American flag. They were attempting to take the
middle of the road and create a dialog between the
antiwar and pro-war organizations. Many felt it was a
pipe dream and that there was no middle ground; you
were either for the war or against it.

Feeling that the organizers had diluted their
message by their soft tactics, Karen was surprised to
see 35,000 demonstrators join the march. Knowing
that it was her last demonstration for a while, Karen
was relaxed and enjoyed herself. She took hundreds of
photographs, many of people she recognized.

The March on Washington was the largest antiwar
protest to date and caught the attention of both sides
of the argument. The demonstrators started at the
White House, then moved to the Washington
Monument where loudspeakers had been set up
around the reflection pool and a platform had been
built for a slate of presenters many of which were
celebrities and well-known lecturers.

Karen knew that even a demonstration of that size
would not change anything until the American public
realized what was really going on in Vietnam. Her new
mission was to reveal the truth on the battlefield and
in Saigon. She wanted to be part of the solution to find
peace and bring troops like her brother home. She
wondered if that was even possible until both sides had
lost enough sons and daughters to bring them to the
negotiating table. She would find out. She would do
her part as Dickey Chapelle had done.

Arlington, Virginia, USA

Looking across the fence where Norman Morrison had chosen to end his life in a dramatic antiwar protest, McNamara starred out the window in his Pentagon office. He had changed. He no longer had the confidence in the reports that his computers churned out at an astounding rate. He was skeptical and felt that he may have unintentionally misled the country and his president. He began to wonder if the war could be won no matter how many troops were sent to protect the South Vietnamese and defeat the communists. Regardless of the personal trauma, McNamara was suffering, the war raged on and it was his duty to analyze and lead to the best of his ability.

The biggest problem he was currently facing was the realization that U.S. Intelligence reports had grossly underestimated the number of North Vietnamese and Viet Cong troops in South Vietnam. Westmoreland was requesting another 200,000 troops which would bring the total number deployed to 400,000. McNamara and Johnson both were floored by the request. Johnson's cabinet was also flabbergasted. They were like deer caught in the headlights. Nobody knew what to say or do. It was Johnson's worst nightmare coming to pass and it seemed there was nothing he could do about it.

McNamara hated the thought of committing more troops to a cause that he was no longer sure could be won. He knew he had to be honest with the president. He owed Johnson that. He owed the American people. He recommended that Johnson lift the troop cap to 400,000 in 1966 and then commit to the possibility that another 200,000 troops would be needed in 1967. He also told Johnson that he estimated that 1,000 American troops per month would be killed in the war and that the odds that the U.S. would be successful at defeating the communists were even at best. Then McNamara did something out of character. He suggested that Johnson order a three to four-week pause in the bombing in hopes of finding a way to end the war before the additional troop buildup. Ambassador Lodge, General Westmoreland, and CINCPAC all opposed such a long halt in bombing for fear that it would give the North a chance to rebuild their supply lines and regroup their reinforcements. PAVN troops would be free to pour into the south unimpeded.

Johnson could see that McNamara had changed. He had softened in his resolve. Johnson had relied on McNamara's stalwartness to boost his own determination in doing what needed to be done to stop the communist expansion. Now, that support was gone. Johnson felt lost at a time when he needed McNamara the most. But McNamara wasn't there anymore. It was like the fighting spirit had drained out of him.

Tiger in the Long Grass

November 14-19, 1965 – Ia Drang Valley in the
Chu Pong Massif, South Vietnam

The majority of South Vietnam's countryside was
already under the control of the Viet Cong and the
rebels had established a strong military infrastructure
from which to resupply and reinforce their troops. The
PAVN were anxious to press that advantage. There
were few reliable roads leading into the Chu Pong
Massif in the Central Highlands of South Vietnam.
This made the area ideal for staging troop buildups in
preparation for the PAVN's coming offensive. If
successful, the PAVN and Viet Cong could cut South
Vietnam in half. Divide then conquer.

This was not the first time the North Vietnamese
had fought in the area. One of their greatest victories
against the French Army during the Indochina War

had been fought in the nearby Mang Yang Pass in 1954. It was the Siege of Dien Bien Phu and the Battle of the Mang Yang Pass that finally convinced the French that they could not win against the Viet Minh and brought about the peace negotiations that divided the country into North and South. After 200 years of ruling Indochina, the French finally left and went home. The Viet Cong and PAVN commanders wanted to repeat their performance, only this time the enemy was the Americans.

After the Battle of Plei Me, the American forces chased the PAVN and VC regiments into the Chu Pong Massif. Once in the shadow of the Chu Pong, the VC and PAVN troops felt relatively safe and began to regroup setting up a new command post in the Ia Drang Valley. Their security was a false hope.

Unlike previous battles with the ARVN forces where the fighting would taper off as the VC and PAVN dissolved into the countryside, the American 1st Cavalry and their helicopters weren't done with them. The Americans were winning, and they would keep on winning until the enemy did something to stop them. The Americans saw each battle as part of a larger effort to destroy the enemy and therefore would continue to rack up enemy casualties as long as possible. It was a war of attrition and American troops combined with air and artillery power would hammer their opponent as long as they were within reach. Unlike the ARVN, the Americans were relentless.

The way the American commanders of the 1st Cavalry saw it, they had trapped their enemy in Chu Pong Massif and just needed to relocate them before they could continue to punish them. Both sides had a lot to learn about fighting each other.

American and South Vietnamese intelligence reports had identified an enemy buildup in the la Drang Valley. Forty-three-year-old Lieutenant Colonel Hal Moore, a Kentucky-born Korean War veteran was the commander of the First Battalion of the Seventh Cavalry Regiment of the 1st Cavalry Division. His orders were to find the enemy and kill him. The Seventh Cavalry was George Armstrong Custer's old outfit and had an aggressive reputation. Moore's outfit was understrength with only 411 soldiers and twenty-nine officers.

There were two clearings large enough to land eight American helicopters at the same time. Each Huey helicopter could carry ten to twelve men with their equipment. Moore chose to use Landing Zone X-Ray because of its proximity to the enemy's suspected location.

Before his helicopters arrived, two batteries of 105 mm howitzers had been airlifted to another clearing, Landing Zone Falcon, five miles away from X-Ray. The howitzer gun crews blasted the surrounding trees and grass to drive off any enemy soldiers that might be in the area of the landing zone which was the size of a football field. Unfortunately, the artillery barrage also warned the enemy commanders that the Americans were coming.

Landing on X-Ray at 10:48 AM, Moore stepped off the first helicopter and sent four six-man teams one hundred yards in all four directions. Moore didn't know it at the time, but he had landed his men only two hundred yards from the position of PAVN 9th Battalion, 66th Regiment. But Moore and his men had been lucky in causing confusion from their swift insertion and the PAVN didn't attack right away but regrouped farther up the mountain slope.

Within the first few minutes, Moore's men captured a terrified PAVN soldier who told his interrogator that the North Vietnamese had three battalions on the mountain, and they very much wanted to kill Americans. Realizing that his understrength battalion would be outnumbered four to one, Moore wanted to get as many of his troops on the battlefield as fast as possible. Even so, it would take several hours to ferry in his entire battalion. Moore knew he couldn't wait. He and his men had to find and attack the enemy before the enemy attacked them. As more troops landed, he sent two platoons of soldiers up the mountain slope in search of the hidden enemy.

What Colonel Moore didn't know was the captured enemy soldier had been wrong. Moore's battalion wasn't facing sixteen hundred PAVN soldiers, but three thousand, seven times Moore's battalion's strength. To make matters worse, the enemy had the high ground. In modern warfare, position didn't matter as much as in the olden days before gunpowder, but it still gave the army on the high ground an advantage when defending as the long slope at Gettysburg had proven.

The PAVN were surprised when the American helicopters landed. They were disorganized and needed time to assemble their forces on the mountain. Reports of American troops coming up to meet them were disconcerting and put them in a defensive posture. This is what Moore had hoped to accomplish… to fix the enemy so that it could not attack his force until it was at full strength.

Moore's strategy quickly fell apart when a North Vietnamese commander of the 66th Regiment ordered two of his battalions, the PAVN 7th and 9th, to fix bayonets and charge down the mountain to meet the oncoming enemy. Hundreds of PAVN troops crashed into the two American platoons marching up the slope. Thousands of bullets flew in all directions as the two sides battled it out on the mountain incline.

One American platoon had ventured too far out and had become surrounded by the enemy. The second lieutenant commanding the platoon was killed and a veteran sergeant took over. He immediately called in a close-in artillery strike that kept the enemy from overrunning the platoon's position. By late afternoon and after having taken heavy fire for several hours, only seven of the platoon's soldiers were still capable of fighting. Everyone else including the sergeant was too badly wounded from flying shrapnel and enemy bullets. Eight Americans had been killed and thirteen had been wounded. The sergeant had been hit in the face by a bullet but was still alive.

In the meantime, Moore had his hands full. The lost platoon had forced him to fix his position until they could be rescued. He had lost the mobility that gave 1st Cavalry the advantage and was forced to slug it out with PAVN troops streaming down the mountain in wave after wave hurtling themselves at his defensive position surrounding Landing Zone X-Ray. His biggest concern was being flanked by the enemy and losing the Landing Zone that was his battalion's lifeline. He sent a platoon to defend a creek bed that most likely would be where the enemy attempted to flank the battalion. He was right and before long the platoon was in a vicious firefight with a company of

PAVN soldiers trying to break through. Moore's own command post was attacked and almost overrun but he and his staff succeeded in fighting the PAVN off. He lost his radioman and several of his staff. He ordered the new radioman to call in air support to hammer the PAVN coming down the mountain.

Called in from all airfields and carriers around South Vietnam, American airpower pounded the PAVN forces with rockets and napalm canisters as they advanced. The two howitzer batteries fired non-stop until their barrels were too hot to continue and needed precious minutes to cool down.

Moore watched as one of the helicopters carrying more of his men was hit and crashed tossing Americans across the landing zone. He knew they would be in deep shit if the helicopters were prevented from bringing in the rest of the battalion. He ordered a platoon to reinforce the landing zone and protect the incoming helicopters. He was running out of men as he shifted his forces back in forth to deal with hotspots.

The gaps in artillery fire allowed the North Vietnamese to advance on the American positions once again. As the PAVN attacked the American battalion, Moore sent a company to locate and rescue the lost platoon. It didn't work. The PAVN were too many and had surrounded the lost platoon. The enemy forces were waiting to attack any American reinforcements that tried to reach the platoon. The American company couldn't break through and eventually pulled back into the battalion's defensive ring. The lost platoon would have to spend the night where they were and fight off the enemy as best they could. Things were looking grim, but the surviving platoon members continued to fight as if their lives depended on it, which they did.

As the sun set, the lead elements of Bravo Company of 2nd Battalion, 7th Cavalry arrived at LZ X-Ray to reinforce 1st Battalion. The new troops were fresh and a welcomed relief for Moore's men that had been fighting most of the day. Just a few minutes to grab something to eat, then close their eyes and clear their heads made a big difference in their effectiveness. The battle would be fought with tiny cat naps on both sides. The additional company had allowed Moore to fully encircle his position which protected his flanks from enemy attack.

The PAVN spent the night probing the American positions using small fire teams looking for a weak spot. Moore ordered the M60 machine gun teams that were tactically placed around the perimeter to hold their fire and not give away their positions.

As the PAVN continued to focus on the 1st Battalion and the lost platoon, the 2nd Battalion, 5th Cavalry was ferried into Landing Zone Victor, three miles away from LZ X-Ray. They would be in a position to reinforce the 1st Battalion if needed the next day.

That night, Joseph Galloway once again convinced a chopper pilot taking ammunition to Landing Zone X-Ray to allow him to tag along. There wasn't much room. He sat on a box of grenades as he rode into battle. As he came closer, he looked out the open doorway and saw hundreds of tiny pinpricks of light weaving their way down the mountain. It was the PAVN moving into position for the next morning's assault.

Like Beckwith before him, Moore was not happy to see the journalist without a weapon in hand. He remedied the situation by handing him a rifle from a fallen American soldier. Galloway knew better than to argue and took the weapon. He would need it sooner than he thought.

Flareships circled above the battlefield all night dropping parachute flares that gave the area an eerie look. The flares and continued artillery barrages discouraged the communists from attacking in full strength, but there were small engagements that kept everyone on their toes. With the enemy so close they could hear their taunts through the darkness, there would be no sleep for the Americans.

The lost platoon survived three additional enemy assaults that night with no additional casualties. The seven Americans that remained in the fight were exhausted but kept the PAVN from penetrating their position.

At 6:30 AM the next morning, the waiting was over. Moore sent out reconnaissance patrols to find the enemy. After advancing a few hundred yards, one of the recon patrols made contact and a fierce firefight broke out. All the patrols quickly retreated inside the Battalion's defensive perimeter.

Hundreds of North Vietnamese rushed through the long grass assaulting the American positions still in the landing zone. The Americans fought back firing waist-high into the grass as the unseen enemy fired back at the same height. It was the blind fighting the blind. The American M60 teams opened fire cutting through the grass in all directions. The communist's heavy mortars were effective at keeping the Americans' heads down, but they were no match for two 105 howitzer batteries and other heavy artillery within range of LZ X-Ray. American air power only added to the Viet Cong and PAVN forces' troubles.

With the sun rising, the American aircraft became far more effective with their rockets and napalm. They poured canisters and rockets into the advancing enemy cutting them down and burning them to death. But the enemy kept coming. Closing on their enemy was their only hope of survival as they ran through the grass searching for the American soldiers. It was a savage fight with dozens of men falling every minute the battle raged. The napalm strikes were particularly effective at demoralizing the PAVN troops. Facing walls of fire taller than the trees made many PAVN dropped their weapons and ran for their lives.

Moore's men marked their positions with colored smoke that let the pilots overhead know they were friendly. But the smoke also let the communists identify and attack the American positions. The North Vietnamese troops would always try to get inside the American's smoke ring where they were safe from enemy artillery and aircraft. The colored smoke was a double-edged sword that cut down men with impunity.

Moore listened to reports over the radio from his company commanders. The battalion's defensive positions were being overrun by the PAVN in a desperate attempt to fight close in and deny the Americans use of their artillery and air support. As the front lines of both sides became entangled, Moore radioed for a "Broken Arrow" which would bring all available aircraft throughout South Vietnam to his battalion's position. Skyraiders, Intruders, Skyhawks, Phantoms, Super Sabres, and Thunderchiefs all came to help the beleaguered American battalion.

As he waited for more air support to arrive on site, Moore ordered artillery to fire on the battalion's position. He ordered his men to keep their heads down and stay in their foxholes. All attacks and counterattacks were to stop so the warplanes and artillery could do their job. Moore's forward air controller did his best to direct the pilots to the enemy's positions but there were aircraft stacked up every thousand feet. It was too much for one man to control. Mistakes were made and some Americans were killed by friendly fire.

As the American aircraft arrived, the PAVN continued to charge and attack the Americans. Napalm canisters, bombs, and rockets rained down sending fire and shrapnel in all directions. Artillery shells exploded all around the PAVN caught in the open. The North Vietnamese did not understand what was happening. Entering the enemy lines had not stopped the American artillery and aircraft. They were being cut down as explosions ripped into their ranks.

The Americans in their foxholes continued to defend their positions and took their toll on the PAVN. It was the most desperate moment for both sides, but it was the PAVN that suffered the most as they had lost scores of men. When the barrage was finally over, over a hundred enemy bodies were scattered around the battalion's foxholes. The Americans had survived and reestablished their perimeter.

MACV authorized a B-52 strike requested by Moore. It would be the first time that long-range bombers would be used in a tactical situation. Moore was informed that the strike was scheduled for 16:00 and that his men needed to be ready. Moore and his forward air controller had picked out the targets. Their focus was on the PAVN 32nd Regiment located three miles to the west of X-Ray.

When the B-52 strike happened, the mountainside blew up in an incredible series of fireballs. The enemy was engulfed by the carpet bombing of their position. Their anti-aircraft guns were of no use against the high-flying American aircraft. Everyone, including the Americans, was stunned by how close the bombs dropped and how many. Hundreds of bombs tore open the jungle and pitted the mountain slope with craters. The B-52s' power was frightening. The psychological effect on the enemy was far greater than the actual damage the bombs had caused. Moore immediately requested a second airstrike. His request was granted, but the bombers needed to return to Guam to refuel and rearm.

Thanks to American aircraft and artillery, the enemy soldiers were beaten back to the mountain. In the early afternoon, the Americans were able to finally rescue their lost platoon. The survivors in the platoon were in shock from having been under attack for a solid twenty-four hours. Dehydrated and exhausted, many had to be coaxed to their feet and helped back to the landing zone where they were airlifted back to the closest combat hospital.

It was the morning of November 16th that saw the final attacks from the Viet Cong and PAVN soldiers. Four times the enemy assaulted Moore's lines and four times they were driven back by artillery and air power. The Viet Cong and PAVN suffered huge losses on the final day of battle on Landing Zone X-Ray. The landing zone was covered with dead enemy soldiers. It was exactly what the Americans had wanted... a chance to use the full power of their military might against the enemy.

Moore received a radio call from Saigon. Westmoreland wanted him on the next chopper. He would be flown to Saigon where Westmoreland would personally debrief him. Moore objected strongly to leaving his battalion while they were still engaged with the enemy. Westmoreland wasn't happy but he yielded, and Moore stayed with his men. The debriefing would need to wait until after the battle.

When the guns were silenced, Moore's men discovered 634 enemy corpses strewn around the landing zone. The defeated North Vietnamese made their way back into the jungle and headed to Cambodia where they knew the Americans would not pursue them. Moore's group had lost seventy-nine killed with another 121 wounded. The Americans estimated that the North Vietnamese had 1,215 killed but there was no way to know for sure since the PAVN and Viet Cong had carried off the majority of the killed at the end of the battle. The Americans had successfully defended the landing zone and the North Vietnamese had withdrawn. In the U.S. commanders' eyes, it was an American victory in both number and position.

Known for leading from the front Colonel Moore was the first to step onto the battlefield of Landing Zone X-Ray and the last to step off once he accounted for all of his men. When asked later how he felt about war and the soldiers under his command, Moore replied, "There's never been a noble war except in history books and propaganda movies. It's a bloody, dirty, cruel, costly mistake in almost every case... But the young soldiers can be and often are noble, selfless, and honorable. American soldiers in battle don't fight for what some president says on TV, they don't fight for mom and apple pie, or the American flag… they fight for one another."

UPI journalist Joseph Galloway was the only civilian awarded a Bronze Star for heroism in the Vietnam War. During the Battle of LZ X-Ray, Galloway had disregarded his own safety and helped rescue two wounded soldiers while under fire. Galloway not only wrote several stories about the battle but co-wrote a book, *We Were Soldiers Once…And Young*, with Lieutenant Colonel Hal Moore that detailed the history of what had happened in the la Drang Valley in November 1965. Moore too had received a medal, the Distinguished Service Cross, for his actions during the battle.

The Battle of Landing Zone X-Ray was the first time the U.S. Army and PAVN met head-on in a major engagement. Westmoreland saw it as a great victory for the U.S. military using superior firepower and mobility. He believed it would be the path forward in Vietnam. The path to victory.

Ho Chi Minh also believed the Americans had won on the battlefield, but the North Vietnamese would use the lessons they had learned to eventually defeat the Americans in the war to reunite his country. The North Vietnamese would grind down the Americans as they had done with the French. Many brave men had been lost to gain that knowledge. Uncle Ho believed it was well worth their sacrifice.

November 18, 1965 – la Drang Valley in the Chu Pong Massif, South Vietnam

The morning after the end of the Battle of Landing Zone X-Ray, all U.S. forces were ordered out of the area. An arc light strike that Moore had requested was coming, and the USAF didn't want any friendly casualties. The key for the Americans was to leave the area as quietly as possible so that any PAVN troops that were hanging around would be caught by surprise by the B-52 carpet bombing. The B-52s were already on their way from Guam when the commanders of the two remaining American battalions received their orders to move their troops outside a two-mile safety zone.

Lieutenant Colonel Robert McDade was in command of the 2nd Battalion, 7th Cavalry Regiment, 1st Cavalry Division, while Lieutenant Colonel Bob Tully commanded the 2nd Battalion, 5th Cavalry Regiment, 1st Cavalry Division. It was decided that McDade's Battalion would advance toward Landing Zone Albany two miles to the north northeast near the Ia Drang River and Tully's Battalion would head for Landing Zone Columbus two miles to the northeast.

At 09:00, Tully's Battalion headed out of LZ X-Ray and ten minutes later, McDade's Battalion started their march. Both commanders knew that PAVN 7th and 9th Battalions were still in the area but were probably in no condition to attack after the shellacking they had received from Air-Mobile at LZ X-Ray. Intelligence reports had the PAVN up on the mountain licking their wounds and regrouping. Hopefully, the PAVN would again attempt to attack LZ X-Ray and the massive arc light strike would take care of them once and for all. It was wishful thinking.

At 11:38, Tully's soldiers made it to Landing Zone Columbus where they rested while waiting for helicopters to pick them up and ferry them back to their base camp. They hadn't slept in sixty hours and were exhausted.

In the meantime, McDade's lead company Alpha was approaching Landing Zone Albany. Alpha's company commander, Captain Joel Sugdinis noticed that the helicopter gunships were no longer patrolling above them. All aircraft had been ordered out of the area during the B-52 strike. Sugdinis heard the distant explosions of the B-52 carpet bombing using 500-pound bombs. Even from where he was standing Sugdinis could feel the explosions tearing into the Chu Pong Massif. He hoped the bombs found the PAVN that had attacked the Americans at LZ X-Ray.

Lieutenant Payne, the recon patrol leader, was walking around a series of termite hills just ahead of the Battalion's main body when he came across a PAVN soldier resting on the ground. Ten yards away, Payne's platoon sergeant came across another PAVN soldier. The two enemy soldiers were taken captive.

As word of the capture reached McDade, he ordered a halt and went to the front of the column to interrogate the prisoners personally. The prisoners were being held 100 yards from the southwest edge of the Albany clearing. The American battalion was strung out over 550-yards in line of march formation in unprepared, open terrain surrounded by chest-tall elephant grass.

After interrogating the prisoners for almost an hour, McDade called the company commander to the head of the column for a meeting. As usual, the commanders were accompanied by their radiomen leaving the rest of the column without radio support. Alpha Company moved onto Landing Zone Albany to provide security for the company commanders and McDade's command group which had crossed the clearing to a clump of trees. There was another clearing on the other side of the trees. The interpreter with the interrogator heard distant voices speaking in Vietnamese. It was the PAVN.

Unknowingly, Payne's recon platoon had walked within 200 yards of the PAVN 3rd Battalion, 33rd Regiment, and the 8th Battalion, 66th Regiment who were bivouacked northeast of the American column. As the Americans rested in the tall grass, they could not see the hundreds of PAVN soldiers silently closing on their position.

The 2nd Battalion Delta Company was holding in place just outside the LZ near the head of the column. Behind it was Charlie Company also holding in place. 2nd Battalion Headquarters was behind Charlie Company and Alpha Company, 1st Battalion, 5th Cavalry Regiment was the next in line after 2nd Battalion Headquarters. The rest of the American column was loosely dispersed east of Landing Zone Albany. The entire battalion was in a terrible defensive position and the individual companies were without their commanders and radios to call in air and artillery support. On top of that, the troops had not slept in sixty hours and had just finished a four-hour march to the landing zone. They were completely exhausted.

At 13:15, PAVN forces began their assault with small arms fire aimed at the head of the 2nd Battalion column, then spread their attack down the east side of the column in an L-shaped ambush. PAVN units peeled off and engaged the surprised Americans in hand-to-hand combat. They had the outnumbered Americans by the belt and would not let go. The tall grass made combat even for both sides. Nobody could see their enemy until they were right on top of them. Even with their radios, the Americans would not have been able to call in effective artillery or air strikes. The enemy was too close. Every advantage that the Americans had was gone and they were in a fight for their lives. Within eleven minutes of the start of the battle, McDade and the company commanders were cut off from the rest of the column. The PAVN were swarming over the American soldiers. Alpha Company was already on Landing Zone Albany. Most of Charlie Company fought their way into the perimeter that Alpha Company had created. Together the two companies had enough firepower to hold off the PAVN who were busy attacking the rest of the column and not focused on the landing zone.

Knowing that his company was under heavy attack, Captain George Forrest left the safety of the landing zone defensive ring and ran the gauntlet down the column being attacked until he reached the troops under his command; Alpha Company, 1st Battalion, 5th Cavalry near the rear of the column. His men were relieved to see their commander.

More PAVN companies poured into the fight down from the landing zone. Many of the Americans broke off from their column to form defensive pockets in which a small number of soldiers could protect each other by shooting in all directions if needed. The danger was obvious. They could not see who they were shooting in the elephant grass and friendly fire casualties mounted quickly as they shot into other American pockets of resistance.

Two miles away on Landing Zone Columbus, Captain Buse Tully, commander of Bravo Company, 1st Battalion, 5th Cavalry, received orders to reinforce 2nd Battalion. At 14:55, Tully's company began marching toward the distant battle. They would approach from the rear of the 2nd Battalion column.

Below LZ Albany, the PAVN, after fighting the 2nd Battalion for an hour, suddenly broke off and their gunfire went silent. The PAVN had been winning and it wasn't like them to back off. None of the Americans in the column thought the PAVN were through and steeled themselves for whatever was to come next. The Americans were right. PAVN mortar rounds began to rain down on the American positions. It was a rolling wave of explosions down the American column as the mortar fragmentation shells took a heavy toll sending hot pieces of shrapnel through the blades of elephant grass.

As mortar rounds pounded the landing zone, McDade and his commanders took cover in the clump of trees between the two clearings. Alpha and Charlie Companies had lost seventy men in the first few minutes of the battle as they attempted to form a perimeter and protect the landing zone and the commanders.

McDade's forward air controller radioed for air support, but there was little he could do except target the PAVN reinforcements east of the American column. It wasn't much, but it was something.

Hearing the American warplanes overhead lowered the PAVN troops' morale as their concerned faces looked up into the sky. Bombs and napalm canisters dropped parallel to the American Column. The PAVN soldiers that had broken off to allow the mortars to assault the Americans, charged forward once again seeking the protection of hand-to-hand combat. Some were caught in a wall of flame as napalm canisters broken open and spread their fiery gel. It was a horrifying sight to see their comrades burn.

Sharpshooters in Alpha and Charlie Companies sniped at the enemy below their defensive positions on Albany. Unsuspecting PAVN were hit and dropped into the long grass screaming in pain. The American commanders were cut off from their companies but did what they could calling for artillery strikes.

McDade watched with dismay as his battalion was gnawed to pieces by the PAVN troops. There was nothing he could do. He had lost control of the battle and his troops were paying the price for his incompetence. When the day had started, he too was exhausted from non-stop fighting and his judgment was impaired from no sleep and the incredible stress of command, yet he had to make life and death decisions. That was a battalion commander's duty… to lead no matter what. He had meant well. His men were exhausted, and he needed to keep them together as they marched toward the landing zone even though some were falling asleep on their feet. But McDade had ignored even the most basic principles of moving through enemy territory. His reconnaissance patrols were minimal. Unit security was lax. The battalion's in-line column formation was an open invitation for the enemy to attack. His compassion for his exhausted men was the battalion's downfall.

At 16:00, Captain Myron Diduryk's Bravo Company, 2nd Battalion, 7th Cavalry, veterans of the Battle for

Landing Zone X-Ray, were loaded into helicopters and flown to Landing Zone Albany. Under heavy fire from nearby PAVN troops, Diduryk's Bravo Company deployed in the long grass next to Albany's adjacent clearing. A few minutes later, Bravo soldiers entered Albany's perimeter where they expanded the defensive ring.

After a one and half hour march, Tully's Bravo Company came into contact with Forrest's Alpha Company at the rear of the column. While reinforcing Forrest's position, Bravo Company cleared and secured a one-helicopter land zone at the rear of the column. A resupply of ammunition and water was flown in and the wounded were flown out. Helicopters in the distance stacked up waiting for their turn.

After giving Forrest's men a much-needed break and a chance to regroup, Tully's company began working their way up the ambushed column to help the other companies. Seeing what they were attempting, the PAVN in a nearby wooded area, fought back Bravo Company's advance driving them to cover. Tully's men turned on the tree line and attacked driving the PAVN away. As darkness descended, Tully and Forrest were ordered to secure a two-company perimeter. Their companies were an anchor on the column's tail and prevented any further PAVN flanking actions.

With Landing Zone Albany's perimeter as an anchor at the head of the column and the two-company perimeter at the tail end of the column, the 2nd Battalion's flanks were protected. Under non-stop attack and still faced with annihilation, the 2nd Battalion column slowly stabilized into defendable defensive positions throughout the night.

As dawn broke on November 18th, the Americans had fought the PAVN at LZ Albany for sixteen hours and had suffered terrible losses. But the PAVN too had suffered losses and were themselves exhausted. Better able to identify the front lines, American warplanes and helicopters flew over the 2nd Battalion providing them air cover. More American artillery targeted the PAVN positions.

Unwilling to turn their victory into a loss, the PAVN commanders pulled their forces back. The Battle of Landing Zone Albany was over.

Air-Mobile forces that had claimed victory at Landing Zone X-Ray were now in disarray and most of the men were in shock by what had happened. The Battle for Landing Zone Albany had been the most violent battle to date in the Vietnam War with the heaviest one-day casualties for the Americans.

Both sides declared victory. The PAVN had 403 killed and 150 wounded, while the Americans had 155 killed and 124 wounded. While the casualty estimates were questioned by both the North Vietnamese and the Americans, there was little question that it was the PAVN forces that could absorb such losses more easily that the American forces which were still greatly outnumbered in Vietnam. Lieutenant Rescorla, the only remaining platoon commander in Tully's Bravo Company said it best when he described the Battle of Landing Zone Albany as, "… one long, bloody traffic accident in the jungle."

December 24, 1965 – Washington D.C., USA

On Christmas Eve at year's end, Johnson decided to temporarily halt the bombing of North Vietnam and seek a diplomatic solution to the war. He hoped the North Vietnamese would see the halt as an olive branch. He had tried before only to be rebuffed for his efforts. But he felt he needed to give American soldiers every possible opportunity before committing them to war.

The leaders in the North saw Johnson's attempt for what it was… a desperate attempt to end a war that the Americans and South Vietnamese were losing. The North was committed to a military victory, and they weren't about to back down now. If the Americans chose to expand the war, they were ready to meet them with their own escalation. More blood would be spilled as the battlefields in the South would determine the ultimate victor.

At the end of 1965, U.S. military personnel in South Vietnam had multiplied over eight times to 184,314 from the previous year of 23,310. American casualties had also increased from 216 in 1964 to 1,928 killed in 1965. South Vietnam's military forces were 514,000 of which 11,242 had been killed and 93,000 soldiers deserted during the year.

The PAVN had 400,000 soldiers at the end of 1965 which was over twice the size of the previous year. 50,000 PAVN soldiers had infiltrated the South. The total tonnage of weapons and supplies transported on the Ho Chi Minh Trail in 1965 was more than the previous six years combined.

Both sides were determined to win. It was going to be a long and bloody war…

Letter to Reader

Dear Reader,

I hope you enjoyed A Savage Joy. While researching the book, I couldn't help but feel that President Johnson and his administration were caught between a rock and a hard place. There was little doubt in my mind that South Vietnam would have fallen to the communists had America not introduced ground troops. As history has shown us, that decision only delayed the inevitable and cost America its very best.

The next novel in the Airmen Series is Beyond Courage. Set in 1966 and based on true events, more American troops are deployed as General Westmoreland grapples with his new strategy – search and destroy. The story includes the largest campaign to date for the Americans, Operation Masher.

Like all books in the Airmen Series, it's full of action, suspense, and historical facts. It's available as eBook and Paperback. Here is the link:

BEYOND COURAGE
https://www.amazon.com/gp/product/B0B6HHCY2B

Sign-up for my never-boring newsletter and you will receive a free ebook – Prophecies of Chaos (one of my favorites) in addition to new release updates, special offers, and my thoughts on history. Here's the sign-up link:

Newsletter Sign-Up
https://dl.bookfunnel.com/5tl2favuec

Reviews and recommendations to friends and family are always welcome. Thank you for your consideration, and I hope to hear from you.

In gratitude,

David Lee Corley

LIST OF TITLES WITH READING ORDER

The Airmen Series
1. A War Too Far
2. The War Before The War
3. We Stand Alone
4. Café Wars
5. Sèvres Protocol
6. Operation Musketeer
7. Battle of The Casbah
8. Momentum of War
9. The Willful Slaughter of Hope
10. Kennedy's War
11. The Uncivil War
12. Cry Havoc
13. When War Dawns

14. A Savage Joy
15. Beyond Courage
16. Flames of War

The Nomad Series
1. Monsoon Rising
2. Prophecies of Chaos
3. Stealing Thunder

Facebook Page:
https://www.facebook.com/historicalwarnovels

Shopify Store: https://david-lee-corley.myshopify.com/

Amazon Author's Page:
https://www.amazon.com/David-Lee-Corley/e/B073S1ZMWQ

Amazon Airmen Series Page:
https://www.amazon.com/dp/B07JVRXRGG

Amazon Nomad Series Page:
https://www.amazon.com/dp/B07CKFGQ95

Author's Website: http://davidleecorley.com/

DAVID LEE CORLEY

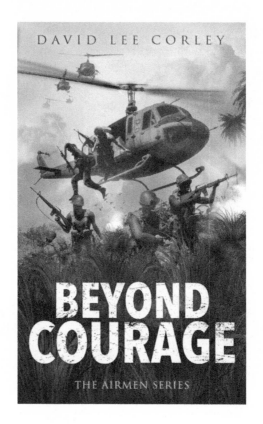

Author's Biography

Born in 1958, David grew up on a horse ranch in Northern California, breeding and training appaloosas. He has had all his toes broken at least once and survived numerous falls and kicks from ornery colts and fillies. David started writing professionally as a copywriter in his early 20's. At 32, he packed up his family and moved to Malibu, California, to live his dream of writing and directing motion pictures. He has four motion picture screenwriting credits and two directing credits. His movies have been viewed by over 50 million movie-goers worldwide and won a multitude of awards, including the Malibu, Palm Springs, and San Jose Film Festivals. In addition to his 24 screenplays, he has written fourteen novels. He developed his simplistic writing style after rereading his two favorite books, Ernest Hemingway's "The Old Man and The Sea" and Cormac McCarthy's "No Country For Old Men." An avid student of world culture, David lived as an expat in both Thailand and Mexico. At 56, he sold all his possessions and became a nomad for four years. He circumnavigated the globe three times and visited 56 countries. Known for his detailed descriptions, his stories often include actual experiences and characters from his journeys.

Made in the USA
Coppell, TX
25 May 2023